Past Imperfect

Joshua Cohen

Kasva Press

St. Paul / Alfei Menashe

Kasva Press
Alfei Menashe, Israel / St. Paul, Minnesota

www.kasvapress.com
info@kasvapress.com

Past Imperfect

ISBNs:
Trade Paperback: 978-1-948403-35-1
Ebook: 978-1-948403-36-8

M 10 9 8 7 6 5 4 3 2 1

To Charlotte, Anabelle, and JoCo

Past Imperfect

One

I SPENT THE morning of Yom Kippur 1957 sprawled on my living room sofa, munching on crullers from Davis Bakery and perusing the Street & Smith's football yearbook. Yom Kippur is the Day of Atonement, the most solemn of the Jewish High Holy Days. By all rights I should've been in synagogue beseeching God's forgiveness for my assortment of sins over the previous year.

But it had been a hell of a week. A member of the Sohio board of directors hired me to find his teenage daughter after she ran off with the carpenter who'd spent the summer building a gazebo on the family estate. After considerable legwork, I tracked the two of them to a seedy boarding house in Lorain. There I used my tact and charm to convince the princess to return to her parents, but not before she doused me in elderberry wine and bit my left hand. Her father showed his appreciation for a job well done by accusing me of gouging him on the bill and shorting me by fifty bucks. After all of that, I preferred to do my beseeching on Yom Kippur in the comfort of my own home.

I was watching *Perry Mason* on television that evening when the telephone rang. "Benny, it's Herb Kline," said the voice on the line.

"Rabbi . . . ?"

"We missed you at services today. I hope everything's all right."

"Who is this?"

"It's really me, Benny."

"Jesus, Herb," I said. "I didn't realize you'd be taking attendance."

"I only knew you weren't there because I went looking for you. We had an incident this morning with one of our congregants. I think I need your professional help to sort it out."

"What happened?"

"This isn't something to discuss over the telephone," he said. "Can we get together?"

"Sure. I guess so."

"How soon can you get here?"

Herb Kline and I grew up on the same block in Glenville. He'd been known as "Rabbi" since the ninth grade, when he cold-cocked a cracker transplant from West Virginia who called him a "stinking Jew boy" in gym class. Herb took the nickname to heart. After high school, he headed downstate to Hebrew Union College in Cincinnati.

I could conceive of only one scenario at Yom Kippur services that might put the Rabbi in immediate need of a private investigator. One of the faithful must have lost a wallet, watch, or something else of value. The owner likely dropped or misplaced his property. Herb, however, must've had some reason to suspect theft. He'd want me to get to the bottom of things as discreetly as possible — a handle-without-scandal assignment. The congregation's reputation could take a hit if news of a pickpocket began circulating.

The Temple parking lot was dark and empty when I pulled my new Edsel in shortly after ten o'clock. I went to a side door and knocked, in keeping with Herb's instructions. A moment later, a light came on. Through the window I saw a Negro janitor walking toward me with a ring of keys.

One

"Yom Kippur services are over," he said as he opened the door. "You're a few hours late."

"I'm here for a bris on Monday morning," I responded. "I'm a couple of days early."

The Temple's membership had long outgrown its building. Most gatherings featured wall-to-wall congregants, giving the place a steamy, claustrophobic feel. My visit that evening was something else again. The emptiness and quiet made the surroundings seem unfamiliar, so much so that I got lost on my way to the Rabbi's study.

Eventually I found Herb. He was sitting at his desk, devouring a plate of baked chicken and mashed potatoes. I startled him when I came in the room.

"Benny, you're here," he said as he stood with a napkin tucked in his belt. "Thanks for coming."

"Not at all, Rabbi."

"I apologize for this," he said, pointing at his dinner. "I didn't have time to go home, so I asked Eleanor to bring me something here."

"If that's your story, Herb, Yom Kippur technically ended at sundown. Presumably you didn't jump the gun in breaking the fast."

The Rabbi started to defend himself but stopped when he realized I was just giving him the business. He returned to his seat and put down his knife and fork. I took the chair on the opposite side of the desk.

"So why don't you tell me who lost what, and why you think it was stolen," I started.

"I don't understand, Benny."

"I figure somebody lost something valuable during services today, and you want me to find out where it went."

"A theft sounds downright quaint compared to what happened this morning. Do you know Mendel Kahn?"

"I know of him," I said. "Big into real estate. He's on your board of trustees if I'm not mistaken."

"Right. He's also a former Nazi collaborator, according to the man who assaulted him during services."

"You better explain that headline."

"Mendel had gotten up to say hello to a friend," said Herb. "As he walked back to his seat, a man sitting on the aisle stood up and blocked his way. 'It's you!' the man screamed. 'It's you! *Farreter! Karsew!*'"

"What does that mean?"

"'Traitor. Butcher.' Then the guy started shoving Mendel around."

"How did Kahn react?" I asked.

The Rabbi shook his head. "He didn't react at all, at first," he said. "Mendel just seemed dazed. Then some members of the congregation got between the two of them and asked the guy what he was screaming about. Services stopped for about half an hour while he explained. Mendel stayed calm. He listened to the allegations, then told everyone why they weren't true."

"What was the guy claiming?"

"He said he and Mendel came from the same town in Poland. According to him, Mendel was part of the Jewish council that ran the ghetto and took bribes from families trying to protect their husbands and sons from forced labor. Later, there were bribes from families trying to avoid deportation to Auschwitz."

"That's pretty serious stuff," I said after taking a deep breath.

"There's more," Herb continued. "The guy said that later, when Mendel showed up at the concentration camp, the Nazis made him a kapo."

"What's that?"

"An inmate flunky who helped in overseeing the other inmates. Mendel got the job, according to the guy, and was absolutely brutal. He hit the other prisoners, and once beat one of them to death."

"Who was the man making the accusations?" I asked.

"Marty Bluestein's cousin from Michigan. He just happened to be here for the holidays."

"An unfortunate coincidence for Mendel Kahn . . ."

"It's a case of mistaken identity, according to him," said the Rabbi. "Mendel's from Poland, all right, and he was in the Nazi camps, but he says he wasn't from that town, and the circumstances were different."

One of the Temple's elder statesmen escorted Bluestein's cousin from the building. Services resumed, and Kahn stayed till the end. As he exited, a few congregants approached to console him for the ordeal he'd endured.

But Kahn's protestations of innocence didn't convince the Rabbi. "I've never completely trusted Mendel," he said. "There's always been something about him that didn't add up."

"Like what?"

"Like how did he have the cash to invest in real estate so soon after emigrating to this country?"

"Just exactly what do you want me to do about this?"

"I've got to stay out in front of this problem," Herb explained. "I've got to know whether Mendel's history is subject to attack."

It came down to a matter of dollars and cents. The Temple was raising three-quarters of a million dollars to buy land in Beachwood for construction of a new building. The board of trustees appointed Kahn as chairman of the committee in charge of the project, and he was aggressively soliciting funding pledges from the bigwigs in the Jewish community. Herb believed those commitments would vanish if Kahn were exposed as a Nazi collaborator.

"No one will want their name associated with a building promoted by a war criminal," the Rabbi said.

"So how am I supposed to find out whether Kahn did the Nazis' dirty work?" I asked. "That was more than ten years ago, on a different continent."

"If this were easy, I wouldn't need a professional to investigate," Herb said. "And by the way, you're going to have to wait for payment, till I figure out where to tuck this into the budget."

The Rabbi shook my hand vigorously as I turned to leave. "Thank you for taking this on," he said. "You're doing the Temple a great service."

"You aren't really giving me much of a choice," I muttered.

"This is a once-in-a-lifetime assignment, Benny. How could you pass it up?"

How could I pass it up? I should've found a way. As I drove home that night, I foresaw only frustration in trying to prove either the sinister past Bluestein's cousin ascribed to Kahn or the benign version Kahn claimed for himself. This was not how I'd planned to spend my fall. I couldn't help but see it as my penance for taking a free pass on Yom Kippur.

Two

I WOULD'VE PREFERRED not to call Marty Bluestein on a Sunday, but I wanted to get in touch before his cousin left town, so I dialed his number the next morning just after ten. Bluestein answered on the third ring. He and I had seen each other around over the years, so I didn't have to explain who I was.

"I heard there was a little excitement at Temple yesterday morning," I said after the obligatory pleasantries.

"Yeah," Bluestein answered. "My cousin ran into a long-lost friend."

"I was wondering whether I could come talk to him about it."

"What's your interest?"

"I have some business with Mendel Kahn," I said. "I want to make sure he's on the up-and-up."

It was a flimsy subterfuge. But I didn't dare reveal that Rabbi Kline had hired me to investigate one of his most prominent congregants.

"Sure, come on over," said Marty.

Bluestein owned a dry-cleaning business on Kinsman near Lee Road. He and his wife lived a couple of miles east of there, on a side street in Cleveland Heights. I pulled up in front right at noon.

"Divina went to visit her niece, to give us a chance to talk," Bluestein said as he showed me into the living room. "Let me go get my cousin."

"What's his name, Marty?"

"Jacob. Jacob Gertner."

A few moments later, Bluestein led a tall, slump-shouldered man in from the back of the house. I estimated Gertner's age at around thirty-five. He wore a dark maroon knit shirt buttoned to the top under his wrinkled black suit. When we shook hands, he smiled just enough for me to see his mouthful of dentures.

"Jacob first came here from Europe but found Detroit better to his liking," Bluestein explained as we sat down. "He still comes back to town for most of the Jewish holidays."

"Ford," Gertner responded curtly when I asked him where he worked. "Tractor manufacture at Highland Park." He spoke with a thick accent, but I could understand what he was saying.

"I heard about the brush-up at the Temple yesterday morning..."

"Ach," Gertner grunted as his jaw tightened and his face turned bright red. He appeared angry that I'd brought up the subject, though he must've known why I came.

"Come on, Jacob," Bluestein said. "Mr. Gold wants to hear what you have to say about Mendel Kahn."

"That is not his name," snarled the cousin. "He is Yitzhak Fried, and he is from the same town in Poland where I am from."

"What can you tell me about him?" I asked.

"Like I said yesterday, Fried was on the Council that ran the ghetto. Then I saw him at Auschwitz. The man is a murderer. He deserves to die."

Gertner spent the next hour and a half giving me the background. He came from Bedzin, a Polish town with around fifteen thousand Jews before the War. The Nazis forced them into a ghetto after invading and crammed in another ten thousand from surrounding areas.

Fried was a lawyer in town. The Germans nominated him to serve on the Council that ran the ghetto. It had responsibility for everything — rationing food, making medical care available, regulating the meager business Jews could still conduct, fulfilling whatever whim the Nazis chose to indulge.

According to Gertner, Bedzin Jews resented the Council, believing it was all too willing to push the Nazi agenda. Fried supposedly took this to an extreme by informing the ghetto police about a surprise attack the Jewish resistance was planning on the local German authorities.

"They should have killed him then," Gertner said.

Fried went on to distinguish himself as the most corrupt member of a notoriously corrupt Council. As the official in charge of employment matters, Fried assigned men and boys to fill the Germans' quota for their various labor camps outside of Bedzin. The conditions were inhuman and the pay often nonexistent. Families gave Fried bribes to keep their husbands and sons from having to go. Fried would take their money or jewelry or whatever they had of value. With the loot in hand, he often chose those very men and boys for the next work detail demanded by the Nazis.

Later, the Council had to designate families for transport to the Auschwitz death camp. Fried and his compatriots would choose twice as many people as the Nazis decreed, then accept bribes from those who still could offer something to buy their way out. This only provided a temporary reprieve for the victims. All the Jews from Bedzin eventually ended up in a cattle car to Auschwitz, including Fried himself and his fellow Council members.

Fried, however, didn't meet his demise in the gas chambers. The Nazis instead put him in charge of a crew working at a big rubber factory, where he again distinguished himself in a notorious way. Most laborers at the factory didn't last more than a couple of months.

"Fried's Jews" (as he called them) had an even shorter life expectancy, given the brutal way he thrashed them when their efforts didn't meet his exacting standards.

Fried made a show of it. He carried a wooden club wrapped in leather and swung it wildly. The Germans on site liked nothing better than to watch him savagely pummel one of his own.

"Did you see this yourself?" I asked Gertner.

"I worked in a different part of the factory. But I talked to the men on Fried's crew, and everybody knew how he treated them."

"I heard you said at Temple yesterday morning that Mendel Kahn once killed a man."

"Yitzhak Fried," corrected Gertner. "A member of his crew spilled a bucket of soapy water at the factory when he went to mop the floor. Fried struck him three times from behind, and the last one snapped his neck. The man fell down and drowned in the puddle."

"So what happened to Fried at the end of the War?" I asked as I lit a cigarette.

"I never knew," Gertner replied. "He disappeared from camp when they were shutting it down before the Russians arrived."

'You mean he escaped?"

"He might have. We all were hoping someone had killed him."

"Neither you nor anyone you know ever saw him again?"

"Not until yesterday."

"That's the sixty-four-thousand-dollar question, Mr. Gertner," I said. "How sure are you that Mendel Kahn in Cleveland is the same man you've been describing?"

"There's no doubt whatsoever. The man at temple yesterday was Yitzhak Fried."

"So what do you think, Marty?" I asked Bluestein after Gertner had excused himself. "Could Kahn really be Herr Fried?"

"I just can't tell," Bluestein answered. "My cousin almost never talks about his experiences in the camp. I don't think he's crazy... I suppose he might be right."

"But what about Kahn? Is he the sort of person who could extort blood money from his neighbors and bludgeon a man to death?"

"I must admit, Benny, I find it a little hard to swallow."

When Gertner reentered the living room, I asked whether there were any differences between the way Fried looked and the way Kahn had appeared the previous morning.

"Fried has put on a lot of weight, and he is a little shorter than I remembered," said Gertner. "Also, he wore a mustache in Bedzin. He does not have one now."

"Anyone you can think of who could identify our man in Cleveland as Fried?"

"Most of the people from Bedzin died at Auschwitz," Gertner said. "Some may have survived."

"How about men from the rubber factory?"

"Again, I am sure there are some survivors, but I would not know how to find them."

I took down Gertner's telephone number and address in Detroit, thanked him for his time, and wished him safe travels back home. I fought off the impulse to give an assurance that "we'll get the bastard," or something to that effect, for several reasons. I wasn't a partisan in this conflict. At least not yet. My charge from the Rabbi was to get the facts—just the facts. Also, I wasn't all too sure Gertner had the right man. His antipathy toward Fried ran so deep he was bound to react viscerally to anyone who even vaguely looked like him. The ID might have resulted more from Gertner's rage than it did from any actual resemblance between the supposed before-and-after picture.

There was another reason I didn't play cheerleader for Gertner's cause. I wanted him to be wrong in fingering Mendel Kahn. In May 1945, I marched into the Ebensee concentration camp as part of the liberating force of the Eightieth Infantry Division. There I witnessed unspeakable horrors I'd spent the years since trying to erase from my memory.

Kahn was no friend of mine. I didn't even know the man. Still, his exposure as a Nazi collaborator would bring the nightmare back to life. As I drove home Sunday afternoon, I found myself hoping that my session with Jacob Gertner had been a complete waste of time.

Three

On Sunday evening, I had dinner with Sylvia Smolens at her apartment on Shaker Square. I'd been seeing Sylvia steadily for nearly three years. She and I had a standing date on Saturdays, but given the holiday, we postponed the weekly rendezvous by twenty-four hours.

Sylvia was a widow. Her husband died in the Battle of Bloody Ridge, in Korea, the summer of 1951. For two years afterwards, Sylvia stayed in bed, staring at the ceiling. By the time I met her, she had pulled herself together. She went to work downtown keeping the books for a jeweler in the Hippodrome Building. I got to know her when I still had my office there.

"How'd the Browns do today?" Sylvia asked as we sipped our coffee with dessert.

"They played last night, in Pittsburgh."

"Who won?"

"What, you lay a bet on the game?" I teased. "Since when do you care about football?"

"You'd be surprised. I told you I was a cheerleader at Heights."

Sylvia could almost still pass as a member of the pep squad. She was of average height and on the slender side, but curvaceous in build. She had dark brown hair, blue eyes, a thimble of a nose, and a clear, unwrinkled complexion. She almost always had her thin lips made up in the same bright red color. Sylvia was the pensive sort, and she often had an earnest-but-concerned expression on her face. When she smiled, she displayed a mouthful of white, perfectly aligned teeth.

"So tell me more about this mysterious new case," Sylvia said, changing the subject. "Who are you investigating, and what did he do?"

"I really can't talk too much about it, Syl. My client could get in a lot of trouble if anyone found out about this job."

"I hope it's all on the up-and-up..."

"It's not illegal, if that's what you mean," I said. "It's just extremely sensitive. The person I'm investigating could have my client fired if he found out what I was doing."

"Well, by all means, don't get caught then."

A short while later, we made our way into Sylvia's living room and played tenuously at a game of backgammon. Between rolls, Sylvia asked whether I'd thought any more about her brother's offer.

"Hon, do we really have to talk about that?"

"Of course not," she replied. "Not if you don't want to."

The truth was, I'd been dodging the question for some time. Sylvia's brother Ronald was a corporate lawyer with his own small firm. Ron wanted to add a litigation practice, and he'd invited me to join him as a full partner to spearhead the effort.

I was an attorney as well as a private investigator. I'd started out exclusively in the law, and did pretty well at it, before the War. But I returned from my tour in Europe with what could charitably be described as an addled brain, and by the time I put the puzzle back together, my trial skills had atrophied to a point where I needed to find a new way to earn a living. Detective work fell into my lap, and

I did at least passably well at it. But I kept my law license, just in case...and after a few years, I got a random chance to return to the courtroom in a high-profile, high-stakes lawsuit. The experiment turned out well—so well, in fact, that I'd taken on several other cases in the ensuing years.

"It's just that you're always saying how frustrated you are with your work," said Sylvia.

And she was right: As a lawyer, I felt like a frustrated private investigator; and when I was working cases as a private eye, I felt like a frustrated lawyer. I always had complaints about whichever job I was working, and pined for the profession that was currently on hold.

I shrugged. "Perpetual dissatisfaction is part of my inimitable charm. I make accentuating the negative into an art form. In my eyes, the glass is always half empty, and ready to spring a leak."

"That sums it up, alright," said Sylvia, "Always the pessimist!"

But of course, this rosy perspective largely explained how even thinking about Ronald Blumenthal's generous proposition turned into a wrenching ordeal. But there was something else at play. The way I saw it, deciding my future with Sylvia's brother meant deciding my future with her as well. Marriage to Sylvia seemed like part of a package deal, along with the corner office and membership at Lake Forest Country Club.

It only made sense. Ron never would've offered partnership to a part-time attorney with a spotty practice who didn't also happen to be a future in-law.

I was convinced I loved Sylvia Smolens. But I couldn't come to grips with the prospect of marriage. I'd had a wife, years earlier, but the marriage crashed and burned, and the divorce nearly destroyed me. Afterwards, I became committed to avoiding a repeat performance, no matter what.

My aversion to wedlock had already scotched one serious relationship — when it came time to fish or cut bait, I chose the latter option, even though I couldn't have adored my then-girlfriend any more than I did. I now found myself in the same bind with Sylvia, the only woman I desired — but maybe not quite enough to have and to hold till death did us part. I just couldn't convince myself to take the matrimonial plunge again.

"I realize I've got to make up my mind about Ron's proposal," I said to Sylvia. "I'm embarrassed about how long I've already taken. I'm just not sure what to tell him."

"It sounds like your heart isn't in it."

"The problem is, I just don't know. I worry I might miss the P.I. work. I also question whether I have it in me to build a litigation practice from the ground up. It's been a long time since I was a full-time lawyer."

Sylvia reached across the backgammon board to grab my hand. "Of course you can do it, sweetheart," she said. "Ron has all the confidence in the world in you. There's no one he'd want more to bring into the firm."

"That may be, Syl. But I don't think it has anything to do with my credentials or my fitness for the job."

Sylvia withdrew her hand as suddenly as she had offered it. "If you're suggesting Ron made his proposal on my behalf, you're..."

"I'm not suggesting anything of the kind, Syl."

But there was no point in denying it. By the end of our conversation in the living room, Sylvia had explicitly leveled the charge: I was hesitant about working with her brother because I didn't want to commit to her.

The back-and-forth became heated. "What are we playing at?" Sylvia barked at one point. "Why are we even spending time together?"

"You know what? If it means so much to you, I'll take the god-damned job with your brother."

"The hell you will," she answered. "There's no way you're putting him in the middle of this."

Barbs about my professional future alternated with barbs about my refusal to commit to marriage. At times I couldn't tell which was which.

"You're a talented lawyer," she declared. "But the law's not good enough for you. You hang onto the P.I. practice like you hang on to your bachelorhood."

"I'm too young to stop working, Syl."

"It's not work with the P.I. practice. You want to be a detective, like Dick Powell or Humphrey Bogart. Part of it's pretending you're a ladies' man."

"This ladies' man hasn't been out with anyone other than you for more than a year and a half," I said.

"But who's counting, right? Face it, Benjamin. At some point, you'll have to decide what you want to do when you grow up, and I'm not going to wait around while you make up your mind."

I couldn't win for losing. The only way out would've been a marriage proposal, then and there, and I briefly considered it, just to end the ugliness. But it wouldn't have made any difference. Given the way the night was going, Sylvia probably would've used my head as a bongo drum if I'd gotten down on one knee.

She eventually excused herself and went into her bedroom, closing the door behind her. Fifteen minutes later, she hadn't returned.

"Are you all right?" I called out but received no response.

After another fifteen minutes, I decided I could take a hint. Just as I stood up to get my hat, Sylvia emerged with a tissue in her hand. I didn't need the prop to know she'd been crying. All her makeup had disappeared, and her complexion had gone completely white, except for her cheeks, which were red and swollen.

"I'm really tired, Benjamin," she said in a quiet, controlled tone. "I think we better call it a night."

"I'm sorry, Syl," I said as I took a step toward her. "I really hate fighting with you. I don't think I should leave until we smooth things over, at least a little bit."

"They're as smooth as they're going to get," Sylvia responded. "I think we understand one another perfectly well."

"Come on, Syl."

"We can talk about it some other time."

I thought I would break her down with a particularly long, particularly firm embrace. I might as well have been hugging a wooden plank.

"Well, see you later, Syl," I said as I turned to leave. "Thanks for dinner."

There was no goodnight kiss. I'd barely exited the apartment when Sylvia slammed the front door.

Four

I CALLED HERB Kline at the temple just after nine o'clock Monday morning to report on my meeting with Bluestein's cousin. He interrupted me as I recited the bill of particulars Gertner had laid out against Mendel Kahn.

"I heard most of this Saturday morning," the Rabbi said. "I'm more interested in your impression of him."

"I don't know, Herb," I said. "The guy certainly believes he's telling the truth. Personally, I'm skeptical, but that may be wishful thinking as much as anything else."

"I remembered something yesterday, Benny. Last year, we had a program commemorating Jewish victims of the Nazis. That included Mendel and another congregant who survived the concentration camps. We praised his heroism and commiserated with his suffering."

"Sounds appropriate to me," I said.

"If he turns out to be a fraud, we'll look like fools."

"If he turns out to be a fraud, that means he duped immigration officials both in Europe and this country with a phony name and a concocted story. You're small potatoes compared to that."

I asked the Rabbi whether he had a photograph of Kahn. "The board of trustees have their pictures taken every year," he responded. "We must have something in our files."

"I also want to interview some of Kahn's friends or acquaintances, if I can do it without too much commotion. I'd like to know if he talks about his time in Europe, and if so what he says."

"The other trustees probably know him the best," said the Rabbi. "I can arrange for you to speak to some of them."

"Great. The sooner the better."

"How about Saturday night? Gordon Feldman and his wife are coming to the house for dinner. You could join us and speak to him then."

"Are you sure Herb? I don't want to be an imposition."

"No imposition," said the Rabbi.

"Can I bring anything?"

"I don't know. How about a bottle of wine?"

"What goes well with pork tenderloin?"

After the call, I immediately dialed Sylvia at the jewelry store. The owner of the shop picked up. I remained on hold for a full two minutes before Sylvia got on the line. Her tone was irritated.

"Benjamin, what is it? You know Mr. Nagelbush doesn't like it when I talk on the phone during business hours."

"Since when do you care? I just called to see how you were doing after last night."

"You don't have to worry," she said. "I'm not going to go to pieces."

"There's nothing to go to pieces about," I replied. "I apologize again, Syl. We had a spat. That's all that happened. I know we've got some issues to decide, but it's nothing we can't work out."

"For months, Benjamin, you've refused to talk about our future. Now I finally get it. Our future is in the past."

"For God's sake, Sylvia. You're overreacting. Nothing's changed."

"That's the problem in a nutshell," she said. "I've got to go, Benjamin. Take care of yourself."

The line went dead. The call ended, and so, apparently, had my relationship with Sylvia Smolens.

"What in the hell happened?" I nearly screamed.

I hadn't managed to bring myself to sign on the dotted line with either Sylvia or her brother, but getting the ax seemed like an excessive consequence. I was deeply hurt and extremely angry, and a little frightened, too. I was deciding whether to redial the jewelry store when my secretary knocked on the door and entered my office.

"Are you all right, Mr. G.?" Evie asked. "I heard you raise your voice."

"No, no. Everything's fine."

"If you say so… Is there anything I can do for you?"

"Not right now. But I've got a memo to dictate about a new case. You can come back in a bit with your steno pad."

"Just let me know," said Evie as she exited the office and pulled the door shut.

I sat wallowing in my misery for around forty-five minutes. I would've wallowed even longer, but Evie buzzed on the intercom to let me know Herb Kline was on the line.

"It's already started, Benny," the Rabbi jumped in without saying hello. "The phone hasn't stopped ringing since you and I spoke earlier this morning."

"Slow down a second, Herb. Who is it that's calling?"

"Everybody. And all they want to talk about is Mendel Kahn. The consensus seems to be that he's guilty as hell, and they want to know what the Temple's going to do about it."

"The Temple isn't going to do anything until all the facts are in," I said.

"We don't have a lot of time, Benny. Like I said Saturday night, we've got to be in front of this story."

Before finishing the call, I promised to give my undivided attention to the Rabbi's case. Then I summoned Evie back into my office to dictate the memo. I laid out all the gory details I'd received from Gertner. Evie didn't flinch, and even asked a few questions about the horrors at Auschwitz.

Evie was intrepid out of necessity. She got married at seventeen to a car mechanic who used her as a punching bag on those frequent occasions he took to drink. He sometimes threatened her with a switchblade and one night cut Evie's brother when he stepped in to protect her. The incident earned him a three-to-five-year stint at Mansfield.

With her husband behind bars, Evie went back to finish high school, put herself through secretarial college, and took a job with me. She still was only twenty-three years old and looked even younger, with her slight build, cherubic face, and bright blonde hair that she wore in a pony tail.

"Evie, what are you doing Saturday night?" I asked after I'd finished with the memorandum.

Evie got a sly look on her face. "Why're you asking, Mr. G.?" she said. "Do you have something... particular in mind?"

I knew she was just teasing me, but it was suddenly difficult not to think... particular thoughts. Reluctantly, I pulled my mind back to business. "The reason I'm asking is I've got to interview an associate of Mendel Kahn's over dinner at my rabbi's house Saturday night, and I thought you might come along as my second."

"What about Mrs. Smolens?"

"As it turns out, she has something else to do on Saturday," I said as blandly as I could manage.

"Sure, I'll go with you, Mr. G. It ought to be interesting."

With the social calendar set, I turned my attention to the matter at hand. I needed to find out whether Mendel Kahn had a rap sheet. I wanted a list of the properties he owned, along with papers from every lawsuit he'd either filed or had filed against him. These things wouldn't directly reveal whether Kahn was Yitzhak Fried, the Nazi collaborator. But they might convey some sense of the type of man I was investigating, and whether he was capable of committing the horrendous acts Gertner accused him of.

I called Sig Danziger, an attorney who'd been a friend since law school. "Sig," I asked, "how many law clerks you currently got on staff?"

"Two, at the moment. Why d'you want to know?"

"Because I'd like to borrow one of them, full-time, for the next couple of days to search some records."

"It'll cost you. What you got going?"

"I'm going to tell you, Sig, because your clerk's going to know anyway," I said after hesitating. "But this is strictly on the QT. My client's anonymous, and I want to keep the investigation a secret as long as possible."

"As far as I'm concerned, whatever you tell me is privileged," Sig replied.

"Good. You ever heard of Mendel Kahn?"

"Known him for years. Used to do his legal work before he got too big for someone like me. We're still friendly."

"Well, I'm sifting through his sordid past."

"Does this have something to do with what happened at the Temple on Yom Kippur?" asked Sig. "My brother- and sister-in-law told me about it."

"You're right on," I said. "I'm trying to find out whether Mendel Kahn was really Mendel Kahn in Europe."

"Now you've got me totally confused. Exactly what kind of records do you want my guy to search?"

"Standard stuff," I said. "Send him over and I'll give him the particulars."

I spent the rest of the day compiling a list of Yiddish and Polish newspapers and periodicals in New York and Israel. I figured I'd need to advertise to find someone who could look at a picture of Kahn and tell me whether he'd been Fried in a former life. I doubted many (if any) survivors of Bedzin and Auschwitz remained in Europe, so I concentrated on locales where they might have emigrated. I went to the library downtown and telephoned various consulates and cultural societies to get the information I needed. The effort proceeded fitfully, but in the end, I came up with a list of six or seven publications that suited my needs.

"I'll write out the texts for the ads in the morning," I told Evie on my way out of the office. "We'll have to rely on the newspapers to translate them."

I headed over to the Theatrical on Short Vincent for an unhappy happy hour. I'd managed to keep Sylvia out of my thoughts since the morning. The timeout had made me more philosophical about the situation, and more self-critical. I realized I couldn't indefinitely waffle about our relationship. She had every right to expect more from me than I'd been willing to give. The time had come to put up or shut up. I needed either to ask her to marry me or disappear.

I debated the pros and cons of the situation as I sipped my rye-and-soda, then its successor, then the successor's successor. But I was all balled up. I didn't know if I was coming or going.

Four

On the way out of the bar, I stopped at the pay phone and impulsively dialed Sylvia's number. After twelve rings, I hung up. I was sure she was home, and she would've known it was me on the line.

But why was I calling? I wouldn't have had a clue what to say if Sylvia picked up. At least she had the good sense to realize that for the time-being, further conversation was pointless.

FIVE

I SAT WITH my five-year-old niece in a booth at Corky & Lenny's in South Euclid, waiting for the waitress to bring us her birthday breakfast. It was Friday morning and not really my niece's birthday, and breakfast wasn't the real reason I'd come to the restaurant. I was waiting for Mendel Kahn to arrive with Sig, who'd set a date for coffee specifically to give me an opportunity to take Kahn's picture. I needed an excuse for having a camera at the breakfast table. My niece's birthday party was the only plausible solution that came to mind.

The Rabbi had struck out in trying to get me a photo of Kahn from the Temple's files. "Kahn didn't show up the last three years when the board had their pictures taken," he told me. "He usually doesn't miss a meeting. That has to mean something."

"A lot of people don't like being photographed," I said. "Maybe he's sensitive about his complexion."

"His complexion's fine."

"We'll just have to get a picture another way."

I went to Kahn's home in Shaker Heights early the next morning to sneak a snapshot on his way to work. The mission failed, mainly on account of the bushes that obscured the pathway from his backdoor to the garage. I trailed him and caught him alone a few times later in the day, but he always seemed to have his head turned. I took a couple of pictures anyway, but none were keepers.

Five

I needed another chance to photograph Kahn, so I decided to manufacture one. Sig had said the two were still friendly. I figured if he took Kahn to a designated place at a designated time, I'd get my shot. I called Sig to explain what I wanted him to do. He was more than willing to help, for future considerations. He contacted Kahn and suggested lunch at a downtown restaurant, near both of their offices, and mine as well. Kahn preferred coffee at Corky's, so here I was.

Sitting in the booth, I knew considerably more about Kahn than I had at the beginning of the week. He had no criminal record, and no litigation history as either a plaintiff or defendant. He came to the United States alone in 1948 and worked as a dishwasher until the fall of 1951, when he quit to devote himself full-time to real estate.

I was surprised by his holdings, or, more accurately, by the limited number of them. Other than his Shaker Heights home, Kahn owned only two modest apartment buildings in his own name. The properties weren't shabby. I'd gone to eyeball both of them myself.

By reputation, however, Kahn was a real estate magnate with a slew of properties around Cleveland. Two suburban apartments does not a magnate make. Kahn bought each of these buildings before he quit working as a dishwasher.

From these facts, I drew two deductions, neither especially incisive. First, Kahn at least initially had access to some unexplained source of money. Second, he owned most of his properties under an assumed name or in the name of some company or partnership. Regarding the latter point, I took a wild shot and had a property search conducted in the name of Yitzhak Fried. It came back empty.

My niece's name was Rachel. I was much closer to her brother, David, who was five years older. I wanted him for the ruse, but he was having trouble with fourth-grade math, and his mother didn't want him to miss any class. Rachel, on the other hand, was in full command of the kindergarten curriculum. Being tardy by half an hour wouldn't jeopardize her education.

I considered it a minor miracle Miriam allowed either of her children to participate in what I had planned. She usually made sure not to upset Jake, who was incredibly straightlaced and strict as a parent. He regarded me as a rogue influence on his children, though my offenses involved nothing worse than slipping them a Hershey's bar or recounting what he regarded as an inappropriate story about his childhood.

I explained to Miriam that I was investigating a regular patron of the restaurant I knew would be there Friday morning. I said the breakfast was a setup to take his picture and assured her that Rachel would be perfectly safe. "I'm shooting with a camera, not a gun," I said.

Your brother's going to kill us both if anything happens," Miriam replied.

"What are you going to tell him?"

"That you're taking Rachel out to breakfast and leave it at that."

"What he doesn't know can't hurt him. Or me either."

On my way home from work Thursday evening, I stopped at F.A.O. Schwarz at Shaker Square and bought Rachel a big stuffed giraffe for our faux celebration. She asked me about it on the ride from her house to Corky's.

"What's this for, Uncle Benny?"

"For your birthday, sweetheart."

"My birthday's not till January eleventh."

"I know," I said. "But we're going to pretend it's today."

"Why, Uncle Benny?"

"I bet sometimes you have make-believe tea parties with your dolls. Today you're going to have a make-believe birthday party with me."

I personally thought it was a clever explanation. But the kid still looked perplexed as she and I went into the restaurant with the giraffe and my Argus C3 in hand.

Rachel had just ordered pancakes and chocolate milk when Sig and Mendel Kahn arrived. I watched as Sig surveyed the dining room until he spotted me, then nodded slightly. The hostess started to show the two of them to a table toward the back, but Sig must've come up with an excuse to ask for the one that had just opened up across from us. He and Kahn returned to the foyer and waited while a busboy cleared the dishes and wiped the table down.

I took the opportunity to size up Kahn while he and Sig chatted. My research told me he was fifty-seven, and he looked right around that age. He was solidly built, a little shorter than average, with square shoulders and a full head of gray hair. He had on a spiffy blue suit with sharp creases, a white shirt and crimson tie, and black shoes so shiny they seemed to emanate light.

This was not my conception of evil incarnate. Kahn looked every bit the upstanding businessman he was supposed to be.

After a few minutes, Sig and Kahn walked back to the table the busboy had cleared for them. Sig made sure to grab the seat on the aisle, leaving Kahn faced directly toward me, albeit on the far side of his table. Sig immediately excused himself and headed toward the washroom. That left me with a clean shot to take my photo.

"Let's get a picture, to show mommy and daddy," I said to Rachel as I pulled the Argus out of its brown case. "Slide out and stand up, sweetheart."

Before Rachel could move, the waitress appeared with her breakfast. "Here you go, birthday girl," she said cheerily as she put the plate of pancakes in front of my niece.

"It's not really my birthday. We're pretending."

"Well, I won't tell anyone," the waitress whispered as she walked away.

I tried to coax Rachel out of the booth to stand next to the table. But the food totally distracted her.

"Uncle Benny, can you help me cut this up?"

"Sure. But first let's take our picture, before we forget."

"I'm so hungry I could eat a horse."

I didn't want to refuse the kid, so I slid over and sliced up the flapjacks as quickly as I could. It wasn't quickly enough. By the time I finished and slid back to get my camera, Sig had returned to his seat.

"I blew it," I said loudly enough for Sig to hear.

"Blew what, Uncle Benny?"

"I was just thinking of something, sweetheart. It's not important."

I tried to watch Sig out of the corner of my eye, so I wouldn't miss the next chance to get my snapshot. Rachel, however, wanted help pouring the syrup. She then spilled a little of her chocolate milk and needed assurance the sky wouldn't fall as a result. Next she asked to try a piece of my toast, with more jelly on top. The commotion lasted for fifteen minutes. Too much time had passed to count on a second chance from Sig.

I shifted in the booth so I was sitting directly across from Rachel. From this vantage point, I had a direct diagonal view of Mendel Kahn, without Sig's head in the way.

"I'm going to take the picture, after all," I said to Rachel. "Smile, sweetheart."

With that, I pointed the Argus at Kahn and took two shots. The process took about fifteen seconds. I was reasonably certain he hadn't seen what I was doing.

"You didn't take my picture," said Rachel.

"Sure I did," I replied. "I just did it in my own special way. Let me take another."

I photographed Rachel with a chocolate-milk mustache and syrup smeared all over her left cheek. The picture wouldn't inspire confidence in my abilities as a chaperon, but I wasn't concerned about Jake's and Miriam's reaction. I'd smoothly accomplished my mission for the morning.

Except I hadn't. Just then, I heard Sig push his chair back. I looked up to see him and Kahn get up from their table and walk straight toward me.

"Hello, Benny," said Sig. "I didn't see you when I came in. Who's your pretty date?"

"Hey, Sig. This is Rachel, my niece. We're celebrating her birthday."

"Well, I'm sorry to interrupt. Benny, this is Mendel Kahn, an old client and friend. Mr. Kahn thought he saw you taking his picture while we sat and had our coffee."

"Nobody takes my picture," grunted Kahn.

"I'm sorry," I said, "but you're mistaken. I took the kid's picture. I wanted a keepsake for the occasion. I had no reason to photograph you."

"I know what I saw," Kahn said. "Now I want the goddamned film."

"Well, you're not going to get it," I said calmly. "There are personal things on this roll, besides my niece's picture."

Kahn and I stared silently at one another. "This is ridiculous," I finally said.

"Mendel," said Sig, "Benny says he wasn't taking your picture, and I think we've got to give him the benefit of the doubt. I've known him since law school. He's not one to lie."

Kahn started toward the door. "I know what I saw," he said again. "You took my fucking picture."

Sig stayed back. "What the hell happened?" he asked. "Did you have to be so obvious?"

"My niece and I got preoccupied. I thought I was running out of time."

"Now I'm in this up to my neck."

"Don't worry, Sig," I said. "Kahn hasn't killed anybody since Auschwitz."

"You don't know that for sure," Sig responded unhappily as he walked away.

And he was right. I didn't.

Six

I WOKE UP Saturday morning with all the gumption of a deflated bicycle tire. I'd been sleeping fitfully the whole week. To remedy the situation, I'd guzzled a bottle of claret right before I turned out the lights Friday night. I thought the wine would improve the shuteye. Instead, it brought on a nasty hangover. The two rye-and-sodas I'd consumed earlier in the evening probably hadn't helped matters.

I waited till mid-afternoon to call Herb, partially to give myself time to recuperate and partially to ensure he'd returned from Saturday morning services. I told the Rabbi I couldn't possibly keep my date for dinner at his home that evening. After my run-in with Kahn the day before, I figured I was pretty much radioactive. Any contact with Herb could arouse Kahn's suspicions.

"I think you're right," the Rabbi said. "Mendel talked to me this morning at Temple. He said he got a call last week from Marty Bluestein, who told him someone came to interview his cousin after the incident on Yom Kippur. Marty didn't tell him who it was, but Mendel definitely knows he has to watch out for himself. And after yesterday morning, Mendel also knows it's you sniffing around."

"Thank you, Marty," I said as I plopped two Alka Seltzers in a glass of water.

"I was about to call to uninvite you. Fortunately, I never told Gordon Feldman you were coming, so your absence won't raise any questions."

"Kahn isn't on to you, is he?" I asked. "He doesn't suspect you're the client who hired me?"

"I don't think so. But I found out something that may make this all beside the point. Mendel told me this morning he has a cousin in this country who can identify him. The guy apparently sponsored Mendel's passage into the country."

"That would certainly end the controversy," I said, "if this cousin could verify that Mendel is really Mendel."

"It would seem so."

I paused for a moment to chug down the medicine. Then I asked for the cousin's name.

"Mendel didn't tell me."

"Where does he live?"

"He didn't say."

"You've got to call him and get that information."

"I can't do that," Herb replied. "Then he'll know I suspect him."

"Well, I can't call. That would tell him you spoke to me."

"You're a private investigator, Benny," the Rabbi said. "You'll have to find the cousin on your own."

"I don't know, Herb," I said, after reflecting on the situation. "It all seems a little too convenient. Marty Bluestein has a cousin who gets Kahn into trouble. Now he comes up with one of his own who's going to get him out of it. You would've thought Kahn would've mentioned it before today."

The fact was that Kahn's cousin could effectively end the intrigue that began on Yom Kippur morning. With a relative to corroborate his identity, Kahn could no longer possibly be Yitzhak Fried's alter ego. The cousin also might have money. That could explain how Kahn financed his spectacular ascension in the real estate world.

Six

The possibility of an abrupt conclusion to the case brought mixed emotions. I still had no hankering to assess Kahn's involvement in gruesome war crimes. But after his profane outburst at Rachel's not-really-her-birthday breakfast, my interest in his exoneration had waned.

He'd certainly had every right to take me to task. I was photographing him without his consent in an obvious, ham-handed way. But he came on like a lout — not the polished professional everyone thought he was. His brutishness didn't make him a Nazi collaborator of course, but it didn't help his defense, either, and for a day, at least, I was willing to entertain the notion he really was Fried.

After hanging up with Herb, I called Evie to tell her our dinner date was off.

"Shoot," she said. "I was really looking forward to interviewing that Mr. Feldman. I went to the library this morning to read up on the Nazi concentration camps. I wanted to ask him some questions about it."

"Evie," I said, "Mr. Feldman got to know Mr. Kahn here in the U.S., not in Europe. He probably doesn't know very much about the camps."

"You never can tell, Mr. G. You never can tell."

I promised Evie she'd get another chance to interview a witness. If she had asked me when, I would've had to tell another fib.

Seven

On Wednesday morning I got a call from Ronald Blumenthal, Sylvia's brother. Sylvia had told him I was declining his offer of partnership and intended to continue my P.I. practice indefinitely.

"I'm disappointed," Ron told me. "Mainly because you didn't have the courtesy to call me yourself with your answer."

"Whoa," I replied. "Sylvia was freelancing on this one. I told her I hadn't made up my mind about your proposal. She took that as a 'no' and interpreted it to mean I had no intention of marrying her, either."

"Sylvia didn't tell me that."

"She's not at her most communicative these days. We haven't talked in a week."

"Jesus," Ron said. "Are you two calling it quits?"

"I wouldn't know," I replied. "Like I said, I haven't heard from her."

Ron used these revelations as an invitation to expound upon Sylvia's impatient streak and her penchant for over-dramatizing situations. "I wouldn't know about that," I said.

"You realize she just turned thirty-six. Our mother asks her all the time when the two of you are getting married. Goddammit! Who needs that kind of pressure?"

"I don't think we can blame this on your mother," I said. "When it comes down to it, Sylvia's right. I've got to make some decisions about my future."

"Well..."

"I'm just wrapping up a case right now. But when it's finished, I promise I'll call you for lunch, and we can hash out where things stand, at least with respect to your offer."

"Thanks, Benny," he said. "You know our group really wants you here, and I think we could make each other a whole bunch of money."

Ron's call gave me a break from staring at the wall. I'd run out of ideas on how I might find Mendel Kahn's cousin. I'd felt certain I could get my hands on some of Kahn's immigration paperwork that would tell me what I wanted to know. I was wrong about that, and wrong in believing that a second review of Kahn's real estate file might uncover a name I'd overlooked the first time.

My frustration notwithstanding, it was still premature to run an obituary on the Kahn case. Until I heard from the cousin's lips that Mendel was really Mendel, I wouldn't know for certain the truth of the matter.

I gave Gordon Feldman a call to see if he knew anything about Kahn's relatives in the U.S., but he wouldn't give me the time of day. "I don't really know you, Mr. Gold, and I don't know why you're asking about Mendel," he said. "I'm sure he wouldn't want me to talk to you."

Another dead end.

I looked through my notes for the name of Kahn's former mistress. Herb had given it to me the morning he invited me to dinner at his house, but I never got around to contacting her. She was Sophie Himmel, and she had an apartment on Cedar Road in Cleveland Heights. If Kahn spoke to someone about his cousin, she was as likely a candidate as any.

I caught Sophie just as she was leaving for a hair appointment. "But I'll talk to you about Mendel," she said. "What are you doing later?"

"I'm free all day."

"Where's your office?"

"You don't want to come down here," I said. "I'm in the Terminal Tower."

"I love a train ride. See you around three."

Sophie arrived fifteen minutes ahead of schedule. She was apologizing for her early appearance as Evie ushered her into my office.

"That's perfectly all right, Miss Himmel," I assured her. "Thanks for coming."

She sat down in the chair in front of my desk. She was a petite woman, both short and slender, wearing a turquoise dress and a white cashmere sweater. I figured she was in her mid-forties, at least, but her short brown haircut made her look several years younger. She had naturally red cheeks and green eyes. Her countenance was alert and lively.

"I'm in the presence of a real live celebrity," she started the conversation.

"What do you mean?"

"You're the Benjamin Gold who married the Forsythe heiress — the Elite Motors family — right?"

"That was me," I admitted.

"And I remember there was some big blow-up with them — divorces, lawsuits, murders, buildings burned down … I didn't follow all the details, but I remember reading something about how brave and smart you were."

All that was pretty much true, except that while it was happening I felt like a half-crazy, more-than-half-drunk idiot a lot more than

I felt like anyone's idea of a hero or a genius. Being admired was embarrassing."Okay, okay," I said. "Enough about my escapades. I want to talk about Mendel Kahn, not myself."

I explained that a client had hired me to investigate the accusations made against Kahn at temple on Yom Kippur. Sophie said she'd heard all about the incident from a friend who'd been there.

"So what do you think?" I asked.

"I have no specific reason to believe any of it's true," she said. "Mendel has always said he was a victim who barely survived the camps. But then again, it wouldn't altogether surprise me, either."

I asked her to elaborate. She hesitated briefly, then said,

"Mendel plays everything close to the vest. What he's thinking or feeling is anybody's guess. He might have deep dark secrets that no one knows about."

"But is he the sort of man who could sell his neighbors down the river? Or kill them in cold blood?"

Again, Sophie paused. She started to say something, then cut herself off.

"Let me answer by telling you a story," she finally offered. "Mendel and I were in Chicago on a weekend getaway. We were walking back to our hotel from dinner when we came across two drunks in a fight. Really only one of them was fighting. He accused the other man of stealing his whiskey and was grabbing his head and slamming it against the brick wall of a building."

"Sounds pretty gruesome," I said.

"Five or six times he slammed the other man's head. When the man collapsed, he began slamming it against the sidewalk. I begged Mendel to do something — break it up, run for help, anything. The one man was killing the other."

"So what did he do?"

"Mendel did nothing," Sophie said. "Nothing but stand and watch. He said the fight was between the two *shikkers* and the one probably had it coming to him. He got mad at me for asking him to get involved, so I stopped."

"What happened to the man whose head was being smashed?"

"He was lying face down on the sidewalk when Mendel and I walked away. I thought for sure he was dead, but Mendel said he was probably just unconscious."

Sophie's voice grew progressively softer as she retold this story. I didn't know exactly what to make of it.

"Maybe he thought he couldn't do anything without putting himself and you in danger," I suggested.

"It wasn't that. Mendel didn't see a need to muss his hair, even if another man was literally being murdered. I don't think I've ever seen anything that cold-hearted in all my life."

"Was Kahn that way at other times?"

"He isn't a particularly warm man," said Sophie. "But he's usually polite and considerate, about small things, at least. That's why the incident in Chicago hit me so hard."

"Did you and he talk about it later?"

"I tried to bring it up a couple of times, but Mendel always got irritated and changed the subject."

Sophie and I talked for another hour, going over the four years she and Kahn had spent together. The affair had ended just a few months earlier, at the beginning of June, when Kahn announced out of the blue that he had fallen in love with someone else.

"With whom?" I asked.

"I don't know. He has an old flame in Utica, New York who he kept in touch with while we were seeing one another. Maybe he's brought her back to Cleveland, and he's seeing her again."

"Who is she?"

"I have no idea," Sophie said. "Mendel never told me anything about her. I only knew she existed because I'd see letters from her on Mendel's desk at home, and letters he was sending to her. He seems to have been supporting her financially."

"Sounds potentially tawdry," I said.

"Maybe she had a sick mother she was caring for."

"So you think the phantom mistress might be back in play?"

"I really couldn't tell you," Sophie said. "It's just as likely he made up his anonymous new love just as an excuse to get rid of me."

It was time for me to ask the question I had contacted Sophie to ask. "Miss Himmel, did Mendel Kahn ever tell you he had an American cousin?"

"No, he didn't," she said.

"Did he talk about other relatives he had in the U.S.?"

"To the contrary, he said none of his family survived the War. Not his mother or father or uncles and aunts. His wife and two sons died in the camps."

"He was married with a family?"

"I can't tell you much about it because Mendel refused to talk about it. But those were the facts."

"I wouldn't want to talk about it either," I said gravely. "Losing your wife and kids in a concentration camp. I can't imagine anything worse than that."

"He really has been through hell," Sophie summarized as she stood to leave. "I tried to keep that in mind during the rough stretches."

As Yitzhak Fried, Kahn was a sadistic menace. In his current persona, he suffered severely at the hands of the Nazis, having lost his family to their killing machine. To discern truth from fiction, I needed verification of who Kahn was, one way or the other. I needed to find his goddamned cousin.

Eight

Sig Danziger telephoned the next morning right at ten. "I shouldn't even be talking to you, after that fiasco at Corky's last week," he said.

"Oh, yeah? Then why'd you call?"

"Just paying my respects."

"I know I'm deserving. But why today?"

"It just so happens I'm going to the *Schvitz* this afternoon with Alvy Mishkin," said Sig. "I'm calling to invite you to join us."

"I don't know Alvy Mishkin," I replied. "Why should I want to sit with the two of you wrapped in a towel, sweating my guts out?"

"You said you wanted information about Mendel Kahn, didn't you?"

Mishkin, it seemed, owned a carpeting warehouse on the near East Side. Most of his business was wholesale, but he dealt directly with certain high-volume retail customers, and Kahn was one of them. Mishkin sold him the carpet he needed at his various apartment buildings.

"You said you were having trouble finding all the properties Mendel owns," said Sig. "Alvy can probably give you a heads-up about some of them."

Since Kahn almost certainly didn't reveal his cousin's identity to his carpet salesman, I was less than overwhelmed at the prospect of meeting Mishkin. But I remained curious about the extent of

Kahn's real estate holdings, and since I suspected that Kahn's cousin was his financier, finding out about his other properties might enable me to discover the cousin's name on a deed or a mortgage.

So I accepted Sig's invitation. At four o'clock, I pulled the Edsel into the parking lot on 116th near Kinsman and headed into the *Schvitz*.

You had to know beforehand where you were going to have any chance of finding the place. It was a brick building with no signs or anything else that hinted at its use or function. It looked more like a small factory than a men's bathing house.

Sig and Mishkin had already entered the steam room by the time I arrived. I found a locker, undressed quickly, grabbed a towel, and headed in to join them.

They were sitting on a wooden bench talking, the only occupants in the room. Sig was already immersed in a sea of perspiration. His arms, face, and head were all dripping. Mishkin seemed to have more-or-less kept his cool. He was a middle-aged man of average height and weight, with a head of thinning red hair and a mustache of the same color.

Sig handled the introductions as I sat down next to them. "Pleased to meet you, Gold," said Mishkin in a high-pitched, squeaky tone. The voice didn't match the body. I thought maybe it was the steam.

"You from Cleveland, Alvy?" I asked.

"Grew up in P.A., forty-five miles outside Pittsburgh. Been here since I got out of the service."

Mishkin was more than happy to give me his history in the carpeting world. Ten minutes into it, I was ready to shoot either him or myself, to end the misery. Fortunately, Sig intervened.

"Alvy, I told you Benny was investigating Mendel Kahn for a client of his," said Sig. "I thought you might be able to share your experience in dealing with him."

"There's not a lot to tell," Mishkin replied. "Kahn hired me to do an overhaul of the flooring in a number of his apartment buildings. He ordered the carpet he wanted, we installed, and he paid. End of story."

"Let me start by asking you what may seem an oddball question," I said. "Did Kahn have any business partners?"

"I wouldn't know that," Mishkin squeaked. "I dealt only with him."

"Did he happen to mention a cousin of his?"

"A cousin? I don't understand..."

"Never mind," I said. "How many buildings does Kahn own in Cleveland?"

"I couldn't tell you for sure. All I know is we installed carpet at eight or nine sites in the area. Some were apartment buildings. Others were smaller than that."

"Are you sure?"

"At least that many, in the city and the surrounding suburbs."

I wiped the sweat that was dripping off my forehead. "Were all of these nice buildings?" I asked.

"Ha!" The shrillness of Mishkin's laugh could have shattered crystal. "I wouldn't let my dachshund go in a couple of those places."

"What do you mean?"

"They were tenements, dumps, whatever you want to call them. There were holes in the walls and the ceilings. There were rats and mice. They stank to high heaven because the plumbing didn't work. My men got in and out of those places as quick as they could."

"It couldn't have been all that bad," I said. "You were putting in new carpeting."

"I was putting in garbage," said Mishkin. "Remnants. Samples. The cheapest stuff I had. We only did it because he was giving us legitimate orders for his other properties."

I turned to Sig. "Did you know Kahn owned places like this?"

"He didn't when I was doing his legal work," Sig answered.

I asked Mishkin the location of Kahn's "tenements." He couldn't tell me, other than to say they were on the East Side, "where the *schvartzes* live."

"Was it Kahn who paid you for the work you did?" I asked.

"Who else?"

"Did he pay you in cash?"

"The invoices were pretty big," said Mishkin. "I'm sure I got checks from him."

"Were they personal checks?"

"I don't recall if they were or not. You're getting pretty specific with your questions."

Just then another man entered the steam room and sat on the bench above ours. The guy was a slab of humanity, square-shouldered and solid all around—a slab with thick black fur from head to toe, except on his face, which was cleanly shaved, and the top of his head, which was bald. He walked in with the *Plain Dealer* folded in his right hand. I noticed he didn't begin reading it when he sat down.

"I'm asking about the checks because Kahn doesn't hold all his properties in his own name," I explained to Mishkin. "He might own them in the name of a partnership or business, and he may have paid you from one of its bank accounts."

"Our books would at least reflect the account name," Mishkin said. "But I don't think I'd be comfortable sharing that information with you. Mr. Kahn has the right to conduct his business in private, just like the rest of us. I don't think he'd approve of my telling you the name of the account."

I was preparing my rejoinder when I saw the Hairy Slab stand up and step down towards us.

"You're tall and skinny," he said to me in what sounded like a Russian accent. "You must be Gold."

"Through and through," I said. I knew I was in for trouble of some kind, but I wasn't sure exactly what it was. "Do you mind telling me..."

"Hey!" the Slab shouted as he slapped my right cheek hard. "I'll do the talking. You do the listening." Then he dropped the folded newspaper to reveal a shiny black thirty-eight.

"You've been sticking your nose where it don't belong," he told me. "You need to learn to mind your own business."

I was a little woozy from the slap and all the sweating. "I don't know what you're talking about," I told him.

He pounded my right shoulder with the butt of the revolver. "Think harder, mister detective," he said. "You know exactly what I'm talking about, and it ends right now." The Slab pounded my left shoulder this time, then turned to leave. "For your sake," he said, "I hope we've seen the last of each other."

I looked over at my companions once I was reasonably certain I wasn't going to vomit. Mishkin held his legs tightly together and was bent over at the waist. Sig sat erect with his hands locked together on his lap.

"Was that from Kahn?" Sig asked nervously.

"Probably. Almost certainly."

"Oh my God," Mishkin squealed. "What if he finds out that we talked?"

"Should we go after him?" Sig asked.

"Not unless you've got a gun hidden under your towel," I said. "I've already taken a beating today. I'd prefer not to get shot on top of it."

Sig escorted Mishkin out of the steam room, then came back to help me. I told him I needed to stay put for another few minutes.

"You're getting too old for this kind of crap, Benny," he said.

"I've always been too old for this kind of crap."

"I've never seen this side of Mendel. I'd leave him alone if I were you."

"You're probably right, Sig," I said. "But think about it. Kahn's a goddamned fraud, regardless of what he did or didn't do with the Nazis. He presents himself as a respectable businessman, a real chamber-of-commerce type. But what he really is is a slum landlord with hired muscle."

"It's just a few of his properties," rationalized Sig.

"As far as we know now."

"His tenants got to live somewhere."

"Come on," I said. "They're *his* buildings. He can afford at least to make sure the plumbing works. And do something about the rats and the mice."

"Benny, I'd leave it alone."

"Would you want to live in a shit hole like that?"

I was in no condition to partake of the steak dinner that usually concluded a visit to the Schvitz. Sig helped me to the showers, where I rinsed myself just enough to put my clothes back on. Then I walked gingerly to the Edsel and drove myself home — no mean feat when I couldn't turn the steering wheel without wincing.

All in all, it could've been worse. The Hairy Slab could've beaten me to a pulp had he wanted to, or even shot me. I had no way to gauge how far Mendel Kahn would go to stop me from investigating his past. After what I learned at the *Schvitz,* I now had just as many questions about his present.

Nine

I CALLED ALVY Mishkin at his warehouse around lunchtime the next day. "Are you doing all right?" I asked him. "You got really upset yesterday when that goon tried to rough me up."

"Listen, Mr. Gold, I've got a family. I can't get involved in things that are none of my business."

"So I suppose you wouldn't even consider telling me the name of Mendel Kahn's company you have listed in your books."

"I checked this morning," he replied. "The name isn't there."

"Come on, Alvy. I'm sure you don't keep your records in disappearing ink."

"I told you, Mr. Gold. I don't want to get involved."

Mishkin's stonewalling didn't surprise me. I really only contacted him as a way of putting off the other, more difficult call I intended to make.

"Mendel Kahn's office," said the woman who answered.

"It's Benjamin Gold. Is he available?"

Kahn waited nearly two minutes before getting on the line. "Mr. Gold," he said in a controlled tone. "To what do I owe the pleasure?"

"I just wanted to let you know I ran into a friend of yours yesterday afternoon at the *Schvitz*."

"I think I may have heard something about that."

"He made sure to pass on your good wishes," I said.

"Well, if you say so."

"I most certainly do," I said. "Mr. Kahn, you and I need to talk. The sooner, the better, as far as I'm concerned."

I thought he'd put up a fight, but he agreed immediately and invited me to meet at his office at three-thirty that afternoon. I thanked him and hung up the telephone.

Over the course of a sleepless night, I had decided I needed to see Kahn. No one liked playing the victim, but I'd done exactly that in offering no resistance to the blows landed by the Hairy Slab. Redemption would come only from confronting Kahn and showing him I wasn't someone he could easily intimidate.

I also wanted a chance to sort out the enigma created by all the contradictions and gaps I'd uncovered in Kahn's background. He was a real estate mogul who owned only a few properties, according to the records. He was a pillar of the business community who exploited poor Negroes by renting them squalid, practically uninhabitable tenements. He'd suffered the unspeakable tragedy of having his wife and children exterminated by the Nazis, but for all I knew, he served as their willing accomplice in other crimes.

Finding his cousin (if I ever managed to do so) could at least resolve this last point. I supposed that would conclude my investigation, other issues notwithstanding. Herb had engaged me to determine Kahn's complicity with the Germans, not his eligibility for sainthood. If he turned out not to be Yitzhak Fried, the rest of it made no difference under the original assignment.

But that didn't entirely make sense. Herb Kline wanted to know about Kahn's history because he worried it might reflect negatively on the Temple. The Temple's reputation would also take a pounding if it came to light that a slumlord served on its board of trustees and acted as its principal spokesman in raising funds for a new building. Either way, the Rabbi needed the truth about Kahn, sooner rather than later. I hoped meeting Kahn would advance that goal.

Kahn's office was in the Hanna Building, at Fourteenth and Euclid. The weather was decent for October, so I decided to walk. The streets were uncrowded when I set out, shortly after three. The lunchtime rush had long ended, and the bustle of Friday evening wouldn't begin for at least an hour.

I arrived at the building right on time and took the elevator to the twelfth floor, where Kahn had his office. A receptionist a few years younger than Methuselah asked my name and directed me to a long gray couch to park myself and wait. The place was nothing fancy. The receptionist's desk sat in front of two oak doors spaced about fifteen feet apart. In between hung a sign that read "Mendel Kahn Real Estate" in navy blue letters. Kahn's name appeared on one of the doors. The other door was unmarked.

Kahn emerged after around five minutes and grunted an invitation for me to join him. I walked into an office that was much smaller than I'd expected. The desk seemed to occupy half the space. It was covered with stacks of papers, some of them neatly arranged, others haphazardly so. In one clearing sat the telephone and the intercom box. In another, the stub of a cigar smoldered in an ashtray of clear glass.

Kahn's office looked out onto Euclid Avenue. He had a clear view of the marquees at the Palace and the State. On the wall across the room, there hung around a dozen color photographs of apartment buildings, each basking in bright sunshine. I walked over to take a closer look.

"Are these all of your properties?" I asked Kahn.

"Oh, no," he answered. "We have twenty-one in total."

"All apartments?"

"About half are boarding houses and two-family residences. We also own an office building in downtown Akron."

"You say 'we', Mr. Kahn. Do you have partners?"

The expression on Kahn's face told me I'd asked one question too many. "I was using it as a figure of speech," he said curtly. "There are others who've invested in the properties, but I'm the owner, more or less."

"The "more or less" made no sense, unless it acknowledged Kahn's use of an intermediary company to hold his real estate. I had half a mind to ask about it but decided not to put him on the spot.

I sat down in a chair in front of Kahn's desk, and Kahn sat in the chair behind it. I hemmed and hawed for a moment, then thanked Kahn for agreeing to see me on such short notice.

"You said on the telephone we needed to talk," he said. "About what, exactly?"

"Mr. Kahn, you obviously know I've been hired to investigate you, and you obviously don't like it, judging from the way your man worked me over yesterday."

"Would you like it, Mr. Gold, if your friends and acquaintances were hounded for information about you? Would you like to have your picture taken in public places against your will?"

"That reminds me," I said as I reached inside my suit and removed a small brown envelope containing the negatives of the photos I shot at Corky & Lenny's. "These are from the other day, at the delicatessen."

I handed the envelope over to Kahn. He removed the negatives one-by-one and held them up to the light.

"I went over the line by photographing you without your consent," I said. "I'm sorry if I embarrassed you."

"Well, okay," Kahn eventually responded. I thought for sure he'd ask me whether I'd had any prints made of the pictures. Since he didn't do so, I didn't have to lie by saying I hadn't. Turning over the negatives was a trick, designed to ratchet down Kahn's antipathy and butter him up for a less guarded conversation.

"Of course, I can't tell you the name of the client who hired me for this job," I resumed. "But I can assure you this only concerns the accusation concerning your history that were made at Temple Yom Kippur morning."

"What kind of assurance is that?"

"I just don't want you to think anything else is at play."

"Listen, those accusations are destroying my standing in the business community," said Kahn.

"So far I've found no evidence that completely closes the book on them."

"You have my word, which is all you should need. Your client needs to mind his own business."

I shifted in my seat. "Mr. Kahn, they say you have a cousin who brought you to this country who can verify your identity."

"So you found out about that," Kahn grumbled. "Certainly he can verify who I am. That's what makes this all so absurd."

"I'm speculating," I said, "but I think your cousin is the one who got you started in real estate."

"Got me started? How?"

"With money," I said.

Spurts of guttural laughter emanated from Kahn's mouth. Each one seemed to rake against his abdomen, threatening his imminent collapse.

"My cousin is a postman," he explained when the fit ended. "I'm not sure he even owns his own house. He's got no money to invest."

"I'd like to meet your cousin," I said.

"He doesn't live in town," Kahn responded.

"I'll go to see him. If we could talk, I could wrap up this whole affair in no time."

"You think so?"

"Once he confirms he's your cousin and he brought you over," I said, "that ends the inquiry in my book."

"My receptionist has his address in Canton. His telephone number also. I'll get them for you before you leave."

Kahn spent the next half hour telling me his story. He came from Krakow, where he owned a tailoring business. The Nazis deported him and his family to Auschwitz, where his wife and two sons were immediately gassed. The Germans assigned him to a work camp, where he survived till the end of the War, then wandered between camps for displaced persons till he landed at one at Cremona in Italy. In the meantime, he had contacted his cousin, who arranged his passage to the United States.

It all sounded well and good, except that it didn't. Kahn recounted his past in a detached monotone, like he was reading from a script. Nothing evoked any feeling — not even the murder of his family. I realized Kahn might've been moderating his emotions to avoid a painful outburst. But he didn't seem to remember the names of his sons, referring to them only as the "older one" and the "younger one", even when the context called for more definite identification.

Kahn just didn't inspire confidence in his truth-telling. Doubt or deception tainted everything that came out of his mouth. He hadn't convinced me of his bona fides as a real estate magnate. He hadn't convinced me he was really Mendel Kahn. And I'd arrived at no benign explanation for why someone in his position would have a henchman on call to menace the people who bothered him.

"Let me get you the information about my cousin," Kahn said as the conversation wound down. He buzzed the intercom but got no response. He buzzed it again with the same result.

"Damn," he said. "I forgot Miss Lillibridge leaves at four on Fridays. I'll have to go out and find it myself."

Kahn walked out of the office, shutting the door behind him. I took this as my cue to see what I could find among the documents piled on his desk. I was looking for something that identified the company or partnership that held title to the properties Kahn didn't own in his own name. I worked as neatly as I could, so it wouldn't be obvious to Kahn that I'd rifled through his papers.

The meticulous approach didn't fit with the clock ticking on Kahn's reappearance. A minute passed, and then another, and I still hadn't found anything with the information I wanted. I was at Kahn's desk, beginning my perusal of a new stack of documents, when I heard the creak of the door.

I jumped back to my seat as quickly and quietly as I could. At the same time, I grabbed the carbon copy that sat on top of the pile, crumpled it up, and shoved into my pants pocket. I had no conception what the paper said — it could have been a dry cleaning receipt, for all I knew. But I wanted to give myself at least a shot at getting something useful out of my sleuthing. If it turned out to be useless, I'd be no worse off.

Kahn walked over and handed me a slip of paper. "Here's what you need to get in touch with my cousin," he said. "His name is Charlie Feigenbaum."

"He's not a Kahn?"

"He's from my mother's side of the family."

"I'll call him and set up a meeting."

I stood up to leave. We shook hands, and he accompanied me out of his office toward the exit. As we walked, the wad of carbon paper in my pants pocket began to rustle. I was sure Kahn would hear it, if he hadn't already. So I pretended to cough, all the way into the hallway.

"Are you all right?" Kahn asked.

"It's nothing," I replied. "I'll be fine."

That prognosis depended upon whether Kahn discovered the page was missing. If he did, it probably wouldn't take him too long to figure out where it went. Then I could expect another visit from the Hairy Slab. That pleasant thought percolated in my head as I walked back to the office.

Ten

I WOKE AT two-thirty the next morning to the sound of anguished groaning. The groaning came from me. I was having a nightmare about Ebensee, the concentration camp liberated by the Eightieth Infantry Division in May 1945, while I was part of the ranks.

The nightmare captured the scene in all its hideous detail. There were corpses on the ground, stacked like kindling. Stickmen in rags barely covering their cankered skin hoarsely pleaded with GIs in unintelligible languages.

I couldn't bear it at the time, and I couldn't bear it now. I found myself curled in a tight ball, fiercely clutching my knees. Cold sweat drenched my tee shirt and pillow. My eyes were wet, too, as though I'd been weeping copiously as I dreamed.

The worst of it was the confusion. I couldn't immediately tell where the bad dream ended and reality began. Even after I realized I wasn't really in Ebensee, I imagined I was locked in the bedroom of my dingy apartment on Euclid Heights Boulevard where I lived when I first got out of the service. Nightmares about the camp came several times a week at that location. The affliction had abated since then, but I'd never completely exorcized the demon. This night it reared its ugly head with a particular vengeance.

I was hardly surprised. I knew that investigating Mendel Kahn as a possible Nazi collaborator would inevitably immerse me in the atrocities I witnessed at Ebensee and the guilt I felt for being a collaborator myself.

I personally killed two prisoners in camp. I did so by feeding them chocolate when their bodies had degenerated to a point where they couldn't tolerate food that rich. I certainly hadn't meant to do it, and others at Ebensee perished the same inadvertent way. But none of that made my victims any less dead. I'd punched their tickets as irrevocably as the Nazis ever could have.

I'd already been teetering on the verge of a nervous breakdown when we arrived at Ebensee. The killings propelled me over the edge. From my lunatic perspective, I myself became a perpetrator of the torture and abuse that afflicted the prisoners. My guilt differed only by a matter of degree from that of the commandants and the flunkies who carried out their orders. There was no defense for what I had done (or, mostly, hadn't done).

The other insanity churning through my head at the time arose from my distorted identity on the home front. Before the War, I had been a Jewish boy who married into Gentile aristocracy, accepted a position at a blue-blooded white-shoe law firm, lived in a segregated suburb, changed my name, and otherwise remade myself in the image of my in-laws, whose unapologetic anti-Semitism would've played well in Berlin. This radical reinvention left me at serious odds with my parents, both of whom passed away before I could mend any fences. My brother, Jake, meanwhile, out-and-out disowned me after he became convinced I was beyond rehabilitation. As for my marriage, the spare correspondence I received in Europe from my alcoholic wife foreshadowed that our impending divorce was a question of when, not if.

The recrimination and misery reached a crescendo in Ebensee, right after I killed the two boys. I simply disintegrated. I couldn't carry on a normal conversation or take care of myself in even the simplest ways. The Army, for once, cut through the red tape. Within two weeks I was checked in at a psych ward on Long Island.

And now the Kahn investigation was triggering a vulnerability I'd thought I had under control. After the years I'd spent on a psychiatrist's couch, I understood the futility of trying to suppress the turbulence over Ebensee that the case had rekindled. I couldn't just forbid my brain to replay the gruesome memories. As long as I had to deal with Kahn, I'd be thinking about Nazi war crimes. And if I was thinking about the Nazi crimes, I'd be reliving that ghoulish experience at Ebensee. Nightmares about the camp would remain a regular on the play bill until I finished the job.

I pulled myself out of bed and straggled to the bathroom for a quick shower, then made my way to the bar in the living room for a rye-and-soda. It was just past three o'clock, but I had no interest in returning to bed and risking more disturbing dreams about Ebensee. I sat on the couch till morning, finishing off a bottle and cursing the fates that crossed my path with Mendel Kahn's.

Eleven

The page I'd pilfered from Kahn's office turned out to be a copy of a letter he wrote to accompany payment to a window-washing service for work performed at apartment buildings in Bratenahl, Westlake, and East Cleveland. Kahn signed the correspondence in his capacity as President of Kandee Incorporated. The letter didn't explicitly say that Kandee owned the three properties, but I didn't see any other way to interpret it. On Monday, I asked Evie to find out everything she could about any company having that name.

By mid-week, I knew that Kandee Incorporated had been formed in Ohio in 1951 by someone named Oscar Eckhardt. In its filings with the Secretary of State, Kandee listed its purpose as "acquiring and holding real estate (primarily residential) in Ohio". The papers didn't say who owned how much of the company, but the pieces seemed to fit together. K and E made "KandE(e)" — the name seemed to be a combination of the last initials of Kahn and Eckhardt. Finally, I'd struck gold. I had found the company that Kahn used to operate his real estate business.

"Call Mark Brandon over at Centennial Title and tell him I need a list of everything Kandee owns in Cuyahoga County," I told Evie. "Ask him to check Summit County and Lake County as well."

"Will do, Mr. G."

"Tell him we need it in a hurry and not to charge us an arm and a leg."

"Got it."

I waited on the results while I waited for my Wednesday get-together with Charlie Feigenbaum. I had telephoned him immediately upon returning to my office from my meeting with Kahn.

"What can I do you for, Mr. Gold?" he'd asked after I introduced myself.

"I got your name from Mendel Kahn. He's a relative of yours, as I understand it."

"Mr. Kahn's mother was my mother's sister," he explained. "I helped him move to this country."

"I'd like to talk to you about that, Mr. Feigenbaum. There are some people who may have confused your cousin with someone else, another gentleman who lived in Poland before the War. To confirm Mr. Kahn is who he says he is, I'm checking up on his background."

"That seems kind of screwy, if you ask me."

"It might very well be. But the sooner I corroborate the truth, the sooner I can put the rumors to bed."

"I don't know how much I can really tell you," said Feigenbaum. "But ask what you want, I suppose, and I'll answer as best I can."

"Actually, Mr. Feigenbaum, I was hoping we could do this face-to-face. Would it be all right if I came and visited you down in Canton?"

"I've got a busy weekend planned," he responded. "Next weekend would be better."

"Is there any way we could do it sooner than that?"

Feigenbaum hemmed and hawed but eventually invited me for dinner on Wednesday. "My wife will whip up something," he said.

Pot roast with noodle casserole was the culinary delight Mrs. Feigenbaum served that evening. The fifty-mile drive down from Cleveland took half an hour longer than usual, given the steady, swirling rain that began mid-afternoon. I pulled up to the small two-story house on Fifth Street just past six-thirty.

"Come in out of the weather," Feigenbaum greeted me at the front door. "It's almost time to eat."

Feigenbaum was tall and lean, with thinning gray hair, distinctly brown teeth, and a bulbous nose. Standing in his corduroy slacks and plaid flannel shirt, he looked not a bit like his putative cousin. That proved nothing, of course, but given my suspicions about Kahn's identity, I was ready to pounce on any possible discrepancy.

I assessed the interior decorating of the place as we waited for Feigenbaum's wife to call us to dinner. It was all clean and tasteful, but it didn't speak of the sort of wealth I'd thought Feigenbaum might possess. Wherever Kahn got the dough for his initial real estate purchases, it almost certainly didn't come from his American cousin.

"Bring him on in, Charlie," Feigenbaum's wife bellowed from the dining room.

Feigenbaum introduced the two of us after he and I answered the call. "Thanks very much for having me to dinner, Mrs. Feigenbaum," I said.

"Call me Rose. I prefer my first name to my last."

"Now, Rose, don't start," cautioned her husband.

Feigenbaum and I sat down. The sniping momentarily chilled the conversation. We passed the serving pieces around the table in silence.

"How long have the two of you lived in Canton?" I finally asked.

"Since 1938," responded Feigenbaum. "That's when I got my first route."

"That's right," I said. "Mr. Kahn said you worked for the Post Office."

"Speaking of Kahn," Rose interjected, "Charlie says he's the reason you've driven all the way down here. What's it all about?"

I finished chewing the leathery piece of pot roast I'd put into my mouth. "It may all be a misunderstanding," I said as soon as I was able. "Someone's raised a question about whether Mr. Kahn is really who he says he is. I'm investigating the matter."

"You some sort of detective?"

"I told you that, Rose," Feigenbaum muttered.

"Well, as far as I'm concerned, Kahn is a big fat impostor," she said. "He presents himself as a big-time real estate tycoon, but he's really just a penny-pinching slob."

"You'll have to forgive my wife," Feigenbaum said angrily. "She holds a grudge against Mendel for not giving our son all the help she thought he deserved."

Rose recounted the plight of son Harold, who'd had an unremarkable military career as a private in Korea and came back without a job or any prospects. After he'd unsuccessfully pounded the pavement in Canton, Rose got the idea that her husband's rich cousin could set him up in business.

"So you and Kahn are close?" I asked Feigenbaum as she told the story.

"Not really," he said. "Not at all. He stayed with us for about a month when he arrived from Europe. We've only spoken a few times since then. But we kept tabs on him — learned about all the apartment buildings he bought and all the work he does for Jewish charities. I'm proud to be his cousin."

"A lot to be proud of," said Rose, "after he treated your son like a louse."

Harold, it seemed, had always dreamed of running his own service station. Rose believed it was practically Kahn's obligation to provide the seed money, after her husband brought him to this country. At the very least, Rose expected her son to receive an offer to work in Kahn's organization, managing one of his buildings or some such position, with a decent salary and room for advancement.

"But that bum pretended to hardly know who Harold was when he called," Rose recounted with disgust. "He eventually took him to Sunday breakfast at some diner and told him stories about growing up in Krakow. Harold could hardly get a word in edgewise. At the end of the meal, Mendel handed him seventy-five dollars in cash and wished him well. That was it."

"We've been over this a hundred times, Rose," said Feigenbaum. "Harold is our headache, not my cousin's. He didn't have to give him anything at all."

"He's a fake, I tell you," Rose retorted. "He's not the high roller he claims to be."

"You misunderstand, Mrs. Feigenbaum," I said. "No one's questioning Mendel Kahn's wealth or his position in the business community. What they suggest is that Kahn literally is someone else, that he's not really your husband's cousin but a Nazi collaborator who snuck into this country under that alias."

"That just can't be true," said Feigenbaum. "We would've seen right through it."

"How so? Had you ever met him, or even seen his picture, before he got here?"

"No, but I'd heard about him since I was a kid. My mother came over with her older brother in 1912. She and Mendel's mother were very close. They kept in touch to the extent they could over the years."

"They wrote to one another?" I asked.

"Once or twice a year. Maybe a little less frequently. The mail moved slow between here and Poland."

"What was in the letters?"

"Family stuff, mainly, I suppose," Feigenbaum answered. "They were written in Yiddish, so I couldn't have read them myself even if I got the chance."

Feigenbaum's aunt had married a jeweler two decades older than she whose first wife had died. Mendel was their only child. The correspondence to Feigenbaum's mother described him as a short, thin kid who turned out to be a prodigy on the violin. By age eleven, Kahn was playing concerts with a chamber quartet in Krakow.

"Did he bring a violin with him from Europe?" I asked Feigenbaum.

"Naw. He had one small suitcase of clothes, and not much else."

I got down to the nitty gritty. "How did Kahn get in touch with you after the War?"

"A letter arrived at my mother's apartment in the fall of '47," Feigenbaum said. "My sister moved in there after my mother died. She took it to a friend to have her father translate it and then brought the translation to me."

"What did the letter say?"

"Mendel wrote that his entire family was dead. Mother. Father. His wife and kids. The Nazis gassed them all. Only he survived, and he was moving from detention camp to detention camp."

"What else did he say?"

"He asked whether there was some way we could bring him to this country," Feigenbaum said. "He wanted to come really bad."

"So what did you do?"

"He did whatever it took, that's what he did," said Rose as she stood to clear the dishes. "He did what you're supposed to do when someone in the family needs help."

Feigenbaum ignored his wife's editorializing. "It took a while to figure out," he said. "Eventually our rabbi directed us to a Jewish agency in New York, which took it from there."

Kahn landed in the U.S. in February of 1948. He moved into the Feigenbaums' basement but didn't stay for all that long. After three and a half weeks, during breakfast, he presented his hosts with a bank check for the cost of his passage and announced he was moving to Cleveland.

"Where'd he get the money?" I asked.

"I don't know," Feigenbaum responded. "He wasn't working, as far as we could tell. He'd disappear for hours at a time but never said where he went."

"Did he speak any English?"

"He spoke it decently enough."

"A lot of good it did us," said Rose as she returned from the kitchen with an unappetizing hunk of apple pie. "He never told us anything. The guy barely talked."

"After what he'd been through, what was there to say?" observed her husband.

"Did he have any photographs of the family; any keepsakes, or things like that?"

"Not that he showed to us," Feigenbaum said.

"Did he say anything that confirmed in your mind that he actually was your cousin from Poland?"

"He didn't say much of anything, like I told you," said Rose. "He could've been almost anyone."

"Now listen," Feigenbaum firmly stated. "I'm sure the authorities checked to make sure Mendel was really Mendel before they put him on a boat to come over here. And whatever he did or didn't say to us, we had no reason to question whether he was really someone else. If you're trying to prove otherwise, Mr. Gold, you'll not get any proof in this house."

"You're probably right," I said.

Feigenbaum had told me as much as he wanted to, and I had no intention of subjecting him to the third degree. So I changed the subject, asking about the current occupation of son Harold (he managed a car wash on Cleveland's East Side) and Feigenbaum's future plans (five years and counting till retirement). I forced myself to eat the miserable pie. I made more small talk. The evening ended around nine o'clock, when I thanked the Feigenbaums for their hospitality and headed to my car for the drive back home.

Twelve

I ARRIVED EARLY at the office the next morning, fully intending to prepare a detailed summary of the news from the night before. I'd forgotten, though, that the Dictabelt was on the fritz, and Evie was busy with other things. I didn't want to write the thing out longhand, so I sat at my desk, cradling a cup of coffee and reviewing the multiple reasons why I thought I could nail Mendel Kahn as an imposter and a fraud.

Not that I had an open-and-shut case. Feigenbaum was undoubtedly right in assuming that Kahn only got permission to come to this country after proving he was who he said he was. There must've been an arduous process for corroborating the identity of would-be emigres. Even before confronting that challenge, Yitzhak Fried would've had to dispose of the real Mendel Kahn without anyone's noticing. And he'd somehow have to pull that off only after Kahn sent his letter to Feigenbaum's mother, or after learning enough about Kahn to forge the correspondence himself.

That was a pretty large helping of maybes and what-ifs for anyone to stomach. But still, the established facts suggested that Kahn wasn't being truthful about his past. He'd presented no tangible evidence of his identity to his cousin in Canton. Nor had he discussed family history or displayed any knowledge of information that only the real Mendel Kahn would possess. The man had a fetish for secrecy, shunning photographs and hiding ownership of his real estate in an obscure corporation. He'd unleashed a member of his personal goon squad when my inquiries about his past hit too close to home. Then there was his former girlfriend, who perceived in him a ruthlessness that (from my perspective, at least) befit a Nazi collaborator like Yitzhak Fried.

The intercom buzzed with news from Evie that Mendel Kahn was calling. "By all means, I'll take it," I told her.

"Mr. Gold, I understand you met with my cousin last evening," he said.

"News travels fast . . ."

"So it went well? Mr. Feigenbaum answered all of your questions?"

"Charlie and Rose were as forthcoming as they could be," I responded. "They told me how you came to live with them after arriving from Europe."

"So you're done now? The investigation's finished?"

"Not quite yet. There are a few odds and ends I've got to deal with before closing the file."

Kahn was not happy. "Mr. Gold, you told me you'd be done after interviewing my cousin."

"I don't recall saying exactly that," I said. "But if I did, I was mistaken. There are really just a few items left. It shouldn't take long."

Kahn started to complain, but I interrupted him. "I've got to tell you, I was very impressed by some of the things I learned about you last night," I said. "Charlie told me you were some sort of prodigy on the piano."

"That was a long time ago," Kahn said.

"Do you still play?"

"I don't own a piano."

"How about another instrument?" I pressed on. "Charlie seemed to recall you played several."

"My cousin was mistaken. I only played the one."

"You mean piano..."

"Yes," he said in a near whisper.

"You held recitals on the piano in your synagogue..."

"Right," he confirmed even more softly.

"You really must've been something."

Kahn was something, all right. His cousin had described him as an aspiring Heifetz rather than a Rubinstein — the violin was his instrument, not the piano. Kahn couldn't explain away this inconsistency. He was either hallucinating an imaginary childhood or blatantly lying about who he really was.

After hanging up, I decided to call Herb Kline to fill him in on what I had learned about his favorite congregant. "Kahn has been flimflamming you," I told him. "The man isn't who he says he is."

"You spoke to the cousin?"

"Yes."

"He didn't back Mendel up?"

"He did," I said, "but he's missing the bigger picture."

"Benny," said the Rabbi forlornly. "Maybe we've taken this as far as we should. If the man is pretending to be someone he isn't, let him go on pretending."

"I thought you were getting pressure from your congregants to do something about Kahn."

"I'm thinking that maybe what they don't know can't hurt them. The yentas can gossip, but without proof, it'll eventually fade. This all will pass, and we'll get the money Mendel's raised for the new building."

"This guy's a nogoodnik, Herb," I told the Rabbi. "Even if he didn't do the Nazis' bidding. He's not an honest businessman. His hands aren't clean."

"I told you I've had my suspicions all along about Mendel," answered Herb. "It's just..."

"Don't back out on me now, Herb. We've got to show the world who this guy really is."

"This guy sits on my board of trustees," said the Rabbi. "He'll have me fired in a heartbeat if he finds out I'm secretly investigating him."

Herb hung up with only a conditional commitment to continuing the case against Kahn. His second thoughts didn't please me, but ultimately they made no difference. With or without the Rabbi, I was going to see the assignment through.

There were several reasons for my persistence. Part of it was sheer curiosity. I wanted to find out who Kahn really was. Part of it was payback. My left shoulder still throbbed every morning from my tête-à-tête with the Hairy Slab.

But the motivation also came from a sense of responsibility. Kahn may have worked for the Germans. He probably defrauded his way into this country, then assembled a real estate portfolio teeming with squalid tenements. A resume like that cried out for investigation. If the charges held up, someone had to expose Kahn and hold him accountable.

I would've preferred not to be that someone. Given my twisted reaction to what I saw at Ebensee, the less I had to think about Nazi atrocities, the better. I never had a hankering to be an immigration cop. And while I abhorred the idea of slumlords, I was no crusader for the poverty-stricken, or crusader of any kind, for that matter.

Still, there was no one else in a position then and there to take on

Mendel Kahn (or whatever his name really was). I'd stick with the job, if for no other reason that relinquishing it would require me to bury my head in the sand all the way to my belly button.

None of this made me noble or heroic. I hoped it also didn't make me a sucker.

Thirteen

The tour of the Kandee apartments began with one on Clifton Boulevard in Lakewood, just east of the park. I'd intended to concentrate my inspections on the inner-city properties and skip those in the suburbs. But I had a meeting at eight o'clock one morning at an architect's office a few blocks away to review a background check I'd prepared on his new office manager. As long as I was in the vicinity, I thought I'd squeeze it in.

The apartment on Clifton was a three-story, brown-brick structure with five windows symmetrically spaced on the second and third floors and three bay windows spread across the first. The building was called the "Bluffington Place", according to the words sculpted above the front door. I didn't much care for the name, though I supposed it was better than "Kandee Manor" or "Kahn Court".

I managed to slip inside the building to look for someone to interview. The halls, however, were empty. Commuters had left the premises at least an hour earlier. I was ready to knock on some random door when a thin middle-aged woman in a plaid housecoat stepped out of Apartment 113 carrying a bag of rubbish. I intercepted her on the way to the incinerator and introduced myself as a field worker for the County Residential Control Board.

"County Residential Control Board?" the woman questioned, a half-smoked cigarette dangling from her lips. "I never heard of it."

That wasn't surprising, since I had made up the agency on the spot. I embellished the hoax by saying I was doing a survey of landlord-tenant relations in suburban apartments. I asked whether she'd sit for an interview.

"I suppose so," she said. "We can talk in my apartment after I dump the trash."

I accompanied the woman to the basement, then followed her into the kitchen of Apartment 113. Breakfast dishes covered almost the entire table.

"Frank just left for work, and I didn't have a chance to clean up," my hostess explained as she cleared the mess and dumped it into the sink.

"That's all right," I said. "Shall I wait in the living room?"

"We can talk right here."

I sat down at the kitchen table and pulled a pad from my coat pocket to take notes. "Now first off," I began, "let me get your name."

"Betty Bristol," said the woman. "Mrs. Frank Bristol. But isn't this survey anonymous?"

"It can be if you want it to. How long have you lived in the building?"

"Since 1952," Betty said. "How ever many years that is. We came here when Frank's company transferred him from the Toledo office."

I asked how much she and her husband paid in rent when they first moved in, and how much they currently paid. Then I asked about the plumbing and the heat and whether the landlord kept up with repairs and building maintenance.

"They do all right," said Betty.

"The place got a manager?"

"The old lady down in 101. She's a real nightmare."

"How so?"

"God forbid you have a conversation in the hallway after nine o'clock," Betty said. "She'll write you up for creating a nuisance. It happens a couple of times, and you get a letter from the landlord."

"Speaking of the landlord," I said, "our files show that a company called Kandee Incorporated owns the property. Is that right?"

"I've never heard that name. I thought the owner was Mr. Conway."

"Conway?"

"He's the one we meet with to renew the lease," Betty explained.

"He claimed to own the building?"

"He and his partner."

"Who's his partner?"

"I'm not sure," she said. "I've never met him."

I pulled a photograph of Mendel Kahn from my coat pocket and placed it in front of her. It was one of the shots I'd taken at the delicatessen during my niece's phantom birthday breakfast.

"Is this gentleman Mr. Conway?" I asked.

Betty glanced at the photograph, then looked suspiciously over at me. "Say," she said. "Are you with the police? Did this guy do something wrong?"

I couldn't immediately come up with a pretext for showing the photo. So I went with a partial version of the truth.

"I thought the man in this picture owned this building, through a company called Kandee," I said. "You've confused me a little, since his name isn't Conway. It's Mendel Kahn."

"Well, that's Conway," said Betty. "I must've misheard the name. He speaks with an accent."

"What do you know about Mr. Conway?"

Betty had very little to tell me. When Kahn came to renew the lease, she and her husband talked to him about the rent or repairs they wanted done in their apartment. That was it. Kahn never spoke about himself. Betty didn't know where he came from, whether he had a wife and family, or anything else.

"So he isn't much on chit chat," I summarized.

"Mr. Conway comes to get a lease signed, not to chew the fat."

Betty pulled a pack of cigarettes from the pocket of her housecoat and lit one up. I asked if I could join her, and she passed the pack to me.

"So what makes you think Conway had a partner?" I asked after taking my first drag.

"He told us so."

"When did he do that?"

"One year, the new lease raised the rent by eight dollars a month," Betty explained. "Frank objected, said that was just too steep, and asked Conway to cut it in half. Mr. Conway refused. He said he and his partner had discussed the matter at length, and they concluded their apartments were underpriced by twelve dollars a month. The partner wanted to raise the rent the full twelve. Mr. Conway convinced him to leave it at eight."

"Did Conway tell you the name of his partner or anything about him?"

"Not that I recall," said Betty.

"Was is Oscar Eckhardt?"

"It could've been, for all I remember. Mr. Conway just mentioned he'd spoken to his partner, who wanted to charge more than Mr. Conway did."

I interviewed two other tenants before leaving the building. Both recognized Kahn from his photograph and identified him as the owner of the apartments. They each described him as close-lipped and distant, just as Betty had, and couldn't offer any insight to his character or personal history. One of them knew Kahn had a "partner" in owning the property. She hadn't ever seen the man, though, and didn't know his name.

The tenants of Bluffington Place confirmed that Kandee Incorporated consisted of Kahn and perhaps a partner, who might've been Oscar Eckhardt, the company's nominal founder.

When I made it to the office, I checked the Cleveland phone directory and found no listing under that name. I called the operator for assistance but drew the same blank.

I half-suspected that Eckhardt didn't really exist. Kahn might've created him as a fictional straw man to do business under a name other than his own. Of course, Marty Bluestein's cousin was accusing Kahn of pulling effectively the same stunt to evade Yitzhak Fried's sinister past and to punch his ticket to the U.S. of A.

This nifty parallel only got me so far. Kahn openly admitted his interest in at least the respectable buildings owned by Kandee. Pictures of them prominently hung on the walls of his office. Anyone who checked the records could identify the company as the actual owner of the properties. These facts established a concrete connection between Kahn and Kandee, which the presence of a phony partner would not obscure.

Kahn might use Eckhardt as a foil for unpopular decisions, like raising Frank and Betty Bristol's rent. He could cite Eckhardt's supposed involvement to mitigate his own personal responsibility for Kandee's tenements, if anyone ever called him on it. But if Kahn were really trying to shroud his interest in the company or its properties, he could've done a lot better than fabricating an off-the-rack partner.

Chances were that Eckhardt was real. If I wanted the truth about Kahn's business, I'd have to find the son-of-a-bitch.

FOURTEEN

I ARRIVED LATE at the office the next morning. Waiting for me was a short, stocky man sitting on the sofa across from Evie's desk.

"This is Doctor Fleischman," Evie told me. "He wants to talk to you."

"Greetings," I said as I extended my right hand to the doc. "What type of medicine do you practice?"

"I'm not a physician," Fleischman responded. "I'm a college professor."

I checked the guy out. He wore a rumpled blue suit over an unpressed white shirt with a plain black tie. A scuffed pair of brown loafers adorned his feet. He had gray hair, which he shaved in an army cut, and brown horn-rimmed glasses with thick lenses. Fleischman was a college professor, all right. He came straight from central casting.

He gave me his personal story after we moved to my private office. He taught European History at C.C.N.Y. in New York City, and had done so for three years, after spending nearly a decade at the University of Minnesota. He originally came from Baltimore and was in town for the funeral of his uncle, Moe Fleischman, a former cab driver who succumbed to failing health at the age of seventy-nine.

Fleischman declined the offer of a cigarette. He did not want a cup of coffee.

"So how can I help you, Professor?" I asked.

Fleischman didn't immediately answer. I posed my question again, but he still said nothing as he repositioned himself in the chair facing my desk.

"Well, I'm just going to come out and say it," he finally blurted. "This may be inappropriate, and if it is, I'm sure you'll tell me so."

"Have at it."

"Last night at dinner, my aunt told me about the incident at her temple on Yom Kippur involving that... Mr. Kahn, was it? Someone has accused him of being a Nazi collaborator during the War. My aunt also said that word on the street is that you're investigating the allegations. I came to ask whether you would tell me what you'd found out."

Fleishman had been justified in his hesitancy. His inquiry was inappropriate, and not by a close margin. I was a private investigator, not the Associated Press. I didn't typically make my work product available for public consumption, on demand or otherwise.

His request flummoxed me for a different reason. I hadn't realized that anyone other than the Rabbi, Evie, Sig Danziger, and Sophie Himmel knew I was looking into the charges against Kahn. I couldn't fathom how my assignment possibly could've become the "word on the street" and reached the likes of Mrs. Moe Fleischman or the anonymous others who told her about it.

If I succeeded in confirming that Mendel Kahn was the war criminal I thought he was, I would share the insight with anyone who cared to hear. But I wasn't keen on having everyone know about my research on Kahn as it was taking place.

Fleischman's intrusion would just be the beginning. I didn't want to answer a constant onslaught of questions, and I didn't want to listen to people's preconceived notions about Kahn's guilt or innocence. Investigating Kahn was difficult enough without having to contend with ardent rooting sections for and against him.

"Professor Fleischman," I said, "I wasn't at that temple on Yom Kippur, and the work I do for clients is strictly confidential. I can't possibly let you know what I'm looking into or what I've found."

"I see."

"You may be curious, but I just can't give you what you want."

"It's not just idle curiosity, Mr. Gold," said Fleischman. "I told you I teach European History. One of the areas of my research is the Nazi extermination of the Jews."

"I didn't realize..."

"How could you?" he replied, "It's a dynamic field. We're learning more and more about the historical roots of German antisemitism. And we're getting a pretty good conception of the protocols the Nazis used to make their killing machine so efficient."

"But why the interest in Mendel Kahn's story?"

"I'm doing a study of the Judenraete, the Jewish councils appointed by the Germans in the cities and towns during the War," Fleischman explained. "Mr. Kahn was supposedly part of that."

I looked over at Fleischman and smiled. The man wasn't just a nosy busybody. He also was a potential expert witness, someone who could educate me about the type of wrongs Kahn had supposedly committed.

"Have you had lunch?" I asked him.

"No, not yet."

"Well, it's on me," I said. "I can't answer your questions, but you can definitely answer some of mine."

"I don't understand, Mr. Gold."

"Let's just say that if I were looking into Mendel Kahn's past, I'd want to have some idea of what I was seeing."

Evie ended up ordering sandwiches from a shop around the corner. We ate at the small table in my office. As Fleischman dug into his turkey on pumpernickel, I asked whether he believed the men who served on the Jewish councils were Nazi collaborators.

"I would say yes, for the most part," he answered. "The Judenraete did the bidding of the Germans. They solved all the practical problems of crowding thousands and thousands of people into small ghettoes and eventually delivering them for extermination. This was an important cog in the genocide."

"How did someone become a member of the Judenraete?"

"There were supposedly elections in each town or district. But really the Germans appointed whoever they wanted. It was mostly rabbis and bigwigs in the community."

"Could a person refuse to serve?"

"Yes," Fleischman said. "That's an important fact. It wasn't easy, but many did decline a position on the Judenrat. In some cities, there was widespread resistance to serving."

I refilled Fleischman's water glass from a pitcher Evie had left on the table. "So what did the councils do exactly?" I asked. "What were their responsibilities?"

"They were the Germans' functionaries," the professor said. "They arranged housing for the Jews moving into the ghetto. They rationed food and medical supplies and oversaw the little business that still could take place. If the Nazis wanted a work detail for some project, the Judenrat would supply the manpower. And when it was time to move the Jews to the camps, they would arrange for that, too."

"Why did people agree to serve?" I asked. "What was in it for them?"

"If you listen to the ones who survived the War, they all tell you they were doing it to help their fellow Jews, to make a horrible situation a little more tolerable."

"But you don't believe that."

"It's a convenient retelling of history," Fleischman said. "The Judenraete helped the Germans perpetrate evil. Who's to say how seriously they would have impaired the Nazi genocide if they hadn't cooperated?"

"So they were all scoundrels?"

"I wouldn't go that far. Some of them probably were really acting out of a sense of civic responsibility, and in some cities, the Judenrat secretly assisted the underground in its fight against the Nazis. But these were the exceptions, not the rule."

Fleischman excused himself to wash his hands, and I cleaned up the debris from our meal. When he returned, I asked whether he'd heard the accusation that Mendel Kahn extorted bribes from people in the community who were looking to avoid labor assignments or deportation.

"Yes," he said. "My aunt told me about that."

"Did that sort of thing really go on?"

"Many members of the Judenraete peddled their influence. They gave preferential treatment to those who won their favor. Sometimes that happened through a bribe."

"So this was widespread?"

"It wasn't uncommon," said Fleischman. "Of course, you can't bribe someone if you don't have anything to bribe them with. The Jews in the ghettos had already lost much of their property by the time they arrived."

"So...?"

"So there were practical constraints on the amount of bribes the Judenraete could get. But rest assured that there were plenty of corrupt members, and some of them undoubtedly did do the sorts of things Mr. Kahn is accused of doing."

Fleischman and I talked for another ten minutes before he stood up to leave. I thanked him for his patience and insights.

"My pleasure," he said. "Glad to help out on the case you may or may not be handling."

"You know, if I *were* investigating Kahn, I probably would've asked if I could call you if some issue arose along the way that required an explanation."

"If that had happened," Fleischman replied, "I would have said you could reach me anytime at my office at the College."

"So long as we understand one another," I said.

Fleischman thanked me for lunch and headed for the elevators.

FIFTEEN

I DECIDED TO call Sophie Himmel to see if she could tell me anything about Mendel Kahn's business partner. I figured she might know something, given how long she and Kahn had been a couple.

But Sophie had a bone to pick with me when I got her on the telephone. "I ran into Mendel at a friend's party last week," she said snippily. "And he was very upset that you and I had talked."

"I'm sorry," I said. "It would've been best if he'd never found out about our meeting."

"I agree. I never would've come if you'd told me you were going to let everyone know about it."

"I didn't," I replied. "The only people privy to that information are on this telephone call."

"What about your secretary?"

"I forgot about Evie. But I can vouch for her. She's got her lip tightly buttoned. Believe me — what happens in our office stays in our office."

"Well, I certainly didn't talk to anyone."

"Kahn must've found out about it some other way."

"You know," Sophie said after a moment, "Mendel had me followed for a while after he dropped me. I called him and raised a stink about it once I realized what he was doing. I was sure that all had stopped by the time I came to your office, but maybe not."

"Why in the world was he having you tailed?" I asked.

"That's the charming side of Mendel's personality. He doesn't trust anyone. I think he expected me to retaliate against him for breaking off the relationship."

"Lovely," I said.

"But I'm pretty sure he stopped having me followed by the time I came to see you."

"You and I made our appointment over the phone," I said. "If he was having you followed, maybe he also tapped your line."

The suggestion resonated with Sophie. "Why, that bastard," she hissed. "That wouldn't surprise me at all. He cuts me out of his life, but he still wants to eavesdrop on my phone calls? I'll tell you what. I'm going to . . ."

"Miss Himmel," I interrupted. "If Kahn was listening then, he may be listening now. I think we should continue our conversation face-to-face, somewhere he doesn't know about in advance."

I arranged to pick up Sophie the next afternoon at four-thirty in front of her building. The call quickly ended.

Mendel Kahn was proving to have remarkable versatility as a low-life. He was a paranoid sneak who spied on his ex-girlfriend, just as he was a bully who had me worked over for asking touchy questions and a slumlord who exploited his tenants by renting out unspeakably wretched apartments. The jury was still out on whether Kahn was a victim of Nazi war crimes, as he claimed, or a fellow perpetrator. But in some respects, it didn't matter. Whatever Kahn did or didn't do during the War, he was a certifiable prick in the here-and-now.

When I picked Sophie up the following afternoon, she was still agitated over the notion that Kahn had tapped her telephone. "I should go to the police," she said. "This can't be legal."

"It's not," I replied. "But your ex-boyfriend's way too clever to let the setup be traced to him."

"Of course he is. Goddamn it! He doesn't have the right to treat me this way."

We drove silently for a few blocks while Sophie stewed. To break the tension, I suggested we drive to the Flat Iron and have a drink.

"The Flat Iron?" she answered. "I'm not sure I've ever been. Is Mendel likely to know the place?"

"Listen. We have to be careful, but Kahn can't hold us hostage. I think we'll be safe."

The Flat Iron was an Irish tavern in the Flats that had been there forever. The regular crowd consisted mostly of steelworkers, sailors, and other blue-collar types, with a smattering of businessmen and suburbanites. Sophie and I would stick out, but not drastically so. I doubted either Kahn or whoever he had following us would expect us to show up at that venue. We would be all right so long as I could lose any tail that might've followed us from Sophie's apartment.

I drove down Cedar Hill to Carnegie and took it to East 105th, then cut over to Hough and headed west. At East Fifty-Fifth, I turned north toward the lake, then slipped onto Perkins Avenue and resumed the trek downtown.

I wasn't through zigzagging. No one could follow the route I was improvising. I myself was having trouble keeping my bearings.

The trip hit a temporary snag when we had to give way to a funeral procession on Superior near Fortieth. I used the break to ask Sophie whether Kahn had ever had a business partner.

"I couldn't say," she said. "He certainly never told me that he did."

"Ever hear the name 'Oscar Eckhardt?'"

"I don't think so."

"So you never had reason to believe there was somebody else who owned a share of his apartment buildings?"

"You have to understand," Sophie said. "Mendel almost never talked to me about business. Or anything else important, really. I was under the impression that he alone owned all his properties."

"I don't know, Miss Himmel," I said when our journey resumed. "You don't go from being a penniless dishwasher to a real estate tycoon in just a few years if you're not getting help from *someone*."

"You've heard of the Alhambra Tavern?" Sophie asked.

"I've been there a number of times. The food is very good."

"You know who runs the place, don't you?"

"Of course. Everybody does. It's Shondor Birns."

"Well, that's where Mendel was washing dishes when he came to this country. Birns hired him and kept him on the payroll for several years."

I pulled the Edsel over to the curb to give myself a chance to absorb this latest news flash. Birns was a gangster, a thief, a murderer — the self-proclaimed Public Enemy Number One in Cleveland. He controlled the policy racket. He ran the whorehouses. He sold protection to businesses that needed protection only from him and his gang. He seemed to have a hand in almost every crooked deal that went down in the city, and he almost never suffered any repercussions, given the broad collection of policemen, judges, and politicians he bought and paid for.

"Why did you tell me this?" I asked Sophie. "Are you suggesting that Kahn has Shondor Birns as his business partner?"

"I'm not suggesting anything," she responded. "Mendel didn't have anything to do with Shondor while I was seeing him, as far as I knew.

But he was very appreciative of the start Shondor gave him, and spoke very warmly about him."

"And...?"

"And nothing. You were wondering how Mendel went so quickly from rags to riches. I gave you information that came to mind when you said so."

"Certainly there's more to it than that," I said.

"You're the detective. You figure it out."

We spoke very little after resuming our route to the Flat Iron. The rush hour traffic was heavy, but it was mostly heading in the opposite direction. We arrived at our destination around ten minutes later.

Sixteen

"Are you hungry?" I asked Sophie as we walked from the Edsel to the front door of the Flat Iron. "They're supposed to have pretty good food here."

"Really? As good as the Alhambra? You're obviously quite the gourmet."

The sarcasm took me by surprise. I knew Sophie wasn't in a chipper mood, but I hadn't realized I'd joined Mendel Kahn on her list of antagonists.

"I suppose we'll just have a drink and be on our way," I said.

The Flat Iron was around half full, about what I would've predicted for an early evening in the middle of the week. The short thick-armed hostess seated us at a small table in the back corner of the tavern and took our orders to the bar.

"You're obviously peeved with me, Miss Himmel," I said as soon as the hostess departed. "I'm sorry if I offended you in some way."

"I'm peeved with everyone right now," she mumbled.

"What is it?"

"Let me ask you one, Mr. Gold. When we first met a few weeks ago, you told me you were trying to find out if Mendel helped the Germans during the War. Now you're asking about his real estate business. What does the one thing have to do with the other?"

"Not necessarily anything," I answered. "I'm still investigating whether Kahn was a Nazi collaborator. That's the primary inquiry. But as I've nosed around, I've learned that his real estate holdings aren't all they're cracked up to be."

"What do you mean by that?"

"Like the fact that his properties include tenements where the conditions apparently border on the obscene."

"That's not true," Sophie said.

"It is so. Kahn is a dicey character. What you've told me about him and Shondor Birns only deepens my suspicions."

"I shouldn't have said anything about that," Sophie replied. "I did so because I'm mad at Mendel and wanted to get back at him for bugging my telephone, if he's really doing that. But it occurs to me that you're no more interested in my well-being than Mendel is. You're going to toss around what I told you so that it gets back to him, and I'll be the one who pays the price."

"I promise you here and now that I'll be discreet with the information you've given me."

Just then the hostess returned to our table with the drinks. "Rye and soda for the gentleman," she announced. "A whiskey sour for the lady. Will there be anything else?"

"We're good for the time being," I said.

I took a sip from my glass. Sophie took what seemed more like a gulp from hers.

"You say you'll be discreet," she then said. "But if Mendel gets wind of what I told you, there's no telling what he might do. And you're not going to be around to stop him."

That was my cue to promise to do whatever it took to keep Sophie safe. But I swallowed the line. To protect Sophie from

Kahn's retribution, I'd have to agree not to follow up on what she'd told me about him and Birns. Then and there, at least, I wasn't ready to make that commitment.

Sophie and I resorted to chit chat to get through the rest of our date. She asked about my Thanksgiving plans. I asked about hers. We both went through the family we had in town and tried to figure out whether our lives had intersected sometime in the past. They hadn't.

I asked if Sophie ever found out whether Mendel had actually rekindled his affair with the mystery woman in Utica. "He was alone when I saw him at the party last week," she told me.

"Have any of your mutual friends told you what Kahn's been up to since you've been out of the picture?"

"The people we both know don't talk about Mendel. It's like his life is top secret. The lady from Utica could be married to him by now, and I wouldn't know it."

I took a direct route up Cedar Hill in returning to Sophie's apartment. To prove that chivalry wasn't dead, I parked the car on the street and walked her to her building. On the front stoop sat the Hairy Slab, with a pistol bulging out of his left pants pocket.

"You two took longer than expected," he said cheerfully. "I been waiting half an hour."

"Who is he?" asked Sophie.

"He's the guy who does Kahn's dirty work," I said. "What're you doing here?"

The Hairy Slab smiled. "You should know better than to run around with the boss' girlfriend," he said.

"I'm not his girlfriend anymore," said Sophie. "He's made that perfectly clear."

"He sent me to assure the little lady we weren't tapping her phones."

"Either Kahn's an idiot, you're an idiot, or you're both idiots," I said. "The only way you could've known she was concerned about having her phone tapped was by tapping her phone."

The Hairy Slab didn't appreciate my observation of the obvious. "So you're a fucking genius, and you saw right through it," he said menacingly as he started to stand.

"Sit back down!"

To make sure he understood the command, I pulled a forty-five of my own from inside my coat pocket and pointed it squarely at his noggin. The Hairy Slab did as he was told.

I'd never been a Boy Scout, but I still recognized the virtue of being prepared. The gun spent most of its time locked in the safe in my office. But I figured there might be rough stuff if Kahn really were listening in and knew that Sophie and I were getting together. I'd brought the forty-five with the specific expectation of running into the Hairy Slab.

"Oh my God," Sophie screeched. "You've both got guns."

No one else was on the street, but I couldn't expect my luck to hold. Even without pedestrians, traffic on Cedar would continue. Inevitably some driver would spot the weapon I was brandishing and alert the police. Then again, a patrol car might cruise by and eliminate the need for a middleman.

I sent Sophie to her apartment, then marched the Slab around the corner to an unlit side street. We stopped near a sewer hole.

I stood behind my companion and jabbed the forty-five into the small of his back. "Okay, pal," I said. "Reach very slowly into your pants pocket, get your gun, and put it on the sidewalk."

"You don't have to..."

"Now," I barked, jabbing him again. "And don't even think of trying to pull something."

The Hairy Slab had a lot of ground to cover to get his arm around his thick torso and into his pants pocket. But he managed to remove the pistol and dropped it gingerly at his feet.

"Thanks," I said. "Now kick it into the sewer."

"No. I'm not gonna do it."

I whipped the back of his head with the butt of the forty-five. The Hairy Slab grunted and doubled over. When he recovered, he stood up and booted his revolver down the hole.

"I'll get you for that," he said.

"Not if I shoot you first."

"Go ahead, mister. You're gonna have to shoot me, or else let me go. Gun or no gun, I'll deliver the message to the boss' girlfriend, just like I'm supposed to."

The Slab had a point. I had nowhere to lock him up, and I couldn't hold him forever at gunpoint on the street in a residential neighborhood. Once I let him loose, he could resume his mission to get at Sophie. To prevent him from succeeding, I'd have to stand vigil at her apartment all night long. I most decidedly didn't want to do that.

"Take off your shoes," I told the Hairy Slab. "Take them off now."

"What?"

I stroked his head again with the butt of the forty-five. "You heard me," I said. "Take off your goddamned shoes."

The Slab sat down on the sidewalk and untied his oxfords. "I suppose you want me to take my socks off, too," he said nastily once he had finished.

"As a matter of fact, I don't. Instead, you need to stand up and remove your trousers."

"You've got to be kidding."

"No joke, pal. Off with the pants."

"You're a sick fuck, mister," opined the Hairy Slab.

"Believe me. I have no hankering to see you in your skivvies. But I've got to make sure that when you're free to go you'll go right to your car and leave this part of town as quickly as possible."

"What prevents me from turning around and coming right back as soon I can?"

"I don't think you will," I said. "Not after I report to the cops on this beat that a man fitting your unique description was running around on the street with nothing on."

"Please, mister," the Slab pleaded. "It's cold out here. What if I promised to leave and not come back?"

"How gullible do you think I am? Would you take your word for it if you were me?"

The man tried to reason with me for a while but finally realized he had no choice. Once he handed the pants over to me, I reached inside the pockets and removed his car keys and billfold.

"I'll give you back your keys, of course," I said. "And you can have the cash from your wallet. I'll keep your driver's license and anything else inside."

"You must have a death wish, mister," said the Hairy Slab forlornly. "You're making an enemy you'd rather not have."

"Are you talking about yourself or your boss?"

"Both of us."

"Mr. Kahn and I already hate each other's guts," I said. "As for you, we'll always have our time together at the Schvitz."

"What the hell you talking about?"

I motioned with the forty-five for the Slab to get a move on. He walked away tentatively. After a few steps, he removed his overcoat and tried to wrap it around his bare legs. He succeeded only in mummifying himself. He might've been more covered, but he also couldn't walk.

"Goddamn it," he cursed. He untied the coat and threw it into the street, then turned and yelled "fuck you, mister" in a voice far too loud for someone who should've been trying not to attract attention.

"I'd hurry up if I were you," I said quietly to him. "You're on borrowed time as it is." I was collecting the Slab's shoes and pants off the sidewalk as he tiptoed his way toward Cedar Road.

SEVENTEEN

IT TOOK ME five minutes to convince Sophie to open her apartment door and let me in. She still was trembling from the confrontation with our gentleman caller.

I tried to reassure her. "They're really after *me*, not you," I said. "If I stay away, Kahn and his goon should leave you alone."

"There's no way you can be sure of that," she responded almost frantically. "This may have nothing to do with you. He was tapping *my* telephone, not yours."

I explained to Sophie how I had disrobed the Hairy Slab. "You're safe for the time-being, at least," I told her. "It'll be a miracle if that oaf isn't arrested before he gets to his car."

"What if he isn't?"

"Then he still has to drive to wherever he calls home and get a new set of clothes."

"He'll do that and come right back," Sophie said.

"It'd probably be late by then. Plus he'd have to think twice about returning after I told him I'd put the police on the lookout for a naked masher who looks just like him."

As it turned out, I didn't make good on that threat. The cops weren't likely to take my report seriously unless I produced the Hairy Slab's pants as proof. Doing so would bring my own conduct into question.

Seventeen

On the way back to Sophie's, I'd found an unlocked Hometown Buick parked on the street and tossed the Slab's trousers and shoes into the back seat. I was reasonably confident no one saw me dump the incriminating evidence.

Sophie didn't want to stay in her apartment alone. She started to dial a friend to see if she could spend the night, but stopped when I reminded her that her ex-boyfriend could be listening in to any plans she made. I ended up treating her to a room at the Alcazar, the ritzy suburban hotel only a few blocks away.

I might as well have arranged for Sophie to stay in a telephone booth. According to the bill I paid the next morning, she spent most of her time at the Alcazar on the line with her cousin Renee in Texas. The two had apparently been close until Renee moved to San Antonio when her husband got a job with a big insurance company in town. Sophie used the person-to-person confab to wrangle an invitation to come to the Lone Star State for as long as she cared to stay.

Sophie was still spooked the morning after the Hairy Slab's appearance on the scene. She wouldn't even return to her apartment to pack a suitcase. Instead, she said she would borrow clothes from Renee and wanted me to drive her straight to the airport.

I stopped at the bank on the way and withdrew three hundred fifty dollars. "Here," I said as I handed the cash over across the front seat of the Edsel. "Build yourself a Texas wardrobe."

I hoped the gift would assuage some of the guilt I felt for Sophie's current state-of-mind. I thought she was overstating the threat posed by Kahn. But I had no doubt that his renewed interest in her sprang directly from her contact with me. He didn't want her to let me know what she knew about his past.

The tidbit Sophie had recounted about Kahn and Shondor Birns exemplified the threat. Even if she couldn't identify him as a Nazi war criminal, she had information that could seriously tarnish the glorious reputation he had cultivated for himself. And as a jilted lover whom Kahn had cut off completely, Sophie had no incentive to mince her words.

Sophie's disappearance into the airport left me alone for the drive downtown. Normally I didn't mind my own company, but I would've preferred some distraction on this day. A nightmare about Ebinsee had interrupted my sleep after I got home from Cleveland Heights, and with it came a special treat — flashes of the old psychotic fantasies about my personal complicity for Nazi war crimes. I long ago graduated from the level of crazy that had me convinced I'd actually committed atrocities in Europe. But just the memory of those thoughts shook me up profoundly, made me feel sinister and dangerous — even though rationally I knew I'd done nothing wrong. Over the years, I'd made an art form out of thinking the worst of myself, but this took self-flagellation to new depths. With company, I could usually avoid the poisonous reminiscing about my troubled past. Flying solo presented a problem.

As I motored toward the office, I tried to force my brain to change the subject. I focused on anything and everything that took me away from my worries: My niece and nephew; Sylvia; the Browns; the Indians; Sid Caesar; Dizzy Gillespie; Sylvia again. I had to paddle vigorously to make it through this stream of consciousness, but it seemed to do the trick. By the time I parked the Edsel, the hobgoblins had retreated a bit, and I could at least pretend everything was back to normal.

Eighteen

Evie was fidgeting at her desk when I arrived at the office around eleven. "You had long distance this morning, Chief," she announced excitedly. "From New York City."

"No doubt the United Nations wants my thoughts on the India-Pakistan question."

"No," said Evie. "Karen Sontag. She was answering one of the ads we placed in the Jewish newspapers."

"The ads about Yitzhak Fried?"

"Right. She says she's got information and wants you to call back as soon as you can."

"All right, then," I said. "Now we're getting some place."

I tried not to make a habit out of counting my chickens, but I had the feeling Karen Sontag was going to bust the Kahn investigation wide-open. Forget trifling discoveries about his cousin and his tenements, his aversion to having his picture taken or his inability to distinguish between lessons on the violin or the piano. If someone affirmatively identified Kahn as Yitzhak Fried, it would corroborate the original allegations made against him on Yom Kippur. His reputation would instantly crater, and the Rabbi could depose him from the temple board without consequence.

I went into my private office and shut the door. I had the operator connect me to the number Evie had written down, and I said hello to Karen Sontag.

"Mr. Gold," Karen said. "I'm the one who called this morning about the Fried matter."

The voice had a pronounced Brooklyn accent. It sounded as though it belonged to a young woman, maybe even a teenager.

"Thanks for getting in touch, Mrs. Sontag. Or is it miss?"

"Miss," she informed me.

"Miss Sontag. Tell me: Did you know Yitzhak Fried?"

"Not me. No."

"Did you live in Bedzin when he served on the Jewish Council?"

"I've never been outside the five boroughs, Mr. Gold," said Karen. "And I personally don't know a thing about this Fried character. I'm calling for my neighbor, Miss Leona Marks. She heard about your ad in *Hadoar* and has some information to pass along."

"Can I speak to her, Karen?" I asked.

"She doesn't like to talk on the telephone, Mr. Gold. That's why I made the call. She told me what she wanted to say and asked that I fill you in."

The needle on my internal bunk detector began to quiver. Offering up an absentee witness seemed like a scam to wheedle me out of the cash reward the ads promised to anyone who could identify Yitzhak Fried or speak to his whereabouts. A wise guy could tell me virtually anything about Fried and attribute it to a source he'd never actually have to produce. Unless the information was patently rubbish, I'd probably end up having to pay out.

"Did Miss Marks know Yitzhak Fried?" I asked Karen.

"Her family lived in the same building as his in Bedzin. She saw him often."

"Were they close?"

"I think so," Karen said.

"Has Miss Marks had any contact with Fried since the War ended?"

"None. She assumed he was dead until she found out about your ad in the magazine."

"But she knew him in Bedzin and saw him frequently," I confirmed.

"Yes."

"And she thinks she can identify Yitzhak Fried if given the chance."

"That's not the reason she had me call, Mr. Gold," said Karen. "She wanted you to know Fried has been seen in Israel."

Karen laid it out for me. Her neighbor had a friend in Tel Aviv named Leah Bloom, a fellow former resident of Bedzin who emigrated after surviving Auschwitz. One evening, Leah spotted a man she was certain was Yitzhak Fried exiting a movie theater. She had plenty to say to him, given his deplorable performance as a member of the Judenrat. But the man wouldn't listen. "Leave me alone," he barked as he walked away. "For God's sake, leave me alone!"

"That was it?" I asked.

"That's what her friend wrote."

"Did the man admit to being Yitzhak Fried?"

"He might have," Karen said. "I'm not totally sure of everything the letter said, to tell you the truth."

I had my doubts about the story I was hearing. Cynicism notwithstanding, I didn't get the sense Karen had conjured up Leona Marks or fabricated the reported sighting of Yitzhak Fried. If that incident really happened, either Marty Bluestein's cousin or Leona's Israeli friend had been dead wrong in identifying the man-of-the-hour.

But Karen's story had my stomach playing limbo, for several reasons. First and foremost, I didn't want it to be true. My research had uncovered a dark and sinister side of Mendel Kahn, regardless of whether he was the same guy who abetted the Nazis during the

War. His exposure as Yitzhak Fried would eliminate any question about his future in Cleveland. He wouldn't have one.

"In what language is the letter from Leah Bloom written?" I asked Karen.

"Yiddish. I'm pretty sure that's right."

"Will Miss Marks let me read it?"

"You're in Cleveland…"

"What if I sent my secretary to New York for a visit?" I said. "She'd have to bring a translator with her, and she'd probably take a picture of the letter so I could get a look at it back here. Would Miss Marks agree to that?"

"I don't know why she wouldn't," Karen answered. "I'll have to check with her."

"Go ask her now. I'll hold on. See if my secretary could drop in the day after tomorrow."

I heard Karen put the telephone down. A few minutes later, she got back on the line and confirmed Miss Marks's consent to the arrangement I proposed. We scheduled an appointment for ten-thirty on the designated date at the Marks apartment in Brooklyn.

"Your advertisement mentioned something about a reward," Karen said just before we hung up.

"It did at that."

"Leona wanted me to ask about it."

"Tell her my secretary will bring a check."

After the call ended, I summoned Evie into my office and asked whether she'd ever been to New York City.

"Nope," she said. "Never."

"Well, you're going tomorrow, and you're going to stay overnight. That long-distance caller — I need to get a statement from a witness in Brooklyn, and you're nominated."

"Karen Sontag?"

"She'll probably be there," I said, "but I'm more interested in the woman Karen was calling for. Leona Marks is her name."

I explained the situation to Evie, who wanted to know why I wasn't going myself.

"There's an appointment in town I intend to make for tomorrow," I explained. "Plus you wanted to do a little field work. Here's your chance."

I sent Evie to make a plane reservation and secure a room at the Hotel Edison. Later in the afternoon, I had her get Professor Fleishman on the line at C.C.N.Y.

"I need someone who can read Yiddish," I told him. "We've heard from someone who heard from someone who might've seen Yitzhak Fried in Tel Aviv."

"I'm fluent in Yiddish," Fleischman said matter-of-factly.

"No fooling?"

"Az me muz, ken men."

"I'll take that as a yes," I said. "You must be allergic to kryptonite, Doc."

By the time Evie left the office, I'd choreographed the whole production. She and Fleischman would rendezvous under the Grand Central clock at nine thirty the morning of the interview and travel together to Leona Marks's apartment in Brooklyn. Upon arriving, Evie would show her hostess one of my snapshots of Kahn to see if she recognized him as Fried. Depending upon what happened, Fleischman would proceed to translate the letter for Evie, who'd transcribe by shorthand the relevant parts. Evie would then photograph the letter with the miniature Minox camera I'd give her, hand Miss Marks the seventy-five dollar check I'd written, and be on her way. She could have lunch with Fleischman in the City and return to Cleveland on a late-afternoon flight.

If Leona Marks recognized Kahn as Yitzhak Fried, Evie's junket to New York would give me the evidence I needed to bring the investigation into the open. If she reached the opposite conclusion, and the letter from Tel Aviv seemed authentic, the case would close unless and until I found another credible witness who could identify Kahn as Fried. It was like waiting for a jury to return its verdict. All I could do was cross my fingers and hope for the best.

Nineteen

The next morning I met Ernie Murtaugh for a late breakfast at the coffee shop in the Hollenden House. Ernie was a crime reporter at the *Plain Dealer* who for years had chronicled the exploits of Shondor Birns. I needed someone who could tell me whether Birns actually had supplied Mendel Kahn with the cash he needed to launch his real estate empire. Ernie was as likely a choice as anyone.

He hadn't hesitated in agreeing to see me. A few years earlier, Ernie covered the Maury Sorin wrongful death lawsuit I brought against members of the wealthy Forsythe family, accusing them of murdering the prominent local attorney. The trial ran three tumultuous weeks, throughout which I fed Ernie a steady stream of inside dope. I certainly had my own agenda in doing so, but he won accolades for his scoops on the case, and he was grateful. He told me at the time that he'd reciprocate with a favor of his own if he ever had the chance. When I called for an appointment, he hadn't forgotten his commitment.

Ernie was sitting at the counter when I walked into the coffee shop. He'd been there for a while, judging from the number of cigarette butts crushed in the saucer underneath his cup.

"Hello, counselor," he said as he stood to shake my hand.

"Not currently a lawyer, Ernie. I'm here today as your friendly neighborhood gumshoe."

Ernie's appearance hadn't changed in the years since I'd last seen him. He was average height and extremely thin, with a ski-slope nose that stood out against sunken cheeks and a sharp chin. Even at eight-thirty in the morning, Ernie had a five o'clock shadow. He probably had on the same blue suit he wore throughout the Sorin trial, and his shirt was of the same vintage. Ernie didn't scrimp, however, when it came to ties. He was wearing a bright red number featuring the image of a big-game hunter in a pith helmet pointing his rifle. I was going to comment on this unusual choice in neckwear but decided to skip the wisecrack.

Ernie sat back down and ordered two eggs over easy, with toast and hash browns. I told the waitress I'd just have coffee.

"So what'd you need to know about Shondor Birns?" Ernie asked as he lit a cigarette. "He's not a guy you want to fool around with."

"I get that. I just want to see if you've ever heard that Birns was mixed up with a guy named Mendel Kahn."

"That name doesn't ring a bell. Who is he?"

"He owns a lot of apartment buildings around town," I explained. "He's almost certainly accumulated his holdings in real estate with somebody else's cash, and a person in a position to know suggested that Birns might be the piggy bank."

"What kind of places does this Kahn own?"

"Mostly respectable ones. A-class buildings, with some notable exceptions."

Ernie took a long drag on his smoke. "I suppose it's not impossible," he said. "Shondor has his hand in a lot of legitimate businesses. But I've never heard he was investing in apartments, or any other type of real estate. It's not his usual racket. I suppose he'll take a piece of anything if it promises easy money."

"So you think it's unlikely," I said.

"I think I'd have heard something if Shondor were invested heavily in high-class real estate. The government would be after it, for one thing, to cover his unpaid taxes."

Ernie's lack of conviction didn't completely douse my hope of connecting Birns's loot with Kahn's apartments. As an immigrant just off the boat, Kahn simply wouldn't have had the capital to acquire these properties, each of which required a hefty down payment before a bank would even consider financing the rest of the deal.

Kahn's partner, Oscar Eckhardt, could have supplied the cash, but his role in Kahn's real estate conglomeration remained a complete mystery. I still wasn't entirely sure whether Eckhardt was a real person or a connivance of Kahn's.

Birns, on the other hand, had all the attributes of a clandestine money man. He had more dough than almost anyone, according to what I'd read. He also had a known ambition to park his cash in enterprises that were above-board, but without creating too much fanfare. And Birns wouldn't necessarily require a mortgage to ensure repayment if he invested in Kahn's apartments. He'd perfected other, more primal means of ensuring his business partners paid what they owed him.

"Ernie," I asked, "how could I find out for certain whether Birns ever had an interest in the Kahn properties?"

"You'd have to talk to Shondor himself and hope he felt like telling you the truth."

"Would he meet with someone like me?"

"A private eye not working for him? Maybe not."

Ernie tried to light a new cigarette with the smoldering stub of the one he'd been smoking. "Listen to what I'm telling you, Benny," he said after giving up. "Shondor is not a shy man. He usually talks openly about the businesses he's mixed up in, at least the legal ones. If he's buying real estate with this Mendel Kahn, and nobody knows about it, that's because Shondor wants it that way. I don't think he'll take too kindly to someone trying to blow his cover."

"Mendel Kahn is my target, not Birns," I responded. "I have no intention of causing Shondor any trouble. I'm just trying to figure out where Kahn gets his money."

"Trouble's in the eye of the beholder, Benny," he said as he pulled a notepad and a pencil from his inside coat pocket. "Your good intentions won't count for a thing."

Ernie ripped a page from the pad and scribbled down a telephone number before handing it to me. "Here," he said. "You usually can reach Shondor in the evenings, after eight. Whatever you do, don't go see him without an appointment."

"Thanks, Ernie," I said.

"You can't say I didn't warn you."

"Wouldn't think of it."

I wondered whether Ernie was discouraging me from seeing Birns as a way of preserving the exclusivity of his access. Only members of the press could talk to Public Enemy Number One. Ordinary humans couldn't risk it.

Whatever Ernie's motivation, I realized I should've had him approach Birns with the questions I wanted answered. That would've at least preliminarily protected me from any rash reaction on Shondor's part.

This brainstorm didn't hit me until after I'd left the Hollenden House and walked halfway to my office. It was just as well. I would've regretted asking Ernie to do my dirty work. Private eyes don't investigate by proxy. I was more-than-leery about approaching Shondor Birns, but if I wanted information from him, I'd have to get it myself.

TWENTY

I SPENT THE rest of the morning wondering how Evie was making out with Leona Marks in Brooklyn. I was hoping she'd ring me long-distance when the meeting ended. I couldn't recall whether I'd specifically asked her to do so. I figured if she didn't call, I could try to reach Fleischman at his office that afternoon for a recap of what took place. Having that option calmed my nerves, even though I knew I probably wouldn't call him.

I was just about to leave for lunch when I received a telephone call from Lieutenant McAllister of the Cleveland Heights Police Department. "Sorry to bother you, Mr. Gold," he began. "But we've got a pretty peculiar situation on our hands."

That certainly had an ominous sound to it. "How can I help, Lieutenant?" I asked cautiously.

"Do you know a man by the name of Jerzy Dudek, Mr. Gold?"

"What?"

"Jerzy Dudek," McAllister repeated. "I think I'm pronouncing that right. Does that name mean anything to you?"

As a matter of fact, it did. It was the name I'd read on the Hairy Slab's driver's license two days earlier before I burned it in the trash can at my office.

The Slab must've filed a complaint about the pilfering of his pants and wallet. That seemed the most likely explanation for the lieutenant's question, though I found it hard to believe. The Slab couldn't tell the cops the truth about our encounter without seriously implicating himself and his boss. He'd come to Cleveland Heights to strongarm Sophie Himmel into clamming up about Kahn's past. The Slab had to realize that his dubious mission would inevitably become the focus of the story if the cops brought me in.

"Jerzy Dudek?" I said. "No, Lieutenant, I can't say I've ever heard of the gentleman. Who is he?"

"It's the damnedest thing. We arrested this guy a few nights ago for public indecency. He was walking down Cedar Road without his pants on."

"That does sound indecent."

"You should see him," said McAllister. "He's one gigantic mass of flesh."

"So where do I fit into the story?"

"Mr. Dudek swears you're the one who had him take his pants off..."

"Hold on one second," I interrupted with an appropriate level of indignation. "I don't go in for that kind of stuff. I'm as regular as the next guy."

"Mr. Dudek wasn't accusing you of that, Mr. Gold. He says you made him undress at gunpoint, on the street, after stealing his wallet."

"So I was holding him up?"

"That's what Mr. Dudek claims," said McAllister. "He says you took his pants so he couldn't follow you."

"Why was I worried about that if I had a gun?"

"He didn't say."

"So how much cash does he say I got away with?"

"None," McAllister said. "He says you stole his wallet but gave him back the money. He had nearly eighty bucks in his shirt pocket when we arrested him. His car keys, too."

"That makes absolutely no sense."

The police reached exactly the same conclusion. As McAllister explained, they didn't give any credence to the Hairy Slab's accusations against me (although they apparently lacked any alternative theory on how he lost his pants). Even if they had believed him, though, they didn't intend to investigate, since the Slab wouldn't go on the record with his charges against me. He gave the cops my name for one reason and one reason only — to get his trousers back.

"If you have them, or know where they are, just bring them to the station," said McAllister. "No questions asked. We just want to get Mr. Dudek dressed and send him on his way."

"You mean he's still in custody?"

"We can't let him go until he's fully clothed," explained the lieutenant, "and with measurements like his, nothing we have comes close to fitting him. We don't want to call in a tailor. We thought we'd call you first."

"Can't you go to his home and pick up something for him to wear?"

"That's the thing," McAllister said. "He won't tell us where he lives. And the Post Office doesn't have a current address for him."

"Does he want to stay in jail?"

"You'd get that impression. He also refuses to call anyone for help. Not a relative, a neighbor, a friend..."

"Does the guy work?" I asked in an effort to implicate Kahn. "Hasn't he called his employer to explain why he isn't showing up?"

"There is no employer. He says he works for himself as a house painter."

"I wish I could help you, Lieutenant," I said after a few more minutes of conversation. "But I have no idea where Mr. Dudek's pants may be."

"I'm not surprised."

"I must say I'm more than a little spooked that he identified me as his supposed assailant. I can't imagine how he even knows my name."

"Don't let it worry you too much," said McAllister. "This gentleman obviously isn't playing with a full deck. He must've heard your name somewhere, and his imagination took it from there."

A few hours after finishing up with Lieutenant McAllister, I received a call from Mendel Kahn's secretary saying her boss wanted to speak to me. "Tell him to hold just a minute," I said. "My girl's out today, and I'm just finishing up the afternoon mail."

Nothing really prevented me from beginning the conversation, but I wanted to let Kahn stew on the line. I didn't know for certain why he was telephoning, but I had a pretty good guess. Since the Hairy Slab hadn't called him (or anyone else) from jail, Kahn had no way of knowing what became of his henchman after he embarked on his assignment to intimidate Sophie.

Sophie's fate also would've been a mystery to Kahn, since her tapped telephone wire had gone silent. And her simultaneous disappearance with the Slab's raised a slew of grisly possibilities. Jerzy Dudek was not a peace-loving, temperate man. For all Kahn knew, the Slab went overboard in roughing Sophie up, then took it on the lam when he saw what he had done.

That, fortunately, hadn't happened — but Kahn had to wonder. I was the only one who could possibly allay his concerns, since I'd been with Sophie that night. For my money, Kahn was calling because he was desperate for information and wanted to find out whether I could answer any of his questions.

"What is it, Mr. Kahn?" I said gruffly when I picked up the receiver. "Did you call to tell me the truth about the war crimes you committed?"

"So that's how it is now?" Kahn responded. "No more pussyfooting around — you openly slander me by accusing me of those horrible things. You better watch it, Gold. I'll beat you to a pulp."

"Well, from what I've heard, you've had plenty of practice at it."

The line went silent for what seemed like a full minute. "Was there something you wanted to talk about?" I finally asked.

"You saw Sophie Himmel the other night," said Kahn.

"Yes. I did. We spent the early part of the evening together. You know all about that because you tapped her telephone."

"Where is she now?"

"I couldn't tell you," I said. "I presume she's at home."

"You know she isn't," Kahn said. "She's been missing since then. I think you've stashed her some place to keep her away from me."

"I left Sophie at her apartment that night. I haven't 'stashed' her anywhere. But you know all about that kind of thing, don't you, Kahn?"

"What's that supposed to mean?"

"I've heard about your lady friend in Utica. You kept that iron in the fire even while you were seeing Sophie."

"Goddamn it!" Kahn exploded. "That's none of your goddamned business."

"It's an awfully brazen arrangement, if you ask me. You're sending her money, paying her bills. All so she's available at your beck and call."

I was making it up as I went along about the woman from Utica, but I saw no need to be accurate. I didn't care a hoot about Kahn's love life. I was just trying to yank his chain, and it seemed to be working.

"You listen to me good," he said in a threatening tone. "You keep away from my friend in Utica. You'll keep away if you know what's good for you."

"I don't know, Kahn. She sounds like something special. I might try to find her and ask her out myself."

"Goddamn you, Gold!"

"With her around, why are you so intent upon finding Sophie Himmel?" I asked. "From what Sophie told me, you dumped her flat months ago."

"Then why are you so interested in her?" Kahn countered. "If she has no current ties to me?"

"Sophie might know things about your past that I'd like to know," I said. "You might've told her what you were really doing during the War."

"Leave her alone," Kahn erupted again. "And keep your goddamned questions to yourself."

"Sophie must know something pretty ghastly for you to be so set on keeping her under wraps."

"I don't want to keep her under wraps," he said. "I just want to find out where the hell she is. She's got to be somewhere."

"I can't argue with that logic," I said.

"You know my man, Dudek?"

"Who?"

"Dudek. Dudek. The guy you spoke to at the Schvitz."

"Oh," I said. "You mean the goon who assaulted me."

"Have you seen him lately?" Kahn asked.

"Fortunately, no."

"You didn't see him the night you were with Sophie?"

"He wasn't invited," I said. "And he didn't crash the party."

The conversation again went to a protracted intermission. I used the time to consider whether I should tell Kahn that the Cleveland Heights police had the Hairy Slab in custody on a morals charge.

I decided I had to do so. The cops didn't believe the Slab's accusation that I disrobed him on the street and took his wallet. Lieutenant McAllister fully accepted my denial of the charge.

But what would their attitude be if they found out I hadn't relayed the news about Dudek after Kahn explicitly asked about him? Only someone with something to hide would remain silent in that situation. I could hope the cops never found out about my telephone conversation with Kahn, but that was a sucker's bet. For all I knew, Kahn the wiretapper was recording the current call as we spoke.

"Did you say your man's name is Dudek?" I asked Kahn.

"Right."

"Jerzy Dudek?"

"That's his name," Kahn said. "You're holding out on me, Gold. You know something."

"I'm about to tell you," I said. I then recounted the high points of my conversation with Lieutenant McAllister.

Kahn was seething by the time I finished. "This is your doing, Gold," he said angrily.

"Well, the police don't think so, and I deny it."

"Dudek isn't a pervert. He wouldn't take his clothes off in public unless someone forced him to. That someone was you."

"Dudek is a behemoth," I replied. "He could crush me with one hand tied behind his back. And he carries a gun, as I recall from our meeting at the Schvitz. How in the world do you figure I forced him to take his pants off on the street?"

"Maybe you had your own gun."

"I don't typically carry one," I said. "But even if I did, you're saying I did all this to steal his wallet — his wallet without any of the cash inside?"

"Dudek will fill me in on the specifics," Kahn grumbled. "I don't believe a word you say."

"Well, believe this: The police want him out of jail. Take him some clothes and bail him out, Kahn. Then you and he could work together in concocting the caper I supposedly pulled."

"Fuck you, Gold," Kahn said. "You're fucking with the wrong guy."

I wanted to comment on Kahn's repetitive use of the ultimate expletive. But he interrupted my observation by cursing and calling me a "fucking moron."

"The third time's the fucking charm," I said. Kahn appreciated the wisecrack so much he slammed down the telephone and ended the call.

Twenty-One

I didn't sleep well that night. I was anxious to hear Evie's report on her excursion to Brooklyn. The time couldn't pass quickly enough. At three o'clock in the morning, staring at the ceiling in my bedroom, I decided I should have indulged my obsessive overbearing impulses and rung Evie at home the previous evening.

I couldn't wait to hear Leona Marks's reaction to the photo of Mendel Kahn. If she identified him as the current incarnation of Yitzhak Fried, it would extinguish the relevance of what her friend in Tel Aviv had to say. I could then bring Leona to Cleveland for a firsthand look at Kahn. While tossing and turning, I plotted out how to stage that confrontation.

The following morning, I was sitting at Evie's desk in the outer office when she walked in at ten-till-nine. "Tell me all about it," I ordered without even saying hello.

She told me all about it, all right. Evie described her conception of the Manhattan skyline from the top of the Empire State Building. She extolled the lavish accommodations at her hotel and the vastness of Central Park, which she toured the evening of her first night in town. She compared taking the subway to a ride at Euclid Beach and expressed her amazement at the different kinds of restaurants she saw.

When the travelogue finally ended, I asked Evie whether

she'd found time to attend the meeting at Leona Marks's apartment. "Of course, Chief," she said. "That's the whole reason I went."

"Did the Marks woman identify Mendel Kahn as Yitzhak Fried?"

With a solemn expression, Evie shook her head.

"Did she see any resemblance at all?"

"No," answered Evie. "Mr. G., you've got to..."

"The guy on Yom Kippur saw Kahn as the spitting image," I said. "I would've expected the Marks lady to at least see some similarity, even if she didn't make a positive identification."

"Boss..."

"Do you think she's on the up-and-up? Maybe she discredited the picture as a way of lending credence to the claim of her friend in Israel."

"Leona Marks is a very nice woman," Evie said. "And she wants nothing more than to find Yitzhak Fried, wherever he is. But she's blind, Mr. G. Completely blind. There was no point in showing her the picture of Mr. Kahn because she had no way of seeing it."

Evie explained that Leona Marks had come down with diabetes a few years after her arrival in this country. For several months, she didn't know what was wrong with her and went without treatment. The doctors eventually gave her the help she needed, but in the meantime, her eyesight began to deteriorate and never recovered.

"How is her health otherwise?" I asked Evie.

"She's very frail and white as a ghost. But Karen Sontag was at the meeting. She said that so long as Leona gets her insulin shots, she stays pretty stable."

"If Leona is blind, she herself couldn't have read the letter from Tel Aviv," I said.

"No. A friend read it to her."

"That couldn't have been Karen, because she doesn't know Yiddish."

"No," said Evie. "It was another woman in her building whose name I can't exactly remember. 'Heller', I think it was. She was there, too, in case we needed someone to translate."

Evie described the letter as several folded sheets of white stationery with handwriting on both sides. Karen helped her smooth out the pages so she could get good snapshots with the Minox.

"Did Doctor Fleischman make it to the meeting?" I asked.

"He and I came together. He was the one who read the letter aloud. It took around ten minutes. Mrs. Heller would say *"daz iz richtig"* when he'd turn a page. Doctor Fleischman told me that meant she agreed with his translation."

Evie opened her handbag and removed a small pad that contained her notes of what Fleischman had read. The transcript showed nothing significant beyond what Karen had told me on the telephone a few days earlier. Leah Bloom spotted someone on the streets of Tel Aviv she swore was Yitzhak Fried. She followed and confronted the man, who dismissed her in a way which suggested he really was Fried but which didn't explicitly confirm as much.

The letter didn't say whether Leah Bloom followed the man when he walked away. If she had any idea where to find him, she left it out of the correspondence.

"Did you get a telephone number for Leona Marks?" I asked Evie.

"Yes, Chief, I did. But she doesn't like to talk on the phone."

"Call her anyway to see if she has a number for Leah Bloom in Tel Aviv."

"Ooh," said Evie. "I didn't think to ask for that."

"Get Leah Bloom's address, too."

"That I did think of."

"Good," I said. "I want you to write a memo to the file describing what happened in New York. You can leave out the parts about the Empire State Building and Central Park."

Evie grinned sheepishly and went to hang up her coat. I walked into my office and closed the door.

As far as I was concerned, Leona Marks turned out to be almost a total bust. She couldn't identify Mendel Kahn as Yitzhak Fried, and the claim of her Israeli friend remained inconclusive at best.

Almost a month had passed since the Rabbi first commissioned me to do the investigation. While my efforts had seriously provoked Kahn, they hadn't yielded any solid evidence he was really some Nazi thug passing himself off as a humble survivor. I had to hope that another witness would answer one of my ads or that Kahn's business partner (be it Shondor Birns or someone else) would have relevant information to share, if and when I managed to find him.

Something had to give. I hoped it wouldn't just be my patience.

Twenty-Two

This was the week for letters. The next morning, I received one from Rose Feigenbaum. The correspondence was not dated. Rose began by reminding me of my dinner with her and her husband in Canton. Then she got to the point:

> I spoke to my son, Harold, who said he has some information about Charlie's cousin that you might want to know. He wanted me to ask whether there was any reward money available.
>
> Rose Feigenbaum
>
> P.S.-Please respond only to me. Do not involve Charlie.

"Well, that's amusing," I said to Evie as I handed her the letter and asked her to file it away.

"What is it, Mr. G.?"

"It's a swindle, or an attempted swindle. That's what it is."

"Huh?"

"Remember Mendel Kahn's cousin in Canton?" I said. "His wife wants to know if I'll pay her son for information."

"Information about what?" Evie asked.

"About Kahn. The letter didn't get into specifics."

"How much does he want?"

"Apparently it's open to negotiation," I said. "But the sale is a no-sale because the buyer isn't buying."

"Don't you want to find out what he has to say?"

"Trust me," I said. "Harold's parents gave me the lowdown on him. He's a grifter looking for a quick buck. He couldn't possibly know something I'd be willing to pay for."

I spent the rest of the day debating that proposition with myself. I certainly had good reason to doubt whether Harold Feigenbaum could be a valuable source of information. His own parents described him as a hapless schmo. I couldn't imagine he knew anything about Mendel Kahn that might justify compensation.

Still, I wasn't a clairvoyant. I couldn't say absolutely that Harold hadn't seen or heard something while Kahn was living at his parents' that betrayed the holes in his cover story. It was the old conundrum: You didn't know what you hadn't known until you knew it.

That bit of wisdom would inform my decision. The investigation of Kahn was proceeding sluggishly, so I'd leave no-stone-unturned and pay to hear what Harold Feigenbaum wanted to tell me.

But I didn't intend to involve his mother in the transaction. Harold would have to talk to me directly. I'd find him and pay him a visit.

The telephone directory gave me all the help I needed. Harold lived in a two-family off Mayfield Road in East Cleveland. At nine-thirty the next morning, I found myself on the front porch, ringing the downstairs bell. When the door eventually opened, a tall spindly woman stepped outside.

"I'm sorry," I said. "I must be in the wrong place. I'm looking for Harold Feigenbaum."

"You're not wrong, mister," she responded in an irritated tone. "I'm Harold's wife. What do you want?"

I gave her the once-over, and it wasn't a pretty picture. Her hair was down in an uncombed tangle and seemed to be thinning on the left side. She wore no makeup to cover the gray tone of her complexion. Her frayed house dress did not cover her knobby knees, and the cracked man's slippers she wore looked one dimension too large for her string-bean figure.

"I'm Benjamin Gold," I introduced myself. "I was wondering whether I could see your husband. I've got some business to discuss with him."

"What kind of business?" Mrs. Feigenbaum asked suspiciously.

"I'd rather go over it with him, if you don't mind."

"Are you selling something? Because if you are, we're not interested."

"Please. If I could just see your husband. It's a private matter."

Mrs. Feigenbaum wasn't having it. "Listen," she said. "Harold minds his p's and q's. He'd better if he knows what's good for him. If you've got business with him, you've got business with me."

"I really need to see him."

"He's not even here," she said. "He's working, like most normal people at this hour."

"I thought the car wash wouldn't open till later in the day."

I recalled what the Feigenbaums told me about their son's place of employment. I figured his wife might soften when I showed her I was in the know. I figured wrong.

"You'd better leave, Mr. Silver, or Gold, or whoever you are." she told me.

"I don't understand your hostility, Mrs. Feigenbaum," I said. "Harold requested this meeting. He could make some money from it."

"Sure he could," she said. "All we have to do is sign up for twelve weeks of dance lessons and convince five of our friends to do likewise. You guys are all the same."

Mrs. Feigenbaum slammed the door before I could say another word. I rang the bell several times and waited five minutes to see if she or Harold would come down, just to get rid of me, if nothing else. When they didn't, I turned around and left.

I caught up with Harold later that afternoon at the Sudsy Car Wash in Euclid. His parents had told me he managed a place on the East Side of Cleveland. After leaving the missus, I returned to Mayfield Road, turned left and started my search. I relied on service stations to point out car washes along my haphazard trek. Sudsy was the fifth place I stopped.

"Does Harold Feigenbaum work here?" I asked the cashier at the end of the line.

"He's working out front today," he responded. "You can't miss him."

I understood what the guy meant when I caught my first glimpse of Harold. He did not inherit his father's angular build. The gene must've mutated. Harold was a human dumpling, almost completely round in stature with a bald crown — the most unlikely counterpart to the stick figure I'd seen at his home that morning.

"Hello, Harold," I said. "I'm Benjamin Gold."

"Listen," he replied angrily. "My wife called about you. You're going to get me in trouble."

"Take it easy."

"I'm not supposed to be on the telephone except for emergencies."

"I thought you were the manager?" I said.

"I still have to follow the rules..."

"Your wife shouldn't have bothered you. There certainly was no cause for alarm."

"You keep her out of this," Harold said. "And leave me alone. Can't you see I'm working?"

"Your mother wrote that you wanted to see me. She asked if I'd pay for information about Mendel Kahn. The answer is yes."

A red-and-white Packard 400 interrupted me by pulling into position for a wash. "Please remove all valuables when you exit the car," Harold recited to the driver. "Make sure that your windows are rolled up tightly. And thank you for using Sudsy, the sudsiest car wash in Northeast Ohio."

"I'll tell you what, Harold," I said when he turned back to me. "I don't have all day. Two fifty-dollar bills in my wallet have your name on them. My car's parked out front. I'll wait fifteen minutes for you to come and talk. If you don't, you've missed your opportunity."

Just then another vehicle pulled up to the car wash. Harold left me to recite his Gettysburg Address to the customer.

"Fifteen minutes," I reminded him upon his return, then walked out.

I was aggravated with myself as I sat in the Edsel. Harold's mealiness had me thinking I was just wasting my time. I hoped he wouldn't come out. Just when I thought I was in the clear, he came toddling up.

For reasons I couldn't figure, Harold got in the back seat instead of the front. There he took a good half minute to get himself situated.

"So, tell me," I finally said. "What makes you think Mendel Kahn really isn't your father's cousin?"

"Oh, I don't think that. I don't think that at all."

"Goddamn it! Then what's this all about? Your mother said I'd want to know what you could tell me. And what I'm interested in is whether Mendel Kahn is who he says he is."

The outburst obviously shook Harold's delicate sensibilities. "Like I told you," he said nervously, "I can't help you there. But Mom said you also wanted to know what Mendel had with him when he came to live in our house. I do have something on that."

I couldn't wait to hear this. I was paying a hundred bucks to find out that Mendel Kahn brought with him from Europe a lucky rabbit's foot, medallion, or some other meaningless knickknack. Perhaps he could tell me Kahn's favorite color, too, so the entry in my catalogue of useless information would have company.

"What is it that Kahn brought with him, Harold?"

"He had a sack of valuables," he blurted. "It was a gray sack, about half the size of a pillowcase. It was gray, like I said, and he kept it hidden in his cardboard suitcase."

"If he kept it hidden, how do you know about it?"

"I found it," Harold said. "I went through his stuff when he was out. I wasn't stealing—I just wanted to see what he had. The sack was tied up in a pair of pants or something. I didn't see it the first couple of times I looked. But then I found it. It was heavy."

"What was inside, Harold?"

"I never looked," he said curtly.

"Harold..." I felt like a parent wrangling a confession from a naughty toddler.

"I swear, I never looked."

"Come on," I said. "You went to the trouble of going through his stuff. Why would you stop the search just when it got interesting?"

"It was jewelry. Jewelry and coins. There was a lot of it."

"What kind of jewelry?"

"I don't know," he said. "Rings and bracelets and things. Maybe some earrings."

"Were there diamonds?"

"I couldn't tell what I was looking at."

"Gold?"

"Probably, that."

I asked Harold whether Kahn ever caught on to his snooping. He said he didn't think so. Harold also said he never let his parents know what he'd discovered.

"They told me to stay away from Mendel's stuff," he sniffled. "They would've been angry if they found out I hadn't listened."

I pulled the two fifties from my wallet and handed them over. For all my grousing, I had to admit it was money well spent. Kahn's hidden treasure raised various intriguing possibilities.

The jewelry presumably was real. If so, it could explain where Kahn got the money to buy the first of his apartments. Harold didn't exactly specify what and how much the gray sack contained, but it could've been sufficient to cover the down payment on a building or two, assuming Kahn figured out how and where to convert it into cash.

I could only guess how Kahn acquired the valuables, though I was certain foul play was involved. My first thought was that Kahn had extorted the jewelry from the Jews of Bedzin under his real name of Yitzhak Fried.

The Nazis, though, largely cleaned out the Bedzin Jews before they arrived in the ghetto. Was there enough jewelry available for Kahn to squeeze out a whole sack of it? And how did he manage to keep hold of it during his exile to Auschwitz, where simply surviving was far less than an even bet? I'd have to resolve these questions.

There was another possibility. Charlie Feigenbaum told me his cousin Mendel was the only child of a jeweler in Krakow. The Germans would have confiscated all his merchandise when they overran the city. But what if Kahn or his father managed to hide some away for retrieval after the hostilities ended? This scenario seemed no less plausible than its alternative. If the jewelry really came from the Kahn family's secret cache, Kahn's possession of it would corroborate his claim that he was who he said he was.

Harold didn't immediately leave the back seat after receiving the hundred. Recounting the raid on Mendel Kahn's suitcase had apparently drained him. He slumped on the seat, his belly protruding, his hands folded in his lap, and his forehead glistening with sweat. For the longest time, he just sat without saying a word.

"Harold, I want to thank you for talking to me," I said to break the silence. "Unfortunately, I need to get a move on."

"Mr. Gold," he answered meekly, "we have to talk about the money."

"The money?"

"My wife said I shouldn't tell you anything, but if I did, I should get two hundred as my reward, or at least a hundred-fifty."

"Whoa, Harold," I said. "That's a lot of scratch."

"She said she better not find out I accepted anything less."

I again found myself believing Harold. It was easy to do so, after meeting his lovely bride earlier in the day. Harold had a heavy cross to bear. He sat in the back seat, looking at me with a forlorn expression, knowing that his big payday wasn't big enough to spare him from misery at home. I had to feel for the guy.

But not fifty bucks worth, and certainly not a hundred. I pulled my wallet from the inside pocket of my suit coat and removed a ten-dollar bill.

"This is all I can do," I said as I handed him the money. "You're taking my last dollar, Harold. Tell her I was going to pay you fifty, and you talked me up from there."

Accepting defeat, Harold hoisted himself from the back seat and exited the Edsel. As I pulled away, he was struggling to stuff the bills I'd given him into the breast pocket of his shirt.

Twenty-three

On Saturday morning, I received a call from my sister-in-law, Miriam, to discuss Thanksgiving. The holiday was less than two weeks away, and she wanted to make arrangements.

"Are you and Sylvia going to be with her family or are you coming here?" she asked. "I really hope you can be with us. My sister's pregnant and can't travel, so as it stands, it's just me and Jake and the kids."

"I'll be there," I said. "But I'll be alone."

"What about Sylvia?"

"She and I... Well, she's decided to stop seeing me for the time being."

"Oh, Benny," Miriam scolded. "What have you done?"

"Nothing."

"There must have been something..."

"No, I mean it," I said. "It wasn't what I did but what I didn't do. Sylvia thought I was taking too long with a marriage proposal."

Miriam started to say something, then cut herself off. After a momentary pause, she began again.

"Benny, I wish I understood what you were doing," she said. "Did you ever intend to marry Sylvia?"

"I suppose I did, or do, eventually, but she got impatient. You can't really blame her. We're not kids anymore. She couldn't wait forever for me to take the plunge."

Miriam proceeded to give me a twenty-minute pep talk about winning Sylvia back. She unquestionably was the right woman for me, Miriam said. It was obvious to her that we loved each other. Jake, too, had commented on it. I'd never forgive myself if I allowed Sylvia to slip away. I needed to do whatever it took to win her back, immediately if not sooner.

It was the Knute Rockne equivalent to advice to the lovelorn. Miriam had me convinced. I told her to hold two seats for Thanksgiving, then hung up to dial Sylvia's number.

"Oh, it's you," she said coolly after she heard my voice. "I never expected you to be calling."

"Come on, Sylvia. Let's not start that way."

"We needn't start any way at all. You've made your choices. There's absolutely nothing left to be said."

I didn't quite understand. Sylvia had broken off our relationship against my wishes. So between the two of us, she was the only one who had made "choices."

"Do you mind telling me what in the hell you're talking about?" I said.

"Don't treat me like an idiot, Benjamin," she replied. "It's no secret what you've been up to."

"It's a secret to me. Please explain."

"Did you or did you not take your secretary on a two-day vacation to New York City?"

"False," I said. "Completely false. Evie went to New York on business alone. I didn't go with her. I stayed in town."

"That's not what I heard. I also heard that you've been seeing that Sophie Himmel woman. Apparently you've put her up in some sort of love nest."

"Did you just say 'love nest?'" I asked incredulously. "Did you honest-to-God just accuse me of hiding some broad in a 'love nest?' Tell me, sweetheart, when did Mendel Kahn feed you this slander?"

It obviously had been Kahn. He'd already expressed to me his twisted notion that I'd "stashed" Sophie away as part of some clandestine tryst. I was certain Sylvia didn't know Sophie, had never met her, and presumably hadn't even previously heard of her. Her scorn for "that Sophie Himmel woman" could only have come from Kahn's distorted portrayal of his former mistress.

I had no idea how Kahn learned about Evie's trip to New York City. But he was someone who illegally tapped telephone lines. When he wanted information about his perceived adversaries, he found a way to get it, by hook-or-by-crook. He added the bit about my accompanying Evie just to make a fraudulent point.

"When did you talk to Kahn?" I asked Sylvia a second time.

"Not that it's any of your business," she said, "but he called me one evening earlier this week. He'd heard from a friend that you and I were seeing each other, and he felt he'd better let me know what you were up to."

"How utterly noble of him."

"He doesn't like you very much, Benjamin," Sylvia said. "He thinks you're purposefully trying to destroy his reputation with this investigation of yours."

"Come on," I said. "You know me better than that."

"I don't know what I know, particularly not after hearing the stories about you and those other women."

"You're not that naïve, Sylvia," I said as I picked a package of Lucky Strikes off the table and pulled one out. "Mendel Kahn had an obvious agenda in calling you up. He was looking to bad-mouth me, and he told you any horrible thing he could think of, the truth be damned."

"Despite what you think, Benny, Mendel's not a monster."

"So it's 'Mendel', is it? You're already on a first-name basis?"

"If you must know," said Sylvia, "Mendel's asked me to dinner tonight."

"Goddamn it!" I burned my thumb trying to light my cigarette.

"I accepted the invitation, Benny."

"Sylvia, Mendel Kahn has no interest in you," I said. "You're just a pawn in his fight against me."

As the words came out of my mouth, I knew I shouldn't have said them. No one wanted to be told they were being played for a patsy, even if it were true. I was on thin ice before I made my thoughtless declaration. Now I had sunk deep into the frigid waters.

"Of course you're right, Benjamin," Sylvia snidely replied. "You're right, as always. Mendel doesn't give a damn about me. You're all he cares about. You're all *you* care about, too."

"Sylvia…"

"Imagine my audacity in thinking that an unmarried man might want to spend time with me, instead of carrying out a vendetta against my moronic ex-boyfriend."

Moronic ex-boyfriend? Now Sylvia had gone over the line. I'd indelicately told her the truth about her dinner date with Kahn, but it was the truth nonetheless. Sylvia needed to get a grip on the situation. She needed to stop acting like a lamebrain.

"Sylvia, I absolutely forbid you from going with Mendel Kahn tonight," I said. "That's for your own good as well as mine."

"Hardy-har-har," said Sylvia. "We're not together anymore, and you're certainly not my guardian. Where do you get off forbidding me to do anything?"

"We had a spat, Syl, and you called it quits temporarily, but I think we both know we'll eventually work it out. I still love you, but so help me—if you go with Mendel Kahn tonight, we're finished for good."

"Finished?" Sylvia repeated angrily. "We were finished when you went to New York with Evie and moved in with that Sophie Himmel."

"I'm dead serious, Sylvia."

"Don't call me again, Benjamin," she said as she hung up the telephone.

I spent the rest of the day discussing the conversation with a bottle of scotch. The booze convinced me the situation wasn't hopeless. It was obvious that Sylvia cared passionately about my involvement with other women. Who I saw and how I behaved still mattered to her. If that were true, then our relationship hadn't irreversibly fizzled, notwithstanding her pronouncements to the contrary.

But I completely misplayed the situation by giving her an ultimatum about seeing Kahn. My arrogance and high-handedness were only part of the problem. I was equally upset about the pointlessness of the command. Petty jealousy aside, what did I care if Sylvia spent an evening with Mendel Kahn? She was the same respectable woman I'd known for years. He was a certifiable louse, whatever his track record with the Nazis turned out to be. Sylvia certainly wasn't going to fall for him. She'd quickly see through the polished façade that had fooled the less discerning.

I had half a mind to go to Sylvia's apartment to take back what I said. I probably would have done so had I not been worried she'd launch a skillet at my head when I stepped inside. Emotions had run high during the call. Best to give Sylvia time to cool off. I could bide my time. The only thing I'd be out was a date for Thanksgiving.

Twenty-Four

"I can't get her, Mr. G. The number's no good."

Evie had tried for three days to reach Leah Bloom on the telephone in Israel. She wanted to check her story about seeing Yitzhak Fried on the streets of Tel Aviv. The first few times Evie placed the call, the operator reported that no one answered. Now the word was the line had been disconnected.

"What do you think it means?" Evie asked.

"I don't know. Probably nothing. Maybe we got the wrong number from Leona Marks. Call her and find out."

The investigation of Mendel Kahn continued on its fitful course. A full week had passed since my meeting with Harold Feigenbaum. While the news of Kahn's treasure trove had all sorts of juicy implications, I still didn't know how I could trace where he got the jewelry in the first place or what he did with it after he left the Feigenbaums' home.

All the theorizing in the world wouldn't give me those answers. It also wouldn't reveal whether Oscar Eckhardt was a real person and if so, whether he or someone else had partnered with Kahn in assembling his portfolio of apartments. I'd hit a dead end in looking at that issue as well.

Of course, I hadn't yet contacted Shondor Birns, who might have been Kahn's deep pocket, according to Sophie Himmel. But upon reflection, I became less than enthusiastic about the idea of directly asking him about it. Why would a notorious gangster willingly tell a perfect stranger what he did with his money? For all Birns would know, I could be fronting for the cops or the IRS. The audacity of my inquiry would probably earn me a broken nose, or maybe something much worse.

While the Kahn case hadn't yet produced results, it was already costing me an arm and a leg. My accountant, Sheldon Lifschitz, delivered that message in a diatribe that afternoon at our bimonthly conference.

"This really is one hell of a job you're on," he complained. "You've worked it for over a month, and you haven't brought in any fees at all. Not one red cent."

"This is an important case, Shelly. Money's not the issue."

"I'm glad it's not the issue, because if it were, you'd have to shoot yourself. The expenses are through the roof. A trip to New York. Honoraria to witnesses. Advertisements in God-knows-how-many newspapers and magazines for weeks on end, and long-distance charges coming out your ears."

"It's not that bad," I said.

"It's worse than 'that bad', because knowing you, I'm not even seeing half of what you're spending on the case."

Sheldon noisily got up from the chair facing my desk. I watched as he began pacing the length of the office, immersed in his aggravation. He was an extremely slender fellow, with slumped shoulders, a gray mustache, and almost no hair on his head. He'd taken off his suit coat and rolled up his shirt sleeves, as if he were preparing to perform some physically demanding task.

"I can afford this, Shelly," I finally said to him. "I don't know what you're trying to tell me."

"I'm telling you that you need your head examined," Sheldon replied. "You're not supposed to work for free, and you're certainly not supposed to pay for the privilege. You're running a business, goddamn it, not a charity."

"Relax, Shelly, relax. This is something I have to do. Just accept it."

"I don't know why you have me on retainer at all," he said. "You need a keeper, not an accountant."

Sheldon's yelping notwithstanding, I wasn't in danger of a trip to the poorhouse. My savings were ample and then some, thanks to the cash I'd finagled years earlier from my investigation into the killing of Maury Sorin, Cleveland's own answer to Clarence Darrow. It turned out that my beloved ex-father-in-law had more than a little to do with Sorin's death; and in commemoration of our loving relationship, I'd fleeced him for more than a million bucks after I learned the truth about the murder. Forsythe didn't even get what he thought he was paying me for. My heart still wept for the poor bastard.

Of course, I hadn't held on to all the wealth that came my way. The taxman inevitably took a sizable chunk, and I gave seventy-five thousand to my brother to put in trust for his children. Two hundred fifty thousand went to the charity Maury Sorin's daughter started in her father's name after the dust settled. And I somehow managed to lose a considerable sum investing in the stock market, despite my broker's repeated assurances that it was "practically impossible" not to trade in the black.

After all that, I didn't have the kind of cash that would've let me dine on champagne and caviar at every meal, or buy a winter home in the French Riviera. But I certainly had enough to live comfortably in Cleveland, Ohio, and indulge a few personal quirks when choosing the matters I handled professionally — even if some of them cost me money instead of the opposite.

Sheldon knew none of the particulars of the Kahn case. I told him only that I was working on a big investigation that would occupy all my time for a month or more.

"You never know, Shel," I said to him. "We might be all right on this one. I know the client's been slow to pay, but I have no reason to believe he won't eventually fork over what he owes."

"Who're you kidding?" Sheldon responded. "It's obvious your client isn't playing this straight. He hired you to work exclusively for weeks on end without having the cash to pay you for it. Either that, or he has the money and he's holding back for no goddamned reason. Whether it's one or the other, you'll never see a dime."

A client who doesn't pay on time isn't always a deadbeat. I wanted to argue the issue with Sheldon, but decided leave it alone this time, since he was dead-on in his conclusion even if it was for all the wrong reasons. Of course I was never going to get paid for investigating Kahn.

That was no surprise to me. Even on the night of my first meeting with Rabbi Herb, I knew for certain I'd be footing my own bill for the work he was "hiring" me to do. I'd fibbed to Sheldon about there being some hope of payment, just to get a temporary reprieve from his harangue.

Herb obviously didn't have the wherewithal to cover my fees himself. As for payment from the Temple, I suspected the Rabbi lacked authority to retain me without approval from the board of trustees, which wasn't going to underwrite an investigation into one of its own, no matter how rancorous the gossip became concerning Kahn's history.

Herb had said he'd try to "tuck" my fees somewhere in the budget. But the expenditure would almost certainly be too large to write off as some conventional charge. I wasn't kidding myself, even if Herb wouldn't acknowledge the reality of the situation. I'd be working gratis on the Kahn case, or close enough.

Sheldon had calmed down only slightly by the time he unrolled his shirt sleeves, put on his coat, and headed out. "You weren't having a great year to begin with," he said as his parting shot. "Stop being a schmuck and get serious about what you're doing."

"Those are words to live by, Shelly. Very eloquent. You could be the new Dale Carnegie, with your own book: *Don't Be A Schmuck and Get Serious,* by Sheldon Lifschitz, C.P.A.."

"If I did write it," he replied as he exited the office, "you could be damn sure I wouldn't give away copies for free."

TWENTY-FIVE

I ENDED THE Thanksgiving weekend in the emergency room at Mount Sinai Hospital near University Circle. I was receiving treatment for injuries inflicted by the Hairy Slab in an attack outside Municipal Stadium late Sunday afternoon. I'd taken my nephew to the Browns-Cardinals game, and the Slab ambushed me when we left after the third quarter. I suffered a moderately severe concussion, a fractured cheekbone, and a broken nose. I managed to get my nephew out of harm's way before the Slab sprang the assault. He came away shaken, with one traumatic story to tell his parents.

Jake was supposed to take David to the Browns game. But Miriam's sister and brother-in-law came to town for Thanksgiving after all, notwithstanding her doctor's advice to avoid travel the last few weeks of her pregnancy. Game or no game, Jake couldn't possibly leave his unexpected houseguests on their last day in town. He was about to cancel the outing with David when I volunteered to go as his replacement. Jake usually bristled at the idea of putting either of his children in my charge, but this time he seemed genuinely grateful.

David and I arrived at the Stadium just before kickoff. The place was half full, which wasn't bad, all things considered. The game wasn't a marquee matchup: The Browns were the best team in the League, Chicago the worst. While the prospect of an uncompetitive game kept some fans away, the weather today was miserable enough to keep even the enthusiasts at home listening to the "contest" on the radio. You had to be a little crazy to show up for this one.

The Cardinals barely put up a fight. The Browns led 24-0 at halftime and added a field goal in the third quarter. Cleveland was going to win in a rout. I knew David would want to stay till the end no matter what, but I couldn't feel my toes anymore and my lips had probably turned blue. Fortunately, he didn't press the issue when I told him after the quarter ended that we had to leave to get home in time for dinner.

I had driven downtown to the game. It seemed easier than taking David on the Rapid Transit. I'd gotten lucky and found a place to park on the street, near East Ninth on Saint Clair. David and I left the Stadium on the east end and headed in that direction.

The Hairy Slab couldn't have possibly known in advance that I was going to the ballgame. He must've followed me downtown when I left my apartment to pick up David right before lunchtime. He also must've trailed us after we went into the Stadium — otherwise he wouldn't have known that we left when we did, or where we were going when we got outside.

The Slab launched the onslaught as David and I made our way through the Stadium parking lot. I caught a glimpse of him skulking behind us and immediately knew there would be trouble, the kind of trouble a kid David's age should never witness.

"I want you to turn around, very quietly and calmly, and walk back toward the Stadium," I told him. "Find a policeman and bring him over here. Tell him your uncle needs help."

"But Uncle Benny, I don't understand," David stammered.

"Please just do what I ask. I'll explain later."

I told David the section and row of the parking lot where we were standing. Then I turned him around and sent him on his way. I watched to make certain the Hairy Slab didn't ambush him in route.

That wasn't going to happen, because the Slab was in the process of ambushing me. He'd gone past us while we were talking, then doubled back. As I was monitoring David's return to the Stadium, the Slab snuck up from behind and whipped my noggin with the butt of his pistol, the same treatment I'd given him on the street outside Sophie Himmel's apartment.

The blow had its intended effect. Everything went black for an instant. When I came to, it felt like a pile of hot coals was smoldering on my skull.

"Not so much fun, is it, smart guy?" said the Hairy Slab as he planted the tip of his left boot squarely into my right knee. "Not goddamned fun at all."

I was bent over trying to catch my breath when the Slab landed an uppercut right above my mouth. I felt something crunch in my nose. As blood started dripping down, I momentarily checked out again.

The Slab wasn't finished. When I returned to an upright position, more or less, he grabbed his gun by its muzzle and thrashed me across my left cheek. The pain was excruciating, and I doubled over a second time.

"Was that your boy?" the Hairy Slab asked. When I didn't answer, he kicked my knee in the same spot he'd hit the first time and repeated his question.

"I don't know the kid," I responded through heaving breaths. "He was lost, and I sent him back to find his parents."

"He's your son, all right," said the Slab as he peered down the aisle David took on his return to the Stadium. "He's got to be your son because he's your spitting image. It's a shame he didn't stick around to watch his old man get humiliated..."

"Stop!" I screamed at the Hairy Slab as he turned back toward me. "Stop, and drop your gun, or I'll blow your fucking head off!"

I was woozy from the Slab's beating, but not too woozy to remember that I had my forty-five holstered inside my coat. I had either the presence of mind or the stupidity to reach for it when the Slab bent me over at the waist a second time. It couldn't have been a smooth move, given the shape I was in, but the Slab apparently didn't notice, occupied as he apparently was in analyzing my genetic connection to David. Now I had my gun pointed straight at his head.

"Don't shoot! Don't shoot!" the Hairy Slab yipped as he threw his pistol to the ground.

"Behave yourself, and I'll give you a chance," I said. "We're going to wait here until my 'son' comes back with the policeman I sent him to fetch. Then I can tell him all about Jerzy Dudek and the dirty work he does for his boss."

A possible arrest scared the Slab more than my forty-five did. He quickly looked around, then took off southward, away from the lake.

I should've at least chased after him, but I was in no condition to do anything, other than sit down and suffer, which is what I did.

After a few moments, I went looking for David. Turned out he'd gotten lost on his return to the Stadium and never found a cop. David was frantically calling out for me when I finally reached him

"Uncle Benny, what happened to you?" he asked when he got a look at my battered kisser.

"I slipped and fell," I slurred. "Hurt my face and my leg, too. But I'll be all right."

No one in their right mind would have driven in the state I was in. But being in that state by definition meant that I wasn't in my right mind, so drive I did, after limping with David from the Stadium parking lot to the Edsel.

I was frantic to get him home. Jake was going to be furious at me for exposing David to the violence practiced by the Hairy Slab. In my defense, I could argue that I did what I could to shield David from the worst of it, but that wasn't likely to earn a reprieve. The best way to protect myself from my brother's wrath was to get his son home as quickly as possible.

I couldn't tell you the route I took from downtown to Jake's house. I also couldn't explain how I managed to complete the trip without crashing my car or smashing up several others. We probably would've been just as well off if David had commandeered the Edsel, but that presumably didn't happen.

Fortunately for me, Jake wasn't home when we arrived. He'd just left to take his in-laws to the Terminal for their return trip to Philly.

Miriam got one look at me and became frantic. "What the hell happened, Benny?" she cried. "Were you and David in an accident?"

"David's fine," I slurred. "There was a little misunderstanding outside the Stadium. Everything's all right now."

Miriam sent David upstairs to wash. Then I gave her a disjointed account of what had taken place.

"I'm calling a cab," she told me. "You're going to the hospital. You look horrible, and you sound even worse. I won't take no for an answer."

I told the taxi driver to drive me home, but he refused. "I've been paid to drop you at Mount Sinai," he said, "and that's what I'm going to do."

"Come on now."

"What you do when you get there is your own business. I'd let them look me over if I were you. You sure must've taken some beating."

I was laying on a gurney in the emergency room shortly after eight o'clock when a uniformed Cleveland policeman approached. "Shaughnessy's the name," he told me. "It looks like someone danced the cha-cha on your face."

"Without the grace of Arthur Murray."

"I've come to see if you have any idea of who did it."

"A hairy slab," I said.

"What do you mean?"

"Sorry, officer, I was making a joke. I got beat up by a guy named Jerzy Dudek outside the Stadium this afternoon during the Browns game. That's Dudek: D-U-D-E-K."

"What did this Dudek fellow have against you?"

"You'll have to ask him," I said. "He's a thug and might've done it on behalf of his boss, a real estate investor named Mendel Kahn. I'm a private eye and I have a case against Kahn. He doesn't think too much of my work."

The police had the Hairy Slab in custody by mid-afternoon the next day. They released him less than 24 hours later without pressing charges.

The Slab, it seemed, had an airtight alibi that shot my story to hell. Four tenants of Kahn's apartment building in East Cleveland swore they had seen him Sunday afternoon working on the furnace in the basement. The cops checked, and the furnace showed signs of recent repair. To make certain the evidence received the proper interpretation, Kahn sent in a lawyer to represent the Slab. The case against him withered and died before it even began.

I stayed overnight at the hospital. The doctors wanted to keep me even longer, but I decided if I had to lie in bed, I might as well do it at my own place. I took a cab to the apartment and fixed myself a rye-and-soda before changing into my pajamas. Not even the alcohol eased the throbbing in my head.

I spent the afternoon thinking bewildered thoughts. I was still punch-drunk from the pummeling I took from the Slab. Periodically I became coherent enough to swear at him and his boss.

Around four-thirty, the phone rang, but I didn't answer it. It rang fifteen minutes later, and again fifteen minutes after that. Finally, I picked up the receiver.

"Chief, it's me."

"Sorry I didn't make it in, Evie," I said. "I had a little trouble over the weekend and need a day or two to recuperate. Hope you had a good Thanksgiving."

"I've got a problem, Mr. G."

As distracted as I was, I could hear the distress in her voice. "What's wrong, Evie?" I asked. "What happened?"

"It's my husband. They're letting him out of Mansfield early, in time for Christmas."

"I thought he isn't up for parole for another year and a half."

"He isn't," she said. "Or wasn't. He's getting an early release. I found out this morning. He got a sponsor who's vouched for him and promised him a good job on the outside."

"Who did that?" I asked as I rubbed my forehead. "Was it some-one in his family?"

"It's Mendel Kahn, that's who," Evie whimpered. "He's agreed to hire him as the superintendent at some apartment building in Euclid."

"Jesus Christ..."

"I'm afraid of my husband, Mr. G., and I don't want him coming home. I don't ever want to see him again for the rest of my life. I thought I'd have some time to take care of things."

Until the call, I'd assumed the Hairy Slab had acted on his own in bushwhacking me outside the Stadium, as payback for his humiliation in Cleveland Heights. But now I wondered whether Kahn had commissioned the assault as part of an offensive he was clearly waging against me and mine.

Intervening on behalf of Evie's husband was not a humanitarian gesture. Kahn had taken the trouble to look into Evie's background and found out her husband was in jail. By reviewing court records, he could've learned that the husband had a drinking problem and a nasty temper that he not infrequently unleashed on Evie. Then, with a few strategic calls, Kahn could've discovered that Evie only sporadically wrote her husband during his time in stir and visited him even less frequently.

Kahn had to know this wasn't some loving couple counting the days till their reunion. My bet was that he figured the husband's release would be a nightmare for Evie, which was precisely why he arranged it. In doing so, Kahn sent the unmistakable message that he'd observe no limits in lashing out so long as he remained under the microscope of my investigation.

The call from Evie ended without any resolution to her problem. I had no idea what to do. I'd never heard of a private citizen successfully lobbying the parole board to release a prisoner before his time was up. I didn't know it could be done. Kahn must've pulled some influential strings and concocted one hell of a sob story to accomplish this feat.

I liked to think of myself as a fighter. When someone got to me, I wanted to return the favor with twice the impact. But the Hairy Slab had laid me low. I couldn't do anything for Evie, much less avenge the attack, until the fuzziness cleared from my head and I could move my jaw and neck without wincing. Till then, I'd just have to wait it out.

TWENTY-SIX

EVIE'S HUSBAND WAS named Murray Brite. Kahn had a car pick him up in Mansfield when they released him the second week of December. Evie frantically scrambled to arrange for Brite to move in with his brother, but Brite had the driver deposit him at her apartment in Tremont. There he delivered a twenty-minute jeremiad on the multiple ways in which Evie had double crossed him.

Brite returned to the apartment the next evening with the priest from the parish where he and Evie had lived before his arrest. They came to work Evie over and make her take Brite in as her lawfully wedded husband.

The Father lectured Evie for nearly two hours on the holy institution of marriage and the Godly virtue of forgiveness. I would've expected Evie to resist this sales pitch, after what her husband had put her through. But she capitulated. Brite moved into her apartment as the man-of-the-house.

I telephoned Herb Kline to let him know about my shellacking at the hands of the Hairy Slab and the ploy Kahn pulled with Brite's parole. I wasn't expecting Herb to come up with some master plan on how to combat Kahn's hostilities. But at least he could listen to my troubles. I couldn't speak openly about the case with anyone else. Herb was my only alternative if I wanted to get something off my chest.

"The assault sounds barbaric," he said. "I'm sorry you had to go through it."

"That makes two of us."

"But the thing with your secretary's husband. I think you may be misreading that. Mendel was bringing him back to his wife after a long separation. It seems like an act of kindness — a peace offering to soften your stance against him, not to antagonize you."

"Come on, Herb," I said. "How did Kahn know Evie was married, and that her husband was at Mansfield? He had to research the situation pretty thoroughly. He had to have known Brite posed a serious threat to his wife's safety."

"The husband can't be that rotten," the Rabbi said.

"He *is* that rotten. That's what motivated Kahn to set him loose on Evie. Don't kid yourself, Herb. Kahn knew he was offering up a curse and not a blessing."

The Rabbi excused himself from the conversation to say hello to a congregant who stopped by his office. Upon returning, he reminded me of his wish to end the investigation of Kahn.

"I can't accommodate you, Herb," I responded. "I've found out too much about your boy Mendel just to drop everything now. If you don't want to be the client anymore, I'll be my own client."

"Mendel's coming after you so hard, Benny. It's almost like an admission of guilt — an admission that if you keep looking, you'll find the proof that he helped the Nazis during the War."

"That's my sense of it," I said. "But don't underestimate Kahn. He'll cover his tracks. I promise you there'll be nothing that ties him to what happened at the Stadium. And you yourself figured out what he'll say if I accuse him of deviling Evie: It was an act of goodwill to reunite her with her husband. He was just trying to help. Who can fault him for that?"

The conversation with Herb continued for another half hour. I told him that according to what Doctor Fleischman heard from his aunt, my investigation of Kahn was common knowledge among at least a certain segment of the Cleveland Jewish community.

"How can that be?" I asked. "I haven't said a word to anyone, and I'm sure you haven't, either."

"The culprit is probably Kahn himself," Herb explained. "He's let more than a few people know you're looking into the accusations made against him on Yom Kippur."

"Why is he doing that?"

"For sympathy, Benny. He says you're persecuting him with horse-shit charges and prying into his business practices, too."

"I can't believe anyone's buying that," I said.

"You'd be surprised. I've had several people call me about it. One board member suggested I contact you to insist you drop the case, given all the harm it was causing Mendel."

"How did you respond?"

"I told him it really wasn't a Temple matter."

"Now, that's ironic," I said.

The phone call wore me out. More than a week had passed since the Hairy Slab pounded and tortured me, and while my condition had improved, I still wasn't a hundred percent. Lying in bed for several days had sapped my stamina. After only a few hours back in the office, I was tuckered out. I thought about going home and was getting up to leave when I remembered something I wanted to do before calling it a day.

From my top desk drawer I pulled out the paper Ernie Murtaugh had given me with a number for Shondor Birns. I picked up the telephone and dialed, expecting the call to be the first step in a drawn-out process of securing an audience with him.

"Hello," answered a deep gruff voice after the fourth ring.

"Yes. I'm trying to get in touch with Shondor Birns."

"You're talking to him. Who is this?"

"You're Mr. Birns?"

"I'm Birns," he confirmed. "Now who the hell is this?"

I took a respectful tone. "Mr. Birns, my name is Benjamin Gold. I'm a private investigator, and I wanted..."

"Gold?" he said. "Ernie Murtaugh told me about a month ago you'd probably be calling. You been in Florida or something?"

"I wish. Mr. Birns, I was wondering if I could take fifteen minutes of your time..."

"No, but you can buy me lunch at the Theatrical tomorrow. I'll tell you what. Be there at twelve-thirty, and I'll buy *you* lunch."

"That was too goddamned easy," I said aloud after I hung up. A longstanding superstition went into high gear: If something began more smoothly than expected, it inevitably turned out to be a disaster.

It was this kind of incisive thinking that explained my elevated status in two professions. It was a wonder I didn't carry four-leaf clovers and commune with psychics.

For the time being, I needed to commune with my pillow. I'd worry about Shondor Birns after I took a good long nap.

TWENTY-SEVEN

THE RENDEZVOUS AT the Theatrical didn't begin on time, even though I showed up fifteen minutes early to make sure I wouldn't keep Birns waiting. Twelve-thirty came and went, and my lunch date hadn't arrived. Half an hour later, I was still sitting alone at the small table in the back I'd requested when I first came in. I was ready to pay for my drink and hit the road when Birns walked through the front door with two muscular companions wearing sports jackets but no ties. Birns motioned to them, and they peeled off to take seats at the bar. Shondor remained standing at the front looking idly around, in no apparent hurry to find me. It was my job to search him out, not the other way around.

I recognized Birns from the pictures that periodically appeared in the papers. Like his chaperons, he came to the restaurant without a tie. He wore a tight gray suit that showed off the sharp contours of his physique. Shondor was around fifty, but he looked at least ten years younger. Puffing on a big cigar, he didn't appear to have a care in the world.

I had to calm myself as I walked over to get him. This was a guy who two months earlier had been on trial for the attempted murder of one of his compatriots in the policy racket. The case was open-and-shut, by all accounts, yet ended in a hung jury. Shondor seemingly got away with everything, no matter how serious the offense or how damning the evidence.

"Mr. Birns, I'm Benjamin Gold," I said when I reached him. "Thank you for coming."

"You already got a table?"

"In the back."

"I'll get better," he said as he summoned the maître d.

We ended up at a booth toward the front of the restaurant that was large enough to accommodate six or seven. Birns apparently was used to conducting business from this spot. I myself would've preferred a more secluded setting, but if Shondor wasn't worried about attracting attention, I guessed I wasn't, either.

"Somebody did a number on your face," he said to me after we ordered our lunch.

"I was sleepwalking and bumped into a door."

Birns ignored my response. "Who did it?" he asked.

"An upstanding citizen by the name of Jerzy Dudek."

"Dudek did this to you?"

"He did," I said. "Do you know him?"

"Dudek's a mutt," Birns said. "He worked for me years ago. I thought he moved back to Pittsburgh."

"No, he still lives around here. He's working for another of your former employees, Mendel Kahn."

"Kahn," Shondor repeated. "He's why you're here. Ernie said you wanted to ask me about him."

"Kahn worked for you as a dishwasher at the Alhambra."

"Yeah, I know."

"And he's gone on to buy a number of apartment buildings," I said.

"What's it got to do with me, Gold?"

"That's what I'm trying to find out, Mr. Birns. It seems impossible that someone could go from being an immigrant dishwasher to a successful real estate investor in as little time as it took Mendel Kahn. He would've needed cash from someone to make the leap. I've tried to figure out who that could've been, and so far I've drawn a blank. I'm wondering whether you were the one who put money into his properties."

Just then the waitress returned with a drink from the bar for Shondor. He thanked her, complimented her outfit, and reached out and pinched her fanny.

"Myrtle's terrific," he said. "She takes care of me always."

I sat in silence as Birns sipped his drink. I didn't want to repeat my question, but I couldn't think of anything else to say. I was about to ask again when Birns spoke up.

"What's your interest in Kahn's business, Gold? Why do you care where he got his money?"

"There was an incident at our temple on Yom Kippur," I said. "Someone spotted Kahn and identified him as a Nazi collaborator during the War. Kahn denies it, but I've been hired to find out who's telling the truth. I'm trying to learn whether Kahn is who he says he is and whether he's the legitimate businessman he claims to be. Investigating his finances is part of that."

The explanation may have been essentially true, but it sounded like a stretch as it came out of my mouth. If I had been Shondor, I very well might've ended the conversation then and there. But Birns had questions about the accusations against Kahn.

"What do they say he did for the Nazis during the War?"

"He oversaw a ghetto for them and ran a work crew at Auschwitz. He supposedly beat one of his men to death."

"A Jew?" Birns asked.

"A Jew. The other workers were Jewish, too, and he treated them as cruelly as the Germans did."

Birns was still stewing over this information when our lunches arrived. Myrtle received no attention this time around, and Shondor seemed no more interested in eating his meal than I was in eating mine. A good five minutes passed before he spoke.

"I'm a linen salesman, Gold. I don't have cash lying around to invest in real estate. If Kahn has a partner, it isn't me or anyone I know."

The proclamation was not convincing. Birns said it in a way that made me strongly suspect the opposite was true. But Birns wasn't the sort of guy I could prod or cross examine. If he denied involvement with Kahn, even in an incredible way, I had no choice but to accept it.

Fortunately, Shondor wasn't finished talking. "I can't tell you where Kahn got all his money to buy apartments," he said, "but I know where he got some of it. He had jewelry that belonged to his mother or aunt or someone that he brought with him from Europe."

"Jewelry?"

"Yeah. Kahn wanted to sell it, but didn't know how, and didn't speak the language all that well. So I helped him find a buyer. I know a lot of people, so it wasn't hard."

"How much jewelry did Kahn have?"

"Oh, I don't know. Two or three rings, maybe, and maybe a necklace. It wasn't much."

Shondor was a notorious fence, not a small-timer who'd bother with a few family heirlooms. The jewelry he sold for Kahn almost certainly came from the sack described by Harold Feigenbaum, which contained far more than a handful of pieces. Birns operated on a scale large enough to dispose of everything Kahn had to offer. And Kahn must've received a generous return from the transaction.

Otherwise Birns wouldn't have said that the proceeds paid for part of his real estate holdings.

"Do you recall how much Kahn got for his jewelry?" I asked.

"You're pressing your luck, Gold. I ain't gonna remember how much he got on a deal from ten years ago."

This time Shondor clammed up for real. But I was satisfied. He certainly hadn't told me everything he knew or everything I wanted to find out. He might or might not have put money into Kahn's real estate ventures. If he knew whether Kahn had a business partner, he'd kept the news to himself. Still, thanks to Birns, I now had the scoop on what became of Kahn's grab-bag of jewelry. Kahn began remaking himself as landed gentry with the cash realized from that loot.

Birns turned his attention to the meat loaf he'd ordered for lunch. Between mouthfuls, he asked whether I was taking on new clients. All I could do was nod cautiously.

"I want to find out about one of my fighters," Shondor said. "I think he tanked a bout at the Arena last week. I got my suspicions, but I got no proof."

"Someone else would be better for that job," I responded. "I really don't know much about boxing."

"Neither did this schmuck, judging from the way they wiped the floor with him."

When Birns finished his meal, he signaled his troops at the bar and stood to leave. The abrupt departure took me by surprise.

"Maybe I should pay the check," I said.

"I told you it was on me, Gold. They'll put it on my tab."

I trailed Shondor on his path out of the restaurant. Before he and his musclemen left, he turned to me with one last message.

"Listen," he said. "I want you to let me know what you find out about Kahn and the Nazis. Either way, I want to know."

I intended to promise Birns that I certainly would do so. But he was already out the door before I could say a word.

Twenty-eight

Nothing much got done at the office in the week following the surprise deliverance of Evie's husband. Evie alternated between frantic rage and inconsolable grief over the resumption of her life as Mrs. Murray Brite. After just a few days, the reality of being with her husband extinguished any illusion that the homecoming could actually work out. Evie spent most of her time at work weeping at her desk or arguing with her sister-in-law on the telephone.

Periodically she'd ask me how she might extricate herself from the crisis. Could she legally lock her husband out of the apartment? What would it take to get his parole revoked? Evie even contemplated the possibility of changing religions so she could pursue a divorce without violating her obligations as a Catholic. Her pathetic desperation put me in a funk of my own.

Evie did manage to complete one task. She got hold of Karen Sontag in New York, who asked Leona Marks about the telephone number she'd given us for her friend in Israel, Leah Bloom. Turned out that either Leona or we had inverted two of the digits. I called Tel Aviv the same day I received the corrected number. This time the call went through.

A lot of good it did. I couldn't get Leah Bloom to recount her story about spotting Yitzhak Fried on the street. I didn't find out whether she'd seen him another time or heard anything about him.

The dialogue never got that far because the only thing Leah Bloom said during our entire conversation that I understood was "No speak English." She repeated the phrase several times, but I didn't decipher it immediately, given her thick accent.

I was reasonably certain Leah Bloom was speaking to me in Yiddish. My familiarity with that language consisted mostly of obscenities and slang, none of which came up in what she was saying. The inability to communicate was almost absolute. I didn't understand her any more than she understood me.

I did say Leona Marks's name several times, as well as Yitzhak Fried's, in hopes that Leah Bloom might put two and two together and figure out why I was calling. But it was a tenuous equation I wanted her to make. She almost certainly didn't know that someone in the U.S. was trying to verify Fried's whereabouts, or that Leona had offered up her letter as proof of the matter. Still, assuming she made out my pronunciation of the two names, she might've surmised that I wanted to ask about the sighting of Fried she'd described to Leona.

It would've been terrific, I supposed, if Leah Bloom guessed my purpose in calling. But she still wouldn't have known who I was or how to get in touch with me. I'd have to telephone again with a translator on the line. I wanted to tell her I planned to do just that, as quickly as I could arrange it. Obviously, though, if I could have intelligibly delivered that message, the reason for the second call would have disappeared.

"Doc, I need your help again," I told Fleischman when I reached him at his office in New York.

"What is it, Mr. Gold?"

"We got a telephone number for our letter-writer in Tel Aviv. But she speaks no English, only Yiddish."

"You want me to give her a call?" he asked.

"What the two of us ought to do is hop on a plane and go over and interview her, face-to-face. That'd be one hell of an excursion. I'd do it, too, except it would probably kill my accountant."

"The cost," said Fleischman.

"I'm an inveterate spendthrift," I said. "So, yeah, I want you to give her a call."

Fleischman and I discussed the advantages and disadvantages of his telephoning Leah Bloom by himself, as opposed to also having me on the line. We decided he knew the facts well enough to handle it on his own. My involvement would only make the conversation more cumbersome. Fleischman could conduct the interview, then send a detailed description of what he'd found out.

"Sounds simple enough," Fleischman concluded. "Give me the number, and I'll try her tomorrow."

"No," I said. "I'll send you the number by air mail, along with a two-hundred-dollar check to cover your expenses and to pay for your services."

"That's not necessary..."

"This investigation is my headache, Doc, not yours. You've got a job of your own, and I've already imposed enough. You've got to get something for your efforts."

"Your accountant won't be happy, Mr. Gold."

"Don't worry," I said. "Once I explain who you are, he'll know we're getting a terrific bargain."

I addressed an envelope to Fleischman that afternoon and went to put it in the mail myself. It was Friday, and I headed home from the post office rather than returning to work. Evie's dire straits had worn me out. I knew she couldn't help it, but we needed at least a temporary return to normalcy if we were ever going to get any work done. I was hoping the weekend would give Evie a chance to reconcile herself to her husband's presence, as miserable as it was.

That wasn't how it played out. Evie showed up at the office Monday morning with a black eye and a cut across her left cheek. After finishing his Saturday shift at work, Murray Brite had gone to a bar in Ohio City for a three-hour toot, then came home and practiced his jabbing technique on Evie's face.

"You should've called the cops," I said as she recounted the ordeal.

"What good would it have done? Besides, he wouldn't let me near the telephone."

"Any idea of what set him off?"

"There's no mystery about that," Evie said. "Murray wants me to quit my job here and go to work as a secretary somewhere else. Maybe as a waitress in a restaurant."

"He thinks you'll make more?"

"It's not the money. It's Mr. Kahn. He says you're trying to destroy him. He doesn't think it's right that the wife of one of his employees is working for somebody who's trying to put him out of business."

"Kahn knew you were Murray's wife when he grabbed him out of Mansfield and gave him a job," I said. "He must've been planning all along to pressure you to quit."

"I don't care what he was planning," Evie said. "I'm not quitting. I got this job on my own and kept it for all this time. I like working here. When I told Murray I wouldn't quit, that's when he started throwing punches."

Brite had continued his assault on Evie till she left to come in that morning. As she was walking out of the apartment, he told her that the beating she'd received so far would be a cakewalk compared to what would happen if she came home without resigning her post, effective immediately.

"Is there somewhere for you to stay tonight?" I asked. "Obviously you can't return to that apartment."

"Murray would find me at the only places I could go... My brother's... My friend Ethel's... He'd come for me wherever I went ten minutes after I didn't show up at the regular time."

"You'll have to go to a hotel, then," I said. "Any chance that Murray will be home this morning?"

"Not that I know of," Evie answered. "He's scheduled to work nine till five."

"Good. I want you to go to the apartment right now and pack a suitcase. Then come back downtown. We'll get you a room somewhere."

"I'm sorry to be such a headache, Mr. G.," she said unhappily.

"This isn't your fault, Evie," I said.

She went home and returned with her bag right around noon. She was less agitated than she'd been earlier, but still looked like she'd been through the wringer. I thought lunch would buck her up, but she barely touched the ribeye I ordered for her at Kornman's.

Later that afternoon, we went to the Hotel Cleveland and booked a room on the tenth floor. Evie registered as Miss Nora Hammett of San Francisco, California. The clerk seemed to sense the phoniness of the pseudonym but gave us no trouble after I paid for three nights in advance.

Evie was safe and sound, but only for the time being. Whenever it came time for her to go home, her husband would be waiting for her, with clenched fists. I could think of no way to force him out.

He'd left jail legitimately, more or less, and had the right to live under the same roof with his wife. The most obvious means of escape was to end the marriage, but Evie's faith gave her an ingrained aversion to divorce, so that route remained permanently closed.

I spent the evening at the Academy Tavern near Shaker Square, imbibing scotch-and-water and pondering other options. There really was only one. I reached this conclusion after my second drink, and it inspired me to have two more.

Murray Brite didn't have to do what Evie wanted him to do, and he certainly had no reason to honor my preferences. But he did have to listen to Kahn, who'd extricated him from Mansfield and given him the job he needed to remain in the good graces of the parole board. If Kahn told Brite he had to take an apartment at the building where he was working, he would have no choice but to comply. Kahn could do any number of things to make the transition sweeter. He could give him extra time off or pay a relocation bonus when Brite moved from Evie's apartment to one of his own.

Kahn naturally wouldn't go out of his way to protect Evie. He sprang Brite from jail for the very purpose of torturing her (and indirectly, me) with the violent cruelty Brite had displayed over the weekend.

I'd have to offer the puppet master an enticement he couldn't resist to move his vicious marionette off the stage. The enticement Kahn so greatly coveted was for me to end my investigation. If I did that, he might become willing to extract Murray Brite from Evie's life and restore the status quo ante.

I didn't equivocate long about what I would do. Evie was a good kid and a great secretary. I couldn't have her life endangered because of a case I was handling. Rabbi Herb wanted to drop the matter anyway, and while I had some alluring leads, I still had found no hard proof that Mendel Kahn wasn't who he said he was.

I'd telephone Kahn in the morning. If he would reign in Murray Brite, I'd leave him alone, forever.

TWENTY-NINE

I GOT TO the office before eight-thirty the next day. Evie got there even earlier.

"What? Did you sleep here?" I asked.

"Not at all," she said. "The room you got me was wonderful. It just was a very short commute."

The Hotel Cleveland sat right next to Terminal Tower. A short passageway connected the two buildings.

"That's right," I said. "You wouldn't have had any excuse if you'd been late this morning."

I waited about an hour before telephoning Mendel Kahn. His secretary answered the call.

"Mr. Kahn isn't in," she told me. "He had an appointment out of the office."

"Will he be back later?"

"After lunch, I think."

"Could you have him get back to me then? It's Benjamin Gold. He has the number."

I took a seat on the couch across from Evie's desk and filled her in about what I'd been doing while she was indisposed. She couldn't get over the fact that I'd actually had lunch with Shondor Birns, as if he were some movie star or Washington V.I.P. She laughed about my international misadventure with Leah Bloom and nodded when I explained that Fleischman was going to act as my surrogate on a second call.

I'd gotten up and walked halfway into my office when the outer door opened. "Oh my God!" Evie shrieked when she saw who was entering. "Murray!"

I'd never seen Brite before. He was on the short side, about five-seven, and seemed very thin. He had on a ragged brown coat that was plainly not heavy enough for winter weather in Cleveland. He didn't wear a hat over his long jet-black hair. Brite hadn't shaved for several days. Thick stubble covered his mug. He was noticeably shivering, and his ears were a luminous shade of red.

"Get your things. You're coming with me." Brite was obviously talking to Evie, but his eyes were fixed on me.

"I'm not leaving," Evie said. "I've got work to do."

"You don't work here no more — not for this bastard. Now get your goddamned purse and coat so we can get going."

When Evie didn't move, Brite walked around her desk and grabbed her arm. Evie yanked it away and curled up in her seat.

"Goddamn it," he said. "You're going to listen if I have to make you."

Brite began manipulating his fingers, in warmup for a slap or a punch. I shouted his last name before he could land a blow.

"You stay out of this, scumbag," Brite growled at me.

"You're reserving yourself a seat on the bus back to Mansfield," I said. "Your parole officer won't like the way you're bludgeoning Evie."

"This is between me and my wife. This doesn't concern my parole officer."

"It does when you beat her up so badly that she comes to work with bruises all over her face. It does when you harass and assault her in public."

"Get up, you whore," Brite said to Evie as he grabbed her hair and pulled.

"Enough!" I bellowed and started toward Brite. I'd only made it a few steps when he pivoted toward me and pulled out a switchblade from his coat pocket.

I heard a click as the blade thrust forward. "Murray!" Evie cried in horror. "For God's sake!"

Brite used his free hand to belt Evie across the jaw. It wasn't a knock-out punch, but it might as well have been. Evie rocked woozily for a few seconds after taking the hit, then fainted. Her limp body slid from the chair onto the floor.

Brite looked briefly at his wife, then turned and started toward me. "This is all your goddamned doing," he snarled. "You're a snake, just like Mr. Kahn says you are."

I tried to keep my cool. "Before you get any closer," I said, "I want you to know I've got a forty-five right inside my coat. A shiv versus a gun — you know what wins that fight. You'd better put your knife back in your pocket."

"I don't believe you for a second," said Brite, although he did stop advancing.

"Okay." I reached deliberately into my jacket and pulled out the gun. "Do you believe me now?"

Just then the office door opened and in stepped the postman whistling an offkey rendition of "When the Swallows Come Back to Capistrano." He stopped dead in his tracks and ended the whistling when he saw the scene playing out in front of him.

Nobody said or did anything for what seemed like an eternity. Then I told the postman he had better turn around and leave. As he backed his way toward the door, Brite made a move toward him.

"Uh uh," I barked. "You stay put." Both Brite and the postman complied with my command.

"Not you," I said to the postman. "Him."

The postman bolted out the door, presumably to fetch the police. "The police," I said out loud. The postman would tell them he came into the office and found Evie unconscious on the floor and me and Brite in a lethal standoff. Brite would claim I instigated the confrontation, but the cops wouldn't believe him — not after Evie and I explained how he'd showed up that morning intent upon resuming the abuse he'd begun over the weekend.

The police didn't usually give much credence to what a private eye had to tell them, but they'd think even less of a story coming from a convicted felon just paroled from jail. The cops would lock Brite up for assault and possession of a deadly weapon, among other possible charges. With any luck, they'd reunite him shortly with his cellmates in Mansfield.

Brite collapsed the blade of his knife. "I'm getting out of here."

"No you aren't," I answered, taking a step closer and pointing the gun squarely at his abdomen. "Drop that knife on the floor and stand perfectly still. The police will be here soon enough."

"You can't hold me up."

"I can and I will," I said. "You've gone way over the line, Murray, and you're going to be here when I tell the cops all about it."

Brite looked at the door, then at me, then back at the door. I took a half-step closer to him and extended my arm holding the forty-five. Brite dropped the knife.

"Can I at least sit down?" he asked.

"No. You'll have plenty of time to sit after this is over. The police should be here within ten minutes."

It didn't take that long. After a few moments, a voice yelled to us through the closed door.

"I'm patrolman Patrick Finnegan of the Cleveland Police Department. Put down your weapons. Put down your weapons now."

"We'll put them down, officer," I hollered back.

"How many of you are in there?"

"There's three of us, including my secretary. She's passed out at the moment."

"I'm going to push the door open," said the officer. "Then I want the two of you to come out, slowly, one at a time, with your hands up above your head. Do you understand?"

"I got it, officer," I said.

"What about the other guy?" Finnegan asked.

"I'm coming out," Brite mumbled belligerently.

"If you don't mind, officer, I'm going to send him out first," I said. "And I'm going to hold my gun on him till he's through the door and in your custody. If I don't, I'm afraid he'll pick up his knife and come for me."

"That's not okay," said Finnegan. "This isn't the Wild Wild West."

"Then come in here and protect me," I said. "This animal is ruthless. I don't want him to have any chance of sticking me with that blade."

We negotiated the point for a good five minutes. Finnegan finally agreed to let me keep my gun while Brite exited after I assured him I'd kick the weapon through the door before I surrendered.

Finnegan's colleagues handcuffed both me and Brite when we finally made it out to the hallway. They then called the postman to come upstairs and identify us as the culprits. "Those were the two I saw," he confirmed. "The guy in the suit works here."

The proceedings moved inside the office. The cops picked up

Brite's switchblade, checked on Evie, and took a rambling statement from the postman.

I then gave my version of the morning's events, spicing up the presentation with details about Brite's thrashing of Evie on Saturday and Sunday.

Evie had pulled out of it by the time I finished. She corroborated my description of events, up till the time the lights went out on her.

Next it should've been Brite's turn, but he chose not to talk. "I want my lawyer," he said. "I've got nothing to say till he gets here."

"Now don't be that way," said the cop conducting the interviews. "There's no need to involve your lawyer in this."

Brite responded by rattling off the name of Howard Resnick, the same attorney Kahn had engaged when Dudek was accused of assaulting me outside the Stadium. The cop tried to convince Brite he didn't need a lawyer, but he wouldn't budge.

"You're leaving us with no choice," the cop finally told Brite. "You can call your counsel from the station. We're taking you in."

Evie and I walked over to talk to Finnegan while another officer led Brite out the door. "I wish this hadn't happened," the patrolman said apologetically. "They obviously let the man out of jail too soon. He just isn't prepared to reenter civilized society."

"What's going to happen to him?" Evie asked.

"He'll face various charges. Almost certainly he's going back to Mansfield."

"That's too bad," Evie dutifully said. I suppressed a grin.

"Don't worry, missus," said Finnegan. "Your husband's not always going to act this way, and he'll come up for parole again. He should be more ready the next time, and you and he can get on with your lives."

Mendel Kahn returned my telephone call around two o'clock that afternoon. I expected him to tear into me about Brite's arrest, but he apparently hadn't heard about it.

"What is it this time, Gold?" he began the conversation. "You calling to apologize?"

"You should be apologizing to me," I said. "Or at least to my secretary, for pulling her scum-of-the-earth husband out of jail to terrorize her."

Kahn chuckled. "It was a act of charity, Gold," he said. "I'm a great humanitarian. That's the way everybody will see it. Everybody but you."

"You're torturing her, Kahn. The man beats her, at your direction."

"I didn't tell him to beat her. I just insisted he make her quit."

"He isn't accomplished at the means of subtle persuasion," I said. "He pounds people into submission or stabs them to get what he wants."

"You know, Gold, you're the one responsible for this. You're trying to destroy me with that investigation of yours. I've got to protect myself any way I can."

"Go after me, Kahn, not my secretary."

"You could protect her from all of this," he said. "I could make this problem disappear if you'd do what you should've done a long time ago and drop the whole thing."

"I might've considered it," I said. "But there's no need now. Your man Brite's in jail, and he'll be back to Mansfield by the end of the week."

I pulled the timetable for Brite's remand out of thin air. The embellishment probably wasn't necessary. Kahn became positively apoplectic when I told him about the morning's events. He swore at me and vowed to have Brite back at home with Evie within 24 hours. Then he hung up.

I called a lawyer I knew in the city prosecutor's office. I wanted to make sure Kahn couldn't make good on his threat. I needn't have worried. As my buddy explained, cons walked on extremely thin ice when they first got out on parole. Brite and his lawyer tried to defend his conduct, but the judge didn't buy it. He ended up celebrating Christmas in the familiar confines of his cell in Mansfield.

Thirty

The Suffolk Apartments sat on a side street near East Seventieth and Superior in the Hough neighborhood. I'd identified it as one of the inner-city abominations in Kahn's portfolio of properties. I decided to go take a look-see. Morbid curiosity piqued my interest — I wondered whether the building could possibly be as squalid and dilapidated as the ones Alvy Mishkin described during our conversation at the Schvitz. But I also had the yips. Sitting around waiting for something to break on the Kahn case was torture, so I decided to do something that was at least relevant, if not necessarily useful.

I picked a swell day for a field trip. Ferocious winds were whipping in off the lake, as the temperature hovered just above the freezing mark. A mixture of snow and rain had begun falling during the morning rush hour and showed no signs of letting up as I drove from the office to the apartments. The Edsel plowed through large accumulations of slush as I made my way eastward.

The weather might've been miserable, but you couldn't tell it from a street view of the Suffolk. Most of the windows were at least partially open. I discovered why when I walked into the building and gagged from the wretched stench.

"Oh my God," I said to an older man who was sitting in a chair near the front door. "What's that horrible smell?"

"Plumbing's been out in the building for five days," he told me. "Water main line's busted."

"What's the landlord doing about it?"

"Oh, he'll fix it, all right," the man gloomily commented. "He'll fix it when he's good and ready, and not any time sooner."

I stepped back outside for a moment for my stomach to settle. The rainy snow bounced off my hat and coat as I looked over the building. It was a three-story wooden house that Kahn had divided into seven or eight apartments, judging by the number of windows. The Suffolk had been painted dark brown, masking the multitude of gaps, cracks, and holes in its façade. Two fractured chimneys jutted out from the roof. A swing on the front porch had fallen off its frame and broken in two. A burned-out jalopy sat on the street directly in front of the building. Cans overflowing with rubbish lined the driveway to the backyard.

After not too long, the weather outside became at least as intolerable as the stink inside. I took two huge gulps of air and reentered the Suffolk, determined to look over an apartment or two, talk to a few tenants, then call it a day.

I hadn't noticed it during my first foray into the building, but the place was jam-packed. The doors of both apartments on the first floor were open. Three or four people congregated in the hallway outside both of them. The temperature was frigid, seemingly colder than it had been out on the sidewalk. Most of the people I saw had on coats and gloves and hats. Steam came out of their mouths when they spoke.

I eventually adapted to the putrid aroma of undrained waste water. At least vomiting no longer seemed like a serious threat.

I confirmed my expectation that the tenants would all be Negroes. While I was trying to decide which of them to approach for an interview, a short middle-aged woman bundled in a blue woolen coat walked over and made the choice for me.

"You got business here, mister?" she wanted to know. "You come to see somebody?"

"I'm here investigating the landlord," I said. "You know him?"

"Yeah, I know him. Is he in trouble with the law?"

"Not right now he isn't, but you never know."

"They ought to throw him in jail for the stuff he's pulling here," she said. "If this ain't criminal, I don't know what is."

Her name was Fanny McGee, and she lived in one of the second-floor apartments with her son, daughter, her daughter's husband, and their new-born baby. Fanny moved to Cleveland from Alabama in 1942 to work in the steel mills. She didn't want to tell me any more about her background, and I didn't press her.

Fanny's apartment could reasonably accommodate two people at most. "We all got to stay here," she said, "cause there's nowhere else to live in this town."

The apartment offered slightly more charm and comfort than a bombed-out flat in London at the end of the War. There was a kitchenette, a living room, a bathroom, and a bedroom the size of an average walk-in closet. Paint peeled from the top of the pock-marked walls. A hole in the living room ceiling went straight through to the apartment above. A tangle of electrical wire sagged down almost a foot from a hole in the bedroom wall. The floors consisted either of dingy yellow linoleum, decaying hardwood, or the remnants of carpeting Kahn has scavenged from Mishkin.

"Are all of the apartments in the building the same size as yours?" I asked Fanny.

"This is one of the bigger ones. Some of them don't have a kitchen or their own bathroom."

"Have you had any trouble with rats or mice?"

"Rats or mice?" Fanny smirked as she thrust her hands in the air. "They should have to pay rent they're here so much. Rats especially."

"Where do they get in?"

"There are holes in the kitchen and the bathroom, next to the pipes. They come in through there."

A thin teenaged girl who must've been Fanny's daughter walked into the apartment with a fussy infant cradled in her arms. The sight filled me with rage. A shit sewer like Fanny's apartment wasn't a fit place for anyone to live, but certainly not for a baby. I wanted to tell Fanny to pack her things and have her family do likewise. Sheldon Lifschitz be damned — I'd put them up in a hotel until I could find a more suitable place for them. It would've been a noble gesture, but ultimately a futile one, when I considered the larger picture. I could relocate Fanny and her crew all right, but the other tenants at the Suffolk would remain trapped in their own disgusting shit sewers.

"You said you know the landlord," I reminded Fanny. "Who is he?"

"You're checking up on him, mister. You must know who he is."

"I just want to make sure we're talking about the same guy."

"It's Kahn," Fanny said. "Mendel Kahn. He owns what's called the Kandee company, and he owns this building."

"How'd you get to know him?"

"Not in any way he'll want to remember. Last winter the furnace in the building started acting up. We were without heat off and on for almost three weeks. We called Kahn, and he said he'd send someone to fix it, but he didn't. So when the first of the month came, we all got together and decided we wouldn't pay our rent until something happened."

"That was dangerous," I said. "He could've kicked you all out."

"We realized that. But we needed to get his attention, and it worked. He came down here with his business partner to talk to us."

"Did they go apartment by apartment?"

"Hell, no," said Fanny. "Kahn didn't really want to talk to anyone. So he gathered all of us together in the backyard, and we talked with him for about twenty minutes, right before dark."

"Who spoke for the tenants?"

"Everybody spoke for themselves, and all at the same time. They were complaining about the furnace and all the other problems at the building. People had a lot to get off their chest."

"How did Kahn react?" I asked.

"He didn't like it. He thought he was only going to have to talk about the furnace."

"Too bad for him."

"Kahn told us he would have the furnace fixed, so long as we paid our rent immediately. As for everything else, he said we were responsible for keeping up our own apartments, not him."

"He was right, legally," I said. "But that doesn't excuse him for renting out apartments that were rat-traps to begin with."

"He said we had nothing to complain about. He said this place was like paradise compared to the camps the Germans sent him and his family to during the War."

My jaw dropped, literally. "He didn't really say that, did he?"

"He sure enough did," Fanny confirmed. "He told us that instead of complaining, we should be thanking him for how good we had it."

Not surprisingly, Kahn's oratory didn't placate anyone. He was damn lucky they didn't string him up.

Thirty

Kahn was chastened enough to have a workman come out the next morning to overhaul the furnace. Fanny and her cohorts then ended their rent strike. "There was nothing else we could do," she said. "It wasn't going to do any good."

"What about Kahn's business partner? Why was he there for the big meeting?"

"Oscar?" Fannie said. "Who the hell knows. Maybe Kahn wanted him for moral support."

"Had you ever seen Oscar before?"

"Never saw him before that day, or since."

"What did he have to say about the condition of the apartments?" I asked. "Was he any more sympathetic than Kahn?"

"He didn't say much. Just mumbled when Kahn would tell us something. Oscar must've said something, though, because I remember he had a thick accent."

I asked Fanny what Oscar looked like. In response, she shrugged her shoulders.

"He looked like nothing," she said. "Average height, average build, average looks. Hair so short it was hard to say what color it was. He looked like nothing at all."

Fanny walked me up to the third floor of the building to see her friend Lula's apartment. It was in even more decrepit shape than Fanny's. As we chatted, Lula showed me a scar on her shin from a rat bite she'd suffered the previous summer.

"I killed the sucker, though," Lula assured me. "With a frying pan and a cleaver."

I asked Fanny and Lula how much they paid in rent. "Sixth five dollars a month," they both told me.

"For these places?"

"Some people pay a little more," said Fanny. "Some a little less. It all averages out to sixty-five."

This information had my blood pressure zooming again. But I kept quiet, to avoid agitating Fanny and Lula about an injustice they could do nothing at all to change.

If all of Kahn's tenements were like the Suffolk, Alvy Mishkin had understated their horror. Kahn was a bona fide slumlord (along with his nondescript partner, Oscar Eckhart, who was a real live person, after all). Bona fide slumlord, and a true son-of-a-bitch — the type who rationalized the suffering he inflicted on others with the suffering he himself had endured.

I was walking down the staircase of the Suffolk on my way out of the building when I heard screaming and moaning coming from the back of the building. By the time I got downstairs, everyone on the first floor was flocking toward the commotion. I followed suit.

"Stay still, Miss Shirley," someone said as I reached the crowd that had gathered just inside the back door. "Stay perfectly still."

"Somebody call her grandson," said another voice.

"We've got to get an ambulance over here right away," intoned a third observer.

Miss Shirley needed prompt medical attention. She was in her late sixties or seventies, I supposed, and lived in the apartment next to Fanny's. She had gone to the store and was hurrying to get back home, out of the rain and snow. But there was a jagged crease in one of the stones of the walkway that led to the backdoor. A build-up of slush apparently obscured it, and Miss Shirley walked right into it, turning her right ankle so severely that it nearly snapped in two.

Fanny came to hold Miss Shirley's hand while they waited for the ambulance to arrive.

"How long has the walkway been broken?" I asked her as I stood nearby.

"Forever," she said. "It was one of the complaints we made when Kahn came over here last winter."

"He never tried to fix it?"

"He did what he always did, which was absolutely nothing. And now this happens."

I wanted to express my sympathies to Miss Shirley, but she seemed too anguished to listen, and I couldn't come up with what seemed like the appropriate words. So I nodded to Fanny and headed for the Edsel.

Thirty-One

The next morning, I called Ernie Murtaugh at the *Plain Dealer* to ask for another favor. "I've spent weeks looking for a guy named Oscar Eckhardt and I've come up empty," I told him. "His name doesn't appear in the Cleveland directory or the directory for any town or city near here."

"Maybe he's a figment of your imagination," Ernie suggested.

"Eckhardt's real all right. Someone verified that for me yesterday. I was wondering whether you could check the paper's archives to see if you have anything on him."

"I'll do what I can."

Ernie called back an hour later. "Today's your lucky day," he said. "We've found your needle in a haystack."

"Eckhardt?"

"The one and only," Ernie confirmed. "On June 25th of last year, we ran a story about a series of petty thefts from vendors at the West Side Market. One of the victims was Oscar Eckhart, who — and I quote — 'has run a candy stand at the facility for several years.'"

"Anything else on Oscar?" I asked.

"Just that he lost twelve dollars from the theft."

"If this is the same guy I'm looking for, he certainly could afford it."

The West Side Market wasn't open every day, so I had to wait 24 hours before going over in search of my prey. The break gave me a chance to reflect upon Eckhardt's situation. I assumed he was an immigrant, given the thick accent Fanny said he displayed during the showdown with tenants at the Suffolk. Exactly where he came from, however, remained a mystery.

So did the source of his wealth. Eckhardt was a man of means, the co-owner of multiple prestigious apartment buildings in the area. At the same time, he ran a candy concession in one of the stalls at the West Side Market. There certainly wasn't anything dishonorable about that, but it couldn't possibly have been the source of his fortune.

Eckhardt worked hard at maintaining a low profile. Obviously, he had something to hide. He might've entered this country illegally or under false pretenses. He might've committed war crimes in Europe, just as his business partner allegedly had. Hell — the two of them might've had some connection all the way back, doing dirty work for the Nazis together.

Eckhardt intrigued me. Even if he couldn't confirm Kahn's identity as Yitzhak Fried, I felt sure he'd have something useful to tell me.

The next morning, I made the short drive from my office to the West Side Market at the intersection of Lorain Avenue and West 25th. The place dated back to the mid-nineteenth century. The concourse inside its brick building featured a hundred vendors selling produce, meats and fish, baked goods, food from every ethnicity in Cleveland — almost anything you could imagine.

As soon as I entered the Market, I started to sweat. The building had no heating, but it was packed with wall-to-wall holiday shoppers, and the horde of humanity raised the temperature on its own. It didn't help that we were experiencing an unseasonably warm December.

I set out to find Eckhardt. The big crowd on the concourse made maneuvering difficult, and none of the people I asked seemed to know anything about a candy stand on the premises. After around fifteen minutes, I finally spotted the place, squeezed between a vendor selling kielbasa and a Hungarian bakery.

Eckhardt wore a white apron over a brown suit with dirty white sneakers on his feet. I immediately saw why Fanny had characterized him as a nondescript nobody. Average height. Average build. No distinguishing features. Bland expression. Standing alone, the man could get lost in a crowd.

When I first arrived on the scene, Eckhardt was waiting on an older woman and a young girl I presumed to be her granddaughter. They bought candy canes, gum drops, and a quarter-pound of milk chocolate from Eckhardt, who filled their order silently with a slight frown on his face. The cash register told the woman how much she owed for her purchase. Eckhardt said nothing even after the little girl wished him "Merry Christmas" as she and her grandmother turned to leave.

"Why so glum, Mr. Eckhardt?" I asked as I approached him. "Buck up. It's Christmas time."

Eckhardt did not respond.

"Come on, man. You have every reason to smile. You own a bunch of beautiful apartment buildings. Even the not-so-beautiful ones are bringing in a ton of cash. Who needs Santa Claus when you're getting presents like that at the beginning of every month?"

"Who are you?" Eckhardt asked sullenly.

"Pardon my manners. I'm Benjamin Gold, the private investigator. I'm looking into…"

"It is no secret what you are up to, Mr. Gold. I wondered how long it would take you to get around to me."

The accent was distinctly German. Kahn's partner hailed from the Fatherland.

"I would've been here a lot sooner if you weren't so secretive about yourself," I said. "I've been trying to find you for almost two months. You're better at hiding than I am at investigating."

"You need not have expended the energy, Mr. Gold. I have no knowledge about Mr. Kahn's history in Europe and no reason to believe he is this other man in disguise."

"Yitzhak Fried?"

"If that is his name," said Eckhardt. "You will have to find the answer to your riddle somewhere else. Now, if you will excuse me..."

"Not so fast, Mr. Eckhardt," I said. "I've got questions I need you to answer. Where, for instance, did you first meet up with Kahn? Where did he get his money to buy the apartment buildings? There are several others."

"Mr. Gold," Eckhardt responded with a slight hint of belligerence, "I have no intention of answering your questions or talking to you any further."

"Oh, you're going to talk to me, Mr. Eckhardt. Believe you me."

"You are an arrogant fool..."

"You're going to talk to me because you won't want me turning you in to the authorities."

I'd struck a nerve with Eckhardt. A frightened expression flashed across his face.

"What are you talking about?" he demanded.

"Of course, I don't know all the particulars," I said. "But I've figured out enough to put you in the soup."

"Again, I ask, what are you talking about?"

"You're hiding something with your obsessive secrecy, and I think it has to do with your finances. You had to have a lot of cash to start Kandee Incorporated and buy all those apartment buildings. And you sure in hell didn't earn it from working here."

"You are guessing, Mr. Gold."

"I am, at that," I admitted. "And my guess is you didn't bring that kind of money into the country when you came here, at least not that the immigration people knew about. The cash had to come from somewhere, and I know some people in the government who'd be very interested in getting to the bottom of it."

I didn't really know any "people" like that. We didn't have a Gestapo in this country to run down one citizen's unsubstantiated suspicions about another. I figured, though, that Eckhardt might not have appreciated the silliness of my bluff. By threatening to squeal, I thought he might become more cooperative.

My hunch proved right. "Please do not discuss my situation with the authorities," he replied quickly. "I will close down for a while, and we can go and talk."

Eckhardt and I left the Market and walked north down West 25th toward Detroit Avenue. Without my asking, he told me that he met Mendel Kahn at the Alhambra Tavern, where he worked as a busboy after coming over from Germany. The two struck up a friendship when they discovered their mutual interest in buying real estate.

"So where'd your money come from?" I asked. "Did you get it from Shondor Birns?"

"No. Birns was my boss, but only my boss. I never spoke to him about financial matters. I do not believe that Kahn did, either."

"If not from Birns, where did you get your cash?"

"My family had money in Swiss bank accounts during the War. I was able to get at it once I arrived here."

There assuredly was more to the story than this headline, but Eckhardt resisted giving me any of the details. He took the same tight-lipped approach in sidestepping my questions about his activity during the War and the circumstances surrounding his emigration from Germany.

I was certain Eckhardt was concealing some juicy secret about himself, but I didn't know what it was. I took a stab in suggesting to him that he'd been an active Nazi who'd used family connections to cheat his way into this country.

Eckhardt responded by offering a bribe. "I will pay you five thousand dollars not to talk to the authorities," he said.

"So I'm right?"

"Five thousand dollars. I will pay more, if necessary."

"I'm not interested in your money, Mr. Eckhardt," I said. "I really don't care what you did or didn't do, so long as you tell me what you know about Mendel Kahn."

"I told you," he said. "I have no reason to think Kahn is this Yitzhak Fried. We never talked very much about his experience during the War. He said he was in a concentration camp, but I do not know which one or how long he was there."

"Did he ever tell you about jewelry he'd brought with him from Europe?"

The question seemed to confuse Eckhardt. "No," he finally said. "I never heard of any jewelry."

"Then where in the hell did he get the money to buy apartment buildings?"

"I believe he got it from his sister in New York," Eckhardt said. "She came here in the Thirties, as I recall. She must have given him the money."

"Wait a minute, wait a minute," I blurted. "You say Kahn has a sister?"

"That is what he told me."

"Where in New York?"

"I think she now lives in Utica."

"That's his girlfriend," I said. "Not his sister. When did Kahn tell you about her?"

"Shortly after we started out. He said we had to include her as an investor in some of our properties. I assumed that meant she had given him money."

I needed a minute to sort out what I was hearing. I'd thought Kahn's woman in Utica was an "old flame." That was the way Sophie Himmel described her, and Kahn said nothing to the contrary when I mentioned her during one of our conversations. Yet Eckhardt found out about the lady while he and Kahn were just beginning their joint venture. Kahn hadn't been in America long enough at that point to have an "old flame." The woman seemingly was someone else — like his sister, perhaps.

But Mendel Kahn — the real Mendel Kahn — didn't have a sister. He was an only child, a point Charlie Feigenbaum made unmistakably in describing his cousin at our dinner in Canton. It stood to reason that if the woman in Utica was really Kahn's sister, then Kahn wasn't really Kahn.

I didn't know for a fact that Yitzhak Fried had a sister in this country, but I was willing to bet he did. Eckhardt hadn't directly confirmed that Kahn was Fried, but in telling me about the sister in Utica, he came damn close.

I turned back toward the West Side Market. Eckhardt followed suit.

"Are we finished?" he asked.

"There's still more I want to know. How much did Kahn's sister give him?"

"I never found out."

"Was it in cash, a check, by money order? How did she get it to him?"

"I cannot tell you," Eckhardt said. "I never knew for certain whether she really gave him money. I believed she did so, but I did not know."

Eckhardt might've been holding back, but I wasn't going to press him on it. He'd provided me with valuable information, more than I ever could've hoped for.

As we approached the Market, Eckhardt asked whether I intended to inform the "authorities" about his situation.

"You have my word I won't," I said. "And I'd like your word that you won't tell Mendel Kahn about what we discussed this morning."

"Pardon?"

"I'd prefer that Kahn didn't know what you told me. You didn't really rat him out," I assured Eckhardt. "All you did was let me know about his sister. I would've found out eventually, anyway."

"I suppose I have no choice but to say yes," he said. "I won't tell Mr. Kahn about our conversation."

Later, as I drove back downtown, I caught myself grinning. There were no two ways about it. The walls were closing in on Kahn. I almost had the son-of-a-bitch. I almost had him.

Thirty-Two

I'd planned to leave the office early the Friday before Christmas to carry out a dreaded mission. I was scheduled to celebrate Hannukah the next night at Jake's and Miriam's, and I had not yet bought presents for the kids. Sylvia typically handled this kind of shopping when she was on the scene. She knew much better than I what was appropriate for David and Rachel and what they might actually like. This year, left to my own devices, I'd put the assignment off as long as possible. Now I would have to fight the hordes at the downtown department stores in a search through unfamiliar aisles, choosing toys I knew nothing about and apparel of unknown size and style.

I was putting on my coat and hat when the telephone rang. "Hold up a second, Mr. G.," said Evie after answering it. "It's Professor Fleischman."

"Were you able to get through to her, Doc?" I asked when I picked up the receiver. "Did you speak to Leah Bloom?"

"I did," said Fleischman. "She had a lot to tell me."

"Did she ever see that guy again?"

"Yes, at least once."

"Does she still think he's Yitzhak Fried?"

"Not only does she think it. She knows it to be the truth."

I sat down at my desk to hear Fleischman's explanation. Leah

Bloom called the police after her sighting of Fried. Israel had what Fleischman called the "Nazi and Nazi Collaborator Punishment Law", which allowed prosecution of former kapos and others who did the Germans' bidding in Europe during the War. The statute applied to perpetrators of "crimes against humanity", "crimes against persecuted persons", and other offenses.

"Leah reported Fried for what he did as a member of the Judenrat in Bedzin," Fleischman told me. "Turns out that two survivors from Auschwitz also spotted him in Tel Aviv and wanted him prosecuted for his atrocities in the concentration camp."

"But are they sure he's the right guy?"

"There's no doubt about it," Fleischman said. "The police ended up arresting Fried. There was no claim of mistaken identity."

"What did he say?" I asked.

"Fried admitted to serving on the council in Bedzin and supervising a work crew in Auschwitz. But he denied doing anything wrong in either situation. He claims he always acted in the best interests of the Jews under his charge. He protected them from the Nazis, in his version of events."

"How did his case turn out?"

"It's not over yet," Fleischman said. "The trial will take place in February or March, I think. Leah's going to have to testify."

Fleischman and I stayed on the line for another ten minutes or so, but I couldn't tell you what we talked about. My head was spinning with the news of conclusive proof that Mendel Kahn the Cleveland business mogul was not Yitzhak Fried the Nazi collaborator.

I couldn't believe it. Eckhardt had told me about Kahn's sister in Utica only a few days earlier. I hadn't yet verified the story, but I had good reason to believe that Kahn was actually someone else impersonating Kahn. And if he wasn't Yitzhak Fried, who in the world was he?

I had a personal stake in being right about this. My investigation of Kahn had turned into a grudge match, and I couldn't stomach the prospect of watching him walk away from it as the self-professed victim of a baseless slander. Kahn would play that angle to the hilt. The story he'd tell would cast me as the one who committed "crimes against persecuted persons" — namely, him.

But Kahn was a degenerate fiend. He was a fraud and a gangster and an imposter, even if he wasn't an imposter for Yitzhak Fried. He deserved no exoneration from the accusations against him, whatever the truth of the matter.

That argument, of course, made absolutely no sense. Kahn didn't have to answer for Nazi war crimes committed by someone else, no matter how consistent they were with his own boundless depravity.

I just wasn't ready to give up the ghost on my investigation. Maybe Leah Bloom and the other witnesses had incorrectly identified Yitzhak Fried. Maybe the trial would reveal some alias identity for the man. I thought through various ways these possibilities might materialize, trying to convince myself that the chances were good.

"Are you all right, Chief?"

Evie's question startled me. "Sure, sure," I responded distractedly. "Everything's fine."

"You've been sitting there for over an hour, with your coat and hat on. I thought maybe Professor Fleischman gave you some sort of bad news."

"No, no," I assured her. "Like I said, everything's fine."

I told Evie she could knock off early, after she brought me the telephone number of Jacob Gertner, Marty Bluestein's cousin. I intended to call him that evening to get his thoughts on the impending trial in Israel. I wanted to hear Gertner repeat his unshakable conviction that he correctly pegged Kahn as the man he had known in Bedzin and Auschwitz as Yitzhak Fried.

I waited until after six to put the call in to Detroit. Gertner got on the line and hesitated when I asked whether he remembered meeting me at his cousin's house the day after Yom Kippur.

"We discussed your confrontation at temple with Mendel Kahn, the man you say is Yitzhak Fried," I reminded him.

"He is Yitzhak Fried. There's no question."

"That's the thing, Mr. Gertner. They've arrested a man in Israel who admits to being Fried. He's going on trial for the very same crimes you said Fried committed during the War."

I told Gertner everything I knew. Much to my relief, he remained unconvinced.

"You say the man admits he's Fried?" he asked.

"Yes, that's what I'm told."

"And he ran the ghetto in Bedzin and a work detail at the rubber factory in Auschwitz?"

"He doesn't deny any of that, though he says he didn't do anything wrong."

"There's some mistake," said Gertner. "The man in Cleveland was Fried. I saw him with my own eyes. They're confusing the man in Israel with someone else."

"That's what I hoped you'd say," I told him. "But to make sure, I want you to speak to one of the witnesses who identified him in Israel. Her name is Leah Bloom. She's from Bedzin, like you are."

"I didn't know her," Gertner said.

"You should hear what she has to say about all of this. Maybe the two of you can figure out how you both spotted Fried on different continents. I'll send you a bank check to cover the long-distance charges."

"Don't bother about the money," he said. "I can afford to make the call and will do so, if you'll tell me how I can reach her."

I gave Leah Bloom's telephone number to Gertner. He agreed to let me know what she had to say when they spoke. Our call ended.

I relaxed somewhat after the conversation with Gertner, but only for about five minutes. Then I started worrying about the hell that would break loose when Mendel Kahn discovered that Yitzhak Fried was in jail in Tel Aviv for the same crimes he himself supposedly committed in that identity.

But how would Kahn find out? The trial in Israel wouldn't start for a couple of months. Upon reflection, I figured that at least until then, the case wouldn't generate much publicity, certainly not enough to catch anyone's attention in faraway Cleveland. Kahn probably wouldn't hear about the Fried spotting in Tel Aviv for the foreseeable future. That would give me time to sort out the facts and devise a plan for proceeding.

I left the office intending to hit the Theatrical for a good long binge. Then I remembered I had shopping to do. Unfortunately for me, the stores had extended hours the week before Christmas. The binge would have to wait. I exited the Terminal Tower and headed across Public Square for the May Company.

THIRTY-THREE

THE CLAMOR OF the telephone jarred me awake on Christmas morning. Actually, it was probably Christmas afternoon when I came to, but I was in no condition to read my wristwatch or even know for certain whether I was wearing it. The previous night I'd put on a virtuoso drinking performance, downing an entire bottle of Dewar's White Label in record time. I guzzled with the specific intention of knocking myself out — I wanted to sleep through Christmas and on until the next morning. I might've made it, too, had the phone not sounded off.

A confluence of miseries explained my wish to remain comatose for Jesus's birthday. Gertner's deafening silence topped the list. When we spoke on Friday evening, I hadn't expected him to call Leah Bloom in Tel Aviv immediately. Doing so would've been inconsiderate, if nothing else, since it was seven hours later in Israel than it was in Detroit, where Gertner lived. Had he contacted Leah Bloom right after we finished talking, he would've rung her up well past one o'clock in the morning.

Gertner might have realized the time difference and waited to place the call. For all I knew, he had elaborate plans for the weekend that caused a further postponement. His work schedule also could've made it tricky to connect with Leah Bloom.

These rationalizations kept me relatively calm until the morning of Christmas Eve. By then Gertner had known for more than three full days about Yitzhak Fried's incarceration and impending trial in the Holy Land. Logistical considerations aside, Gertner wouldn't have waited that long to see what he could find out, given the utter loathing and contempt he felt for the man and his steadfast belief that Fried was pawning himself off in Cleveland as a solid citizen with an unblemished past.

I was betting Gertner had already spoken to Leah Bloom. The information he received must've been such that he didn't want to repeat it to me.

That fear that had me climbing out of my skin the morning before Christmas. In the hope that I was dead wrong, I waited all day by the telephone for his call. It never came.

I took a pack of cards from my desk and went to continue the vigil at Evie's station once she left for the day. After what seemed like my fiftieth game of solitaire, I looked up at the wall clock to discover that it was already past seven-thirty.

"To hell with it," I said. "To hell with Jacob Gertner."

He had started the whole ruckus over Mendel Kahn's past with his accusations about Bedzin and Auschwitz. Under the circumstances, the least he could do was grace me with a goddamned telephone call. I eventually would have no choice but to call him back myself, much as I hated to let on how desperate I was to hear about his conversation with Leah Bloom.

I tried to tell myself I didn't really have any urgent need for this intelligence. The real Yitzhak Fried either was or wasn't behind bars in Tel Aviv. That ultimate truth wouldn't change, regardless of what Gertner had to tell me. Whether I found out on Christmas Eve or New Year's Eve or some later date, the consequences would remain exactly the same.

This realization didn't prevent the sick feeling I had when I headed out for home. I'd given Gertner my telephone number at work but not the one for the apartment. That meant he couldn't possibly contact me after I left for the holiday. I briefly considered camping out at the office on the off chance he'd call on Christmas. The foolishness of that idea made me feel even sicker.

Sweat beaded on my forehead as I drove toward Cleveland Heights, even though the temperature had suddenly turned frigid. The Kahn investigation was disintegrating. My bleak mood permitted no other conclusion. The Israel authorities couldn't have possibly arrested the wrong guy — not after Yitzhak Fried admitted who he was. When he did so, Mendel Kahn slipped right off the hook.

I caught myself cataloguing the things I'd learned about Kahn, separate and apart from his suspected history as a Nazi collaborator. He stole a cache of jewelry from somewhere and sold it off with the fond assistance of Shondor Birns, Public Enemy Number One. He employed thugs like the Hairy Slab to intimidate people who didn't do what he wanted. He illegally spied on his girlfriend after ignominiously dumping her. He unleashed Evie's violent husband upon her in a cynical ploy to get at me. He rented indecent apartments for obscene amounts at wretched properties like the Suffolk. And he almost certainly was some anonymous person who had faked his way into the country under the name of Mendel Kahn.

A track record like that qualified Kahn for the hair shirt, or something equally punitive. But in my current state, I couldn't help believing that no one would care about any of it, if Kahn proved not to be the man Gertner said he was at Yom Kippur services. "Leave him alone," would become the community's rallying cry. "He's been through enough."

I had these deep, dark, depressing thoughts, and more than a full day to ruminate upon them, all by myself. Christmas had always been something of a dead day for Jews. The City essentially shut down; there was nothing really to do other than go out for Chinese food at dinner time.

I didn't want to do even that alone. The holiday made Sylvia's absence an acutely sore subject, particularly since I couldn't stop thinking about our Christmas together the previous year.

I'd gone over to her apartment mid-morning to kill some time. She wasn't yet dressed, so she had me sit on the living room sofa and chat from there while she prepared herself in the bedroom. I took the opportunity to serenade her with a tribute to her namesake from the latest Belafonte album:

Bring me little water, Sylvie.
Bring me little water, now.
Bring me little water, Sylvie.
Every little once in a while.

After my third rendition of the chorus, Sylvia came out of her bedroom wearing nothing but a sheer powder-blue negligee. She walked over and stook right in front of me with a hand firmly planted on her right hip.

"Are you sure water's all you want, Benny?" she asked as she reached out to me with her other hand. "Isn't there anything else I can get you?"

I swallowed hard before answering with mock severity.

"I must say I'm shocked, Sylvia. I've never seen you behave in such a — well, there's no polite way to say it — such a lascivious manner."

"Sure you have," she laughed. "Several times, in fact."

"That may be... but never on a holiday. What will the

neighbors think?"

"The neighbors are mostly at church," she said. "And they're not invited where we're going. Come on."

"Ho ho ho," I said. "Merry Christmas!"

I followed Sylvia into her bedroom, where we spent the better part of the day. It was unhurried but passionate. We'd attained a perfect equilibrium, where inhibitions disappeared but the sex still sizzled.

A year later, I ached for that kind of intimacy as I sat at my kitchen table with my bottle of White Label. I had a hard time accepting that Sylvia and I still hadn't worked out our differences. I couldn't stop thinking about the previous Christmas at her apartment, except when I was thinking about Gertner's failure to call, and the likelihood that my case against Kahn had flamed out. The booze, as I said, went down the hatch in record time.

I couldn't have answered the telephone that woke me on Christmas even had I wanted to. I promptly fell back asleep, for several hours, I think, only to have another call awaken me in the same way. I must've been dreaming about the previous Christmas, because I was convinced it was Sylvia who was on the line. I dragged to the telephone, only to have it stop ringing the moment I arrived.

I gathered myself, then dialed Sylvia's number. "Have you been calling me today?" I asked when she answered the call.

"Benjamin, it's you," she said in a surprised and unfriendly tone. "What makes you think I'd be calling you today, or any day?"

"Syl, do you remember last Christmas?"

"Not specifically, no," she said.

"Come on. Last Christmas at your apartment?"

"What are you driving at, Benny? The circumstances were quite different then."

"Not for me," I said. "Don't you ever think of that day? Doesn't that memory get to you at all?"

"Benny, I've got to go..."

"I bet you do," I said, not knowing exactly what I meant but feeling compelled to respond.

"Go take a cold shower. You'll think more clearly after you do."

Sylvia hung up. I was about to dial her again when the telephone started ringing. I knew it wasn't Sylvia this time.

"Hello," I answered listlessly.

"Jesus, Benny, where have you been? I've been trying to reach you all day." The voice belonged to Herb Kline.

"I've been here, Herb, roasting chestnuts on an open fire. What's so important that you're interrupting my Christmas?"

"This is no laughing matter," said the Rabbi. "He knows, Benny. He knows all about the arrest and trial."

"Whoa," I said, "Who is 'he', and what are you talking about?"

"Mendel. Mendel knows about Yitzhak Fried. He got a call from Marty Bluestein's cousin in Detroit who told him all about it."

"Gertner? Why did Gertner call Kahn?"

"To apologize, I guess. He said you told him that Fried was in custody and about to go on trial in Israel. He checked on it, and you were right. Fried is in Israel. Identifying Mendel as a Nazi, or as that particular Nazi, turned out to be wrong."

I swore under my breath. Gertner had found time to call Kahn but wrote me off completely.

"Herb," I said, "this had to have happened in the last few days. How is it that you know all about it?"

"Mendel called me. He's naturally livid, and he says he's preparing to sue."

"Gertner?"

"You, Benny. He intends to sue you for defaming him. He mentioned some other claims, too, but I didn't fully understand what he meant."

"So why is he telling you about it?"

"Because he knows you're a fellow congregant, and he knows we grew up together," said the Rabbi. "I'm sure he wanted me to pass on his sense of outrage and the threats he was making."

"Tell him to go ahead and sue me," I said angrily. "That won't be the end of the world."

"Mendel says the publicity will put you out of business."

"The publicity won't do him any good either. A trial would give a chance to air all the dirty little secrets I've learned about him: A thief; a slumlord; a charlatan, regardless of whether he's Yitzhak Fried..."

"Enough, Benny, enough," Herb interrupted. "We've reached the end of the line. The war's over, and our side lost. I had a feeling we should've dropped this, and now we're paying the price for not doing so."

"What do you mean 'we', Herb?"

"We're going to have to tell him, Benny. Mendel needs to know I'm the one who hired you to do the investigation. I think it's the only possible way to save your skin, and it's certainly the only way I can live with myself. He's got to know the truth."

"You can't be serious, Herb," I said. "There's no need to sacrifice yourself."

"I've never been more serious in my life."

"We need to talk, Rabbi."

"That's why I called," he said.

Thirty-four

On the Saturday between Christmas and New Year's, I telephoned Jacob Gertner in Detroit. Afterwards I regretted just how badly I'd wanted to wring his neck for not calling me.

"I'm sorry, Mr. Gold," he said pitifully. "I was too embarrassed to talk to you, after the trouble I'd stirred up. I don't know how I could have made such a horrible, horrible mistake about Mr. Kahn. It's unforgivable."

"So Leah Bloom convinced you that Yitzhak Fried is in Israel."

"There's no question. She saw him in Tel Aviv and described him in great detail. The man she spotted was Fried, all right, and two or three others in Israel identified him as such. Fried also admits he is Fried. Why would anyone do that if it weren't the truth?"

"I understand you've spoken to Kahn," I said.

"I called him to apologize. I wouldn't have blamed him if he hung up on me. But he was very gracious."

"Good for him."

"I humiliated the man," Gertner said. "I accused him of treachery and called him a murderer. All at Temple, in front of the entire congregation."

"I wouldn't beat yourself up too badly," I said. "Kahn's a rough customer with a calloused hide. He can take it, and then some."

The conversation quashed the last vestiges of hope I had for a miracle, one where Kahn turned out to be the real Yitzhak Fried notwithstanding the goings-on in Israel. The verdict was in. I'd devoted two months to chasing down a completely bogus lead. Kahn had made no secret of his intention to punish me for pursuing the case against him. Now he'd have the chance to make good on his threat.

For the time being, the impending showdown with Kahn worried me less than the Rabbi's avowed determination to self-destruct. I couldn't talk him out of his insistence upon coming clean with Kahn, even though doing so would certainly end his tenure at the Temple, and maybe his career, depending on how ruthless Kahn became in his response.

"I'm guilty, Benny," Herb told me during our conversation on Christmas. "Guilty as charged."

"You haven't been charged with anything, Herb," I said. "It's me Kahn is after."

"That's only because he doesn't know the whole story."

"What's the horrible thing you think you did? You're not the one who accused Kahn of being Yitzhak Fried. You didn't campaign for his removal from the board of trustees or ask the Temple to revoke his membership. You didn't start some whispering campaign about his criminal past. You didn't do a goddamned thing."

"I hired you, Benny," the Rabbi said when my rant ended. "I hired you, and you hounded Mendel, and pushed him around."

"You've got the pushing-around exactly backwards. I was the one who ended up in the hospital. All I was doing was investigating Kahn. God knows he was fair game after the accusations from Marty Bluestein's cousin."

"You defamed him," said Herb.

"Maybe I didn't. I only talked to a few people about this case, and even then, I made sure not to say a hell of a lot. I certainly don't remember telling anyone point blank that Kahn was really Yitzhak Fried, or that he committed war crimes in Europe."

"I'm going to let Mendel know about my role in this, Benny," the Rabbi said. "You shouldn't have to take the heat alone."

"I don't need your company," I said. "This is all in a day's work for me. People generally don't like peepers. Part of my job is dealing with the ones who want to make an issue of it."

"Still..."

"Kahn's a vindictive asshole, Herb. If you confess, you'll regret it, immediately and forever more."

Herb remained unconvinced. He insisted he had to "level with Mendel", as if Kahn were some moral authority whose jurisdiction included Herb's soul. My efforts to dissuade him fell flat. Conventional arguments were insufficient to move a rabbi with a vexed conscience.

So I made something up, out of thin air. I told Herb that the confidentiality privilege between private investigators and their clients went both ways: Just as a PI couldn't reveal who his clients were, clients couldn't reveal the identity of a PI working for them if the PI asked them not to do so.

Of course, there was no such thing as a confidentiality privilege. Private detectives had no prerogative to withhold information about their clients, and clients certainly could say whatever they wanted about an investigator working for them, regardless of his preferences. My homemade jurisprudence was patently ludicrous.

The Rabbi was a smart cookie. Normally he would've seen right through the smoke I was blowing. But with all his tribulations,

Herb somehow accepted the notion that he'd need my consent to tell Kahn he'd hired me to look into the accusations raised against him. The rabbi reluctantly agreed to hold his tongue.

The commitment lasted less than 24 hours. Overnight, Herb again became fixated on the "moral imperative" of honestly squaring things with Kahn.

"Don't be a schmuck, Herb," I told him. "Telling the truth just for the sake of telling the truth isn't a virtue. It's stupid, is what it is. Nothing good will come of it."

"At least I'll be able to sleep."

"I doubt it. Unemployment and poverty have a way of keeping people awake at night. You tell Kahn, and you'll end up selling Fuller brushes door-to-door."

In urging Herb not to commit harikari, I was trying to protect myself as much as I was looking to protect him. The earnest confession he planned could hurt me considerably, since it would suggest my investigation hadn't been justified or fair. The Rabbi would convey exactly that impression by seeking absolution for ordering it up.

Kahn was already enraged about the inquiries I had made. Herb's admission of guilt would reinforce his belief that I improperly subjected him to an inquisition.

Eventually I got Herb back under control. Or so I thought. On New Year's Eve, he called to tell me he'd scheduled a face-to-face meeting with Kahn and me at the Temple two days later. My attendance was mandatory.

"This has to be done," he said. "We've got to try to clean up this mess."

"Herb, I have no interest in..."

"I won't take 'no' for an answer, Benny. You want me to keep quiet about my deal with you. Okay. I'll honor your wishes, for now. In exchange, though, you're going to sit down with Mendel to see if some sort of resolution is possible."

"He's going to want a boatload of cash," I said.

"If he does, I'll have to find a way to pay my fair share behind the scenes."

"Seriously, Herb," I said. "This isn't a good idea. "Kahn's a viper, and a con artist, if you'll pardon the pun. He's not going to play this fair and square."

"I'll be there to referee," Herb said. "I'm sure he'll behave himself."

"Right."

I had a different response in mind, but I didn't think the Rabbi liked it when I cursed.

THIRTY-FIVE

I DINED ALONE on New Year's Eve at Stouffer's at Shaker Square. I'd made reservations for two earlier in the month, when for no particular reason I became optimistic that the Cold War between Sylvia and me was about to end. She never called, however, and neither did I, except for the once on Christmas. That left me to spend the most festive night of the year by myself in my apartment, contemplating the impending wreckage of my practice once the Kahn investigation imploded. Better to park myself in a tony restaurant, sulking over the same thoughts, surrounded by revelers oblivious to my suffering as they welcomed in 1958.

The roast beef and asparagus I ordered sat untouched at my table under the glistening chandelier. I was far more attentive to the parade of rye-and-sodas the waiter brought me from the bar. This continued for nearly two hours, when he told me as politely as he could that "the table was needed for other patrons."

"I can take a hint," I slurred as I pulled a fifty-dollar bill from my wallet and handed it to him. "Happy New Year to all," I proclaimed, "and to all a good night."

The booze had pickled my brain, but not enough to impede my obsessive worries about the fallout from the Kahn case. I didn't place much hope in Herb's efforts to mediate a resolution of Kahn's grievances. Compromise and settlement became impossible for a party motivated exclusively by spite and revenge. Kahn wasn't really looking to remedy some harm caused by my investigation; instead, he wanted to punish me (and punish me severely) for having the audacity to question the version of himself he presented to the world. If his threatened lawsuit against me ever got traction, he would litigate my professional life into oblivion.

This forecast was genuinely frightening. Still, I had no great enthusiasm for negotiating a truce with Kahn. The accusation that he was Yitzhak Fried might have misfired, but I had proof of other deviant sides of his character. I still wanted to expose him for who he was.

And who he wasn't. I strongly suspected that Kahn wasn't really Kahn, regardless of whether he was Yitzhak Fried in disguise. I got that impression after Kahn displayed only a sketchy understanding of his own personal history. He couldn't tell me much about his wife and children. He claimed prodigy status on the piano when he'd really played the violin. Oscar Eckhardt's insight about a sister that the real Kahn never had was the strongest evidence yet that I was dealing with a phony.

I had real hope that with a little time and a little leeway, I could conclusively prove that Mendel Kahn was a bogus construct of a human being. But the crush of his impending lawsuit would probably prevent me from delivering the goods. Kahn had me right where he wanted me after Fried surfaced in Israel.

I was sitting at the kitchen table having a nightcap around eleven-thirty when the telephone rang. I picked up to hear Sig's voice on the line.

"You're still awake, I take it," he said.

"As a matter of fact, I'm sound asleep on my living room couch.

This conversation must all be a dream."

"Come on, Benny. It's not even New Year's yet. You'll be up at least another hour."

"You got me there, Sig," I said. "So why exactly are you calling?"

"To say I'm sorry. I heard what happened to the case with Mendel Kahn. That's a bad break for you."

"He just wasn't who they thought he was," I said. "There's never a guarantee on how an investigation's going to turn out."

"You needed to be right on this one," said Sig. "Mendel's got a hot rod up his tuchus about all of this. He's been at your throat from the start, from the incident with your brother's kid at Corky's to the trouble at the Schvitz."

"The man lacks a certain refinement," I said. "He needs to rethink his diplomacy skills."

"This is no laughing matter, Benny. He's going to come after you now. Come after you hard. You can count on it."

"Don't you worry your pretty little head, Sig. I've got nothing to fear but fear itself. Truth and justice are on my side."

"When the hell did that ever make any difference?"

"Probably never," I said. "But better to say that than to admit I'm in a hell of a jam."

"At least you realize it."

""The spirit of the season calls for looking on the bright side, Sig, even if there isn't one."

"Gevalt," Sig said. "You're drunk."

"Most assuredly so."

"Happy New Year, Benny. Get some sleep."

"How can I sleep, Sig, if you keep calling?" I hung up the telephone and went back to my bottle.

"Should auld acquaintance be forgot," I sputtered a few hours later as I crawled into bed. I was trying to get into the spirit of the new year, but hope wasn't springing eternal. There was no getting around it. Kahn's defamation case gave him a nearly invincible means of retaliating against me for the assault he thought I'd waged against his good name. Sig was right to express his condolences. I was, for all intents and purposes, a dead duck.

THIRTY-SIX

KAHN WAS NOWHERE to be found when I showed up the day after New Year's for the meeting at the Temple. Instead, sitting with Herb on the sofa in the Rabbi's study was a man I knew to be Jules Braverman, attorney at law.

"Rabbi, what's he doing here?" I asked.

"I'm Mr. Kahn's legal representative," said Braverman as he stood to greet me. "I don't think I've had the pleasure, Mr. Gold."

"Oh, we've met, Braverman, several times," I said. "Where's your client this morning?"

"I advised Mr. Kahn not to come. I didn't want to risk some sort of confrontration between you two, so I came in his place. I have full authority to speak on his behalf."

"This is bullshit," I said. "Kahn agreed to show up personally for a meeting, then sends a mouthpiece instead. That's bad faith as far as I'm concerned."

"I'd watch myself, if I were you," Braverman replied as he wagged his right index finger at me. "Anyone who's done what you did shouldn't accuse anybody else of bad faith."

"Don't take it personally, Braverman. I was impugning your client's integrity, not yours."

"I can leave right now, if that's the way you want it," he snorted. "My client didn't request this little get-together. He only agreed to it to accommodate the Rabbi, out of respect for their longstanding friendship. If it were up to me, I'd say to hell with you."

Braverman started for the door. He stopped and turned around when Herb called out to him.

"You can't quit before you even start, Mr. Braverman," said the Rabbi. "Please, the both of you take a seat. Rather than bickering, you should at least see if there's some way to resolve this unfortunate situation."

I myself would have preferred the bickering. Given Braverman's charming personality, any attempt at genuine conversation would inevitably degrade into the same thing, or worse. He was a reasonably competent trial lawyer, I supposed, and he'd scored some decent victories in the courtroom over the years. But Braverman was also an incorrigible bully, with a reputation for needling, badgering, and humiliating anyone who stood in the way of whatever outcome he was trying to achieve. You paid a heavy price when you had a case against Braverman, even when you managed to win.

Braverman slinked back to rejoin the party. He was in his late fifties and stood around six-foot-one. In the few years since I'd last seen him, he'd put on some serious weight, particularly across his midsection. His white dress shirt strained to impound his flaccid belly. I tried not to stare at the buttons at the bottom. It was only a matter of time before they popped.

"It's going to cost you a lot to get rid of this case," Braverman said as he parked his carcass in a chair across from the sofa. "You fraudulently portrayed my client as a Nazi war criminal."

"I didn't fraudulently portray him as anything," I replied. "I was trying to find out whether he was really Yitzhak Fried."

"Kahn told you he wasn't Fried. Now Fried turns up in Israel. You should have checked your story before you disseminated it."

"Disseminated it to whom, exactly?" I asked. "I'd like specific names and dates. I think you're making all of this up."

An arrogant grin came across Braverman's face. "I'm not going to try my case here in the Rabbi's study," he said. "The evidence will come out in due course."

"So how much in reparations does Mendel...Mr. Kahn have in mind?" Herb asked apprehensively.

"At least fifty thousand," Braverman answered. "That's a fraction of the business he's lost from the slander committed by Gold."

"That's a ridiculous number," I said. "I wouldn't pay that much even if I had really defamed him, which I didn't."

"Oh, you defamed him, all right," said Braverman. "Listen, Gold, I understand your handicap."

"What's that supposed to mean?"

"Your delusions sometimes get the best of you. I know all about your Section Eight from the service. I know you spent time in the loony bin and years on a headshrinker's couch. You might have genuinely believed the charges you trumped up against my client. You might have genuinely believed he was Yitzhak Fried, and that you were justified in saying as much to anyone who'd listen."

Braverman paused to clear his throat. "But delusions aren't reality, Gold," he resumed. "The things you said about my client — first of all, you really said them, no matter how your mind reworks the history now. And they were false and defamatory, as a matter of fact. So you're going to have to pay."

Braverman didn't really surprise me with his ambush on my psychiatric past. As one of his signature tactics, he dug up some embarrassing tidbit on his intended target, embellished it, then worked it into his schtick at every turn — subtly or unsubtly, on-the-record or otherwise.

The routineness of Braverman's attack didn't lessen its sting. I didn't like to think about (much less hear about) my crackup under any circumstances. Braverman sprung the topic on me in an unlikely context and highlighted its ugliness, and then some. He intended to rattle me, and it worked. I wanted to stand up, walk over, and pound in his face.

I restrained myself from committing the felony. But my self-control was at an end. I'd taken more than enough from Kahn's corpulent lawyer.

"There was no Section Eight, Braverman," I barked at him. "I was honorably discharged from the Army."

"That's not what I heard," Braverman responded calmly.

"What you heard is garbage, if you really heard it. And so are your accusations. The only person who committed slander was your client. He defamed me, not the other way around."

"More delusions, Gold?"

"Kahn told people I took another man's wife to New York for some lurid tryst," I said. "At the same time, he said I was sequestering his former girlfriend in a secret lovers' hideaway. These were out-and-out lies, utter fabrications. Your client falsely made me out to be some sort of sex fiend."

"Section Eights are often deviants," Braverman said.

"Kahn's lies severely damaged my reputation. Now that's something really worth some cash."

Braverman paused for a moment, presumably to come up with a suitably nasty response. Before he could speak, I went back on the offensive.

Thirty-six

"Another thing, Braverman," I said. "I want to know what compensation Kahn is offering for the times he sent his goon to beat me up."

"'Goon?' You must be joking..."

"I'm not, and I've got the bruises to prove it. The man's name is Dudek—Jerzy Dudek. Ask your client about this model employee of his."

"Delusions," said Braverman. "There is no 'Jerzy Dudek'."

"Ask the cops in Cleveland Heights. They recently arrested him for public indecency. Talk about your sexual deviants..."

"I'll be leaving," said Braverman as he heaved himself up from his seat. His gut threatened insurrection under his shirt as he leaned over to smooth his trousers and straighten his suit jacket.

"You should know that my client didn't wait to begin his lawsuit," he said. "The case of Kahn vs. Gold was filed in common pleas court on New Year's Eve."

"That's truly unfortunate, Mr. Braverman," Herb said glumly. "I thought you came here willing to work out a settlement."

"There's only one settlement that's possible, and I'll tell you what it is. The deal has two parts, one of which is the fifty thousand bucks. The other part is an apology to my client."

"An apology?" I said. "That's what Kahn wants? Well, you can tell him I'm sorry, no hard feelings, and all of that."

"Even if you were being sincere, that's not what he has in mind," said Braverman. "He wants a public apology—an acknowledgement to the press that your investigation was ill-conceived and baseless from the start."

"I won't say that," I said. "The accusations against Kahn turned out to be wrong, but I still had legitimate grounds for looking into them."

"Well, that's what he wants. He also wants you to publicly name the person who hired you to go on this wild goose chase. Mr. Kahn thinks it was a business competitor of his who was maliciously out to get him. He wants the culprit identified."

"That's completely out of the question," I said. "No way I'm revealing my client."

I didn't dare look at Herb to see how he reacted to this demand. I worried he'd confess, right then and there. Fortunately, the rabbi remained silent.

"Finally," said Braverman, "you have to publicly announce that your investigation confirmed Mendel Kahn's identity and turned up no wrongdoing or questionable conduct on his part."

"You've got to be kidding."

"That's non-negotiable. Without a statement to that effect, there can be no deal, and we'll litigate the case to the hilt."

"Why don't you ask for my first-born son?" I said. "You have as much chance of getting that as you have in convincing me to give Kahn the public whitewash he's requesting."

Braverman turned to Herb. "I'm sorry this wasn't fruitful, Rabbi," he said. "I could have told you it wouldn't be."

"You can negotiate a lower number," Herb said after Braverman left the study and began his trek down the hallway. "And it won't kill you to make the apology Mendel wants."

"What about naming you publicly as the client who commissioned the investigation?"

"I'll handle that part of it privately with Mendel," he replied dejectedly. "It was pie in the sky to think I'd simply be able to walk away from this."

"Kahn's dirty, Herb. You know it and I know it. There's no way

I'm giving him the Good Housekeeping Seal of Approval."

"Braverman's got all the compassion of an executioner," the Rabbi observed. "He wants your head on a platter."

"He's a saint compared to his client."

"Seriously, Benny, these guys mean business."

"It'll be fine," I said.

I frowned in delivering the line. These Section-Eight delusions were going to get me in trouble someday.

Thirty-seven

The following Tuesday the Cuyahoga County Sheriff's Department served me with Kahn's lawsuit. The petition showed that I'd turned down quite the bargain in foregoing the fifty-thousand-dollar settlement. Kahn was suing for five times that amount, based on losses supposedly suffered from two real estate acquisitions that tanked after his lender caught wind of the accusations about his cozy relationship with the Nazis.

The lawsuit charged me with "publicly and purposefully propagating" falsehoods all over Cleveland that compromised or destroyed Kahn's reputation as "an honest and upstanding citizen and pillar of the business community." The petition supported this allegation by listing various people who'd purportedly heard me describe Kahn as a Nazi stooge. Included were Sig Danziger, Charlie Feigenbaum, Sophie Himmel, and Shondor Birns.

The first two of these names didn't trouble me. I'd recently spoken to Sig and knew exactly where he stood on the issues at hand. He wasn't going to verify Kahn's version of events. As for Feigenbaum, he presumably didn't believe the aspersions I cast on his cousin and still thought highly of him regardless of what I had to say. Since my comments (whatever they were) hadn't damaged Kahn's reputation in Feigenbaum's eyes, they didn't add much to the claim for defamation.

I couldn't so easily dismiss the appearance of Sophie's name in the petition. Kahn wouldn't have listed her without getting some idea beforehand of what she'd be willing to reveal about her conversations with me. That meant he'd either found her in San Antonio or she'd returned from her hideout in the Lone Star State. Either way, Kahn was undoubtedly pressuring her to say exactly what he wanted to hear. I needed to find Sophie immediately, to protect both her and myself from Kahn's coercion.

The mention of Shondor Birns in the petition also signaled potential trouble. I never would've expected Kahn to involve him to substantiate his defamation claim. The high-minded, principled man Kahn pretended to be simply wouldn't ordinarily associate with lowlifes like Shondor. Forget about the falsehoods I "publicly and purposefully" spread — Kahn inflicted a serious hit on his own reputation by explicitly acknowledging that Public Enemy Number One's perception of him actually made a difference. Kahn must've believed that Shondor's corroboration of the slander was so compelling that it overshadowed his sliminess as a witness.

Birns had necessarily consented to the use of his name in the petition. Kahn otherwise wouldn't have gone near it. The two of them must've spoken about my conversation with Shondor, who apparently had a soft spot for his former dishwasher and agreed to help him vanquish the evil private eye who was spreading scurrilous rumors about him.

In mulling this over, I remembered that I owed Shondor Birns a telephone call. When our lunch at the Theatrical concluded, he directed me to contact him when I found out for certain whether Kahn had really been the Nazi stooge I suspected.

I couldn't let Shondor think I was ignoring his command. He had a way of expressing disappointment that could land me back in a Mount Sinai hospital bed for another, more intensive stay.

This potential threat notwithstanding, I dreaded making the call. I'd gotten off easy in my first go-round with Shondor Birns. No one had ever accused him of being tactful or understanding. I'd just as soon skip a tongue-lashing from him. Sticks and stones might break my bones, but so might Shondor's vitriol, depending on whether he backed it up.

I generally tried to place the telephone calls I didn't want to make immediately, to give myself less of an opportunity to talk myself out of calling at all. With this in mind, I retrieved the number Ernie Murtaugh gave me for Shondor Birns as soon as I made it downtown Wednesday morning.

"Is Mr. Birns available?" I asked the gentleman who picked up the call. To my dismay, he answered in the affirmative and asked me to hold on.

"Who is it?" Shondor grunted when he got on the line.

"This is Benjamin Gold, Mr. Birns. I wanted to..."

"You the detective asking me about Kahn?"

"That was me," I admitted.

"Where are you, Gold? You and I need to talk, face-to-face. I'll have one of my boys come pick you up and we can meet."

"That's all right, Mr. Birns," I said. "I've got my own car. Tell me the restaurant or coffee shop you prefer, and I'll drive right over."

Shondor didn't run a limousine service. He obviously wanted to arrange an impromptu surprise party for me, and it wasn't for my birthday. I preferred to meet him in public, with my own means of transportation if I wanted to leave.

"You sure I can't give you a ride?" Shondor asked.

"I'm absolutely certain."

"Okay. We'll talk on the phone for now."

"Mr. Birns, I resumed, "I wanted to let you know that..."

"You gave me a bullshit story about Kahn, Gold. He wasn't carrying the Germans' water like you said he was."

"That's what I called to tell you. I was investigating Kahn to find out whether he was Yitzhak Fried, the Nazi collaborator. Well, Fried turned up in Israel. Kahn couldn't be him."

"You lied in saying that he was," said Shondor. "It was a bullshit story, through and through."

"I told you Kahn was accused of being Yitzhak Fried, not that he was Fried as a matter of fact."

"I know what I heard. You fucking lied to me about Kahn, and you lied about Dudek, too."

"The Hairy Slab?"

"What the hell're you talking about?" Birns responded. "Dudek—Kahn's employee. You framed him in Cleveland Heights. You got him thrown in jail as a pervert. Don't think you won't pay for that little scam."

"Dudek got himself arrested," I said.

"Fucking liar..."

"And he's already beaten me up for what he thinks I did to him."

"The score's not even, Gold," said Shondor. "Just so you know."

"I can deal with Dudek," I said.

"And the score's not even with me either. You tricked me into telling you about Kahn's jewelry by lying about him and the Nazis."

"What about jewelry?" I asked with as much innocence as I could feign. "I don't know what you're talking about."

"Cut the crap, Gold. You know what I told you."

"I honestly don't. I remember our conversation vividly, and the topic of jewelry never came up. I didn't even know that Kahn wore any."

The line went silent for a moment. Then Birns told me I wasn't as stupid as he'd thought.

"Just make sure there's no sudden cure for your amnesia," he said. "As long as you got no memory, we've got no problem on that score."

"That, I'll remember," I said.

I breathed a small sigh of relief. Shondor's irritation with me seemed to have as much to do with what he'd revealed about fencing Kahn's jewelry as it did with what I'd supposedly told him about Kahn's dirty work for the Germans. I supposed it came down to a matter of honor among thieves: Birns didn't want to implicate a guy when he'd done nothing (as it turned out) that justified ratting on him. I figured that by assuring Shondor I'd keep my mouth shut about his sale of Kahn's jewelry, he'd let me go in peace.

But Shondor immediately crushed that illusion. "You're still in a lot of hot water, Gold," he said . "You lied to the wrong person."

"I didn't lie to you, Mr. Birns. This is all a misunderstanding."

"Save your breath," Shondor said. "You can explain it in person when we get together."

"Mr. Birns..."

"We'll pick you up some other day, Gold," Shondor concluded. "Till then, try keeping your nose clean."

So Shondor Birns wanted to take me for a ride, in retaliation for my suspected deception in telling him about the investigation of Kahn. I'd have to keep an eye out for his involuntary shuttle service at the same time I was guarding against a new attack from the Hairy Slab, who apparently believed he still had a score to settle with me. Through all of this, I'd have to devise a strategy to avoid financial and professional ruin from the defamation lawsuit Kahn was prosecuting for a quarter of a million bucks.

I could've thought of happier ways to start the new year. I particularly didn't like the feeling of inevitability about Shondor's pledge to nail me. But the solution both to this and to the other threats boiled down to the same thing: I had to make my case against Mendel Kahn. I needed to prove him to be an imposter and a bastard, regardless of whether he was Yitzhak Fried in disguise. I'd deflect the heat directed at me by turning it on Kahn, or whatever his name really was. All I'd have to do was hang on long enough to finish the job.

THIRTY-EIGHT

THE NEWSPAPERS DIDN'T waste any time in reporting on Kahn's lawsuit against me. Before the end of the week, the *Plain Dealer* ran a story under the headline, "Real Estate Mogul Claims Slander over False Identification as Nazi Collaborator". The article named me as the purported wrongdoer and described some of my former work as both a detective and an attorney. Similar stories appeared in the *News* and the *Press*.

The reporters from the papers called to interview me for their articles. I told them that while I couldn't comment on the case right now, I'd have plenty to say in the coming weeks. They each wanted to know whom I had chosen as my attorney. I indicated that I hadn't yet hired anyone.

The truth was that I'd decided to serve as my own lawyer. I fully recognized the peril in doing so. The old joke is that an attorney who represents himself in court has a jackass for a client. In this case, I didn't think it would make any difference. The odds of winning would be slight, even with Clarence Darrow at the podium.

Kahn wouldn't have too hard a time in proving defamation. Sophie, Shondor, or someone else would testify that I'd publicly accused him of being Yitzhak Fried, a coopted member of the Germans' brigade of war criminals. The damage to his reputation would be all-but-presumed, given how horrible the charge was. Kahn could gin up sympathy for himself by claiming to be the victim of what he'd characterize as my crusade to hold him responsible for atrocities committed by a completely different person.

To have any chance of winning, I knew I'd have to violate the normal rules of engagement. Parties to a lawsuit were supposed to keep a low profile. They were supposed to avoid any interaction with the opposition until the judge gaveled the matter closed. Lawyers also typically warned their clients not to talk about the case publicly and to shun any inquiries from the press about what was going on.

I myself put clients in this kind of lockdown when I acted as trial counsel in my other profession. I wholeheartedly believed in the wisdom of the protocol. But I didn't have the option of retreating into a protective shell. The strategy that gave me the best chance against Kahn would require extensive legwork in advance.

Claims for defamation address the injury the plaintiff's reputation suffered when defendants made false statements about him. If the plaintiff had a bad reputation to begin with, he doesn't stand to recover much, regardless of what the defendant might have said. Kahn, of course, had a stellar reputation, principally because no one knew what he was truly like.

But what if they did? His reputation would disintegrate, and so would his defamation claim — since the inaccurate accusations I had supposedly made wouldn't have portrayed him in an appreciably worse light than the truth of the matter.

My job, therefore, was to tell the world about the real Mendel Kahn before the trial began. His reputation would then reflect the slumlord and gangster he truly was... Slumlord, gangster, and outright fraud. Someone who wasn't really Kahn, but had pretended to be for more than a decade.

This last point was critical. While Kahn might try to explain away his other aberrant conduct, there'd be no rationalizing his theft of another man's identity to slip into this country and make a life for himself.

At this point, that crime remained mostly a hypothesis. I'd need more proof to tell a conclusive story about Kahn's impersonation of Kahn. His supposed sister in Utica gave me the most hope of corroborating the point. But exactly how I would find her, I didn't know.

I also had no clue where to find Sophie Himmel. I wanted to talk to her about her reconciliation with Kahn. The appearance of her testimony in Kahn's court petition meant the two of them had reconnected. It also obviously meant that Sophie (voluntarily or otherwise) was lending assistance to Kahn's campaign against me. I needed to know the whys and wherefores behind that story.

Before she left town, Sophie had given me the telephone number for her cousin Renee who'd be hosting her in San Antonio. While Sophie had probably already left Texas, I thought Renee might have some idea where I could find her, so I called person-to-person.

"Sophie told me all about you," Renee said when I finally got ahold of her. "She said you helped her out of the mess with Kahn."

"Do you have any idea where she might be now?" I asked.

"Unfortunately, she's in Cleveland— with him."

"How'd he find her?"

"I'm not sure," Renee said. "She didn't really tell me."

Renee said that Sophie had left San Antonio just before Christmas. Kahn brought her home by train and put her up in an apartment building he owned on the West Side.

"Sophie's a lifelong East-Sider, isn't she?" I asked.

"She sure is. It's like he's holding her prisoner there."

Thirty-eight

Renee gave me the address where Kahn had Sophie holed up, and it was a building I knew. I told Renee I'd be paying her cousin a visit.

"Go rescue her, Mr. Gold," she said. "Kahn's a rotten apple. He's been trouble for Sophie since the word go."

It was mid-afternoon when I parked the Edsel in front of the Winter Haven Estates on Detroit Road near West 110th. The three-story brownstone came from the reputable side of Kandee Incorporated's portfolio. I estimated the building housed six or seven apartments.

In fact, eight mailboxes lined the wall just inside the front door. Each had a label that matched a tenant and apartment number with the box. Sophie's name did not appear. The mailbox for Apartment 3C, however, was assigned to Landlord — Private Suite." I was betting that was Sophie's unit.

I trudged up the stairs and knocked at the door. When no one answered, I knocked again, and then another time. I was getting ready to turn and leave when the door cracked open and I heard Sophie sleepily ask who it was.

"It's Benjamin Gold," I said. "I was hoping we could talk for a few minutes."

"Benjamin Gold," she repeated a little more alertly. "Mr. Gold. I've been meaning to call you since I got back to town."

"I've saved you the trouble. May I come in?"

The door creaked open, and I entered. Sophie was off to the side, so I didn't see her immediately. Instead, I surveyed the apartment's living room. The place was freshly painted a bright shade of white. The floors were covered by a thick gray carpet, no doubt a recent purchase from Alvy Mishkin's warehouse. There was almost no furniture. An unilluminated reading lamp stood in one corner.

The only place to sit was a solitary folding chair facing a card table backed against the wall adjacent to the front window. The room was otherwise empty.

"I wasn't expecting anyone," Sophie said as I turned to look at her.

Her apparel confirmed she was telling the truth. Sophie wore a sheer tan nighty that left absolutely nothing to the imagination. The negligee looked more like a prop from a burlesque show than something an ordinary woman would actually wear.

The undress had my blood percolating. Sophie's firm, petite body looked like it belonged to a woman in her twenties or thirties. Chivalry demanded that I avert my eyes, but the view was far too titillating. My excommunication by Sylvia had deprived me of this sort of stimulation for three months running. I just couldn't look away.

In her grogginess, Sophie initially seemed oblivious to my ogling. After a short moment, though, the skimpiness of her outfit apparently dawned on her.

"Oh, Mr. Gold," she said as she pressed her legs closely together and crossed her arms. "You'll have to excuse me for a minute."

Sophie disappeared inside the apartment and came back with a turquoise silk robe wrapped snugly around her. The added attire ended the peep show but still smartly displayed her assets. I remained agitated but had enough presence of mind to begin a conversation.

"You ratted me out," I said.

"I really did mean to call you when I got back to Cleveland."

"To apologize, no doubt. You surrendered to the enemy."

"You're talking about the court filing," she said gravely. "Believe me, Mr. Gold, I didn't have any choice."

"What does that mean?"

"I didn't have any choice. Mendel told me what to say, so I had to say it."

"Kahn threatened you in some way?"

Sophie smiled grimly. "You don't understand," she said.

"Let's start from the beginning. Your cousin Renee told me that Kahn sent you a train ticket home from San Antonio. Do you know how he found you in the first place?"

"I called him," Sophie said.

"What?"

"I was flat broke, with no prospects. I had no choice but to call Mendel, and he agreed to help me come home."

The revelation had my head spinning. Sophie went to Texas specifically to escape Kahn, then enlisted him to bring her back. It didn't make any sense.

"In exchange, he got you to tell him about our conversations," I said. "Was that it?"

"Essentially. It was no secret even before I called that Mendel was interested in what you and I talked about. That's what started all the fuss to begin with. When he helped me out, I told him what he wanted to hear. Like I said, I didn't really have any choice."

"How much do you owe him?" I asked testily. "Tell me, and I'll lend you the money to pay him back. Then you won't be beholden to him."

"You don't understand, Mr. Gold," Sophie quietly said. "Mendel and I are together again, in a way."

"Meaning what?"

"He's supporting me now."

"What the hell. You were supporting yourself before you left for Texas. Why can't you do it again?"

"I wasn't supporting myself," she said. "I lived off my savings after Mendel dumped me, and the well just ran dry."

"I didn't realize..."

"I haven't supported myself for years. I think it was during the War when I last had a job. It's a little late for me to get back at it now."

"Jesus," I said. "What would you have done if Kahn hadn't come through?"

"If you want to know the truth," she said, "I was planning on calling you."

Sophie silently awaited my response. When I didn't give one, she started to explain.

"You and I always seemed to understand one another," she said. "And when you gave me money for my trip to Texas, I took that to mean our relationship ran a little deeper... I thought we might have a future together."

"A future? Really?"

"I'm not proposing marriage, Mr. Gold," she said. "It's just that we got along so well together, and it might've gotten even better if we'd let things develop."

I wasn't proud of what happened next. Sophie's appearance in the scanty nightwear still had me revved up, and her talk of a "future together" suggested she was looking for something more.

Whatever it was, I couldn't restrain myself. I strode toward Sophie till I was right on top of her, wrapped her in my arms, and kissed her hard.

There was nothing romantic about it. This was a hungry kiss, a voracious one, a prelude to something more. Sophie didn't resist. When we separated after the first smack, she leaned in for another.

My left hand slipped inside her robe and grabbed a fistful of lingerie at the back, which I squeezed and twisted back and forth.

The kisses became longer and more adventurous. When we finally came up for air, Sophie invited me to join her in the bedroom.

I was ready to go, and almost went, but at that instant my conscience returned from its vacation below my belt buckle. What the hell did I think I was doing? I awkwardly untangled from Sophie and took a step back.

I was the monogamous sort at heart, not a dealer in easy virtue. In my fit of passion, I'd lost sight of the difficult judgment day I was setting up for myself when I'd have to explain to Sylvia exactly what went on here. It was Sylvia, still and always. I was a one-woman man, though currently without the woman. I hadn't stopped believing our rapprochement was imminent and inevitable.

Of course, when the reunion finally happened, nothing would obligate me to fill Sylvia in about absolutely everything I'd done since her departure. There hadn't really been anything to tell before my turn as Lothario with Sophie. I supposed I could keep the smooching session (such as it was) to myself. But with anything more involved, I knew I'd end up confessing and having to beg Sylvia for absolution. I got ahold of myself just in time.

"I'm really sorry," I said to Sophie after I caught my breath. "I don't know what came over me."

Sophie frowned. "I wasn't expecting an apology," she said. "You certainly didn't owe me one."

"It won't happen again."

"That's really too bad, Mr. Gold. If you're worried about what Mendel will say..."

"God...I didn't even think of that."

"There's no need to worry," she said. We're not a couple of teenagers, and he's not my father. He'll never know about today."

"Thank you for that."

My indiscretion put a strain on further conversation. I did manage to ask Sophie to go lightly on the testimony about my accusations against Kahn. "If this goes to court," I said, "I'll have to cross examine you, and it might get pretty uncomfortable."

"I'll keep that in mind," she responded. "I'm hoping it'll never get that far."

As I turned to leave, I thought of one more thing I wanted to mention.

"You remember telling me about Kahn's former mistress in Utica?" I asked.

"Yeah, what about her?"

"She might not have been his mistress. She could've been his sister."

Sophie was incredulous. "Mendel didn't have a sister," she said. "He denied having any living family at all."

"Did he tell you explicitly the woman in Utica had been his lover?"

"No," she said after considering the proposition. "He never came out and said so. He never even really acknowledged her existence. I assumed she was his mistress when I found out about her. Why else would he have been sending her money?"

"Well, that's why I think she may have been his sister," I said. "Do you have any idea of the woman's name?"

"It started with a B, I think. Bella or Bertha or… Beryl. I think it was Beryl."

"Any last name?"

"Not that I ever heard," she said.

I suggested to Sophie that she not tell Kahn about our discussion of the woman in Utica.

"Mendel's never going to find out you were ever here," she said, "much less what we talked about. And I'm not sure he's even aware I know about his girlfriend in Utica. I'm certainly not going to tell him."

Sophie opened the door for me as I was leaving her apartment.

"Take care, Mr. Gold," she said.

"You, too, Miss Himmel."

The formality of our goodbyes almost made me chuckle, given what'd happened only a few moments earlier. But the sad expression on Sophie's face made laughter inappropriate. She watched me from the doorway as I headed for the stairwell.

Thirty-nine

I FILED MY own lawsuit against Mendel Kahn the first week of February. I was the attorney on the case, not the plaintiff. I was suing on behalf of Shirley Brown — "Miss Shirley", the tenant from the Suffolk Apartments who fractured her ankle when she stumbled on a large crack in the outside walkway obscured by the slush and snow.

Kandee Incorporated stood as the principal defendant in the case. As landlord at the Suffolk, it had a duty to keep all common areas safe and free from hazard. The longstanding crevice in the walkway embodied a clear breach of Kandee's obligation. I added Kahn as a defendant in his capacity as the company's controlling officer.

Filing the suit was a master stroke, I thought. The case would expose Kahn's disreputable real estate holdings for all the world to see, along with his exploitative tactics in dealing with the unfortunate tenants at those places.

To ensure I got the publicity I wanted, I sent a photostat of the petition to Ernie Murtaugh at the *Plain Dealer*, then telephoned him to discuss it. Ernie at first didn't grasp why I was soliciting his help.

"I'm a crime reporter," he said. "I don't do real estate. And in any event, this seems rather run-of-the-mill. Why should the paper care about this particular case?"

"You may not have caught it, but one of the defendants in the lawsuit is Mendel Kahn, the same guy I was telling you about last fall. He's known as a muckedy-muck in the real estate world, but the lawsuit shows he's really a piker."

"But Benny, this is just a negligence case."

"The *PD* ran a story about Kahn only a few weeks ago," I said. "It concerned his defamation lawsuit against Yours Truly and how I'd destroyed his reputation with certain things I supposedly said. Well, his reputation won't be so great if word gets around that he's a slum landlord. People need to know the truth about this guy when they're assessing his claims."

"So you have a personal interest in this case," said Ernie.

"I certainly do. Which is why I sent it to you. I've got to make sure this story hits the press, so I'm asking a friend to shepherd it through."

"I'll see what I can do," Ernie said coolly.

"You ever heard of a mug named Jerzy Dudek?"

"Dudek?"

"Yeah, that's right," I said. "He used to work for Shondor Birns."

"The name sounds familiar. Why do you ask?"

"Because he now works as muscle for Mendel Kahn."

"Why does a muckedy-muck in real estate need muscle?" asked Ernie.

"It makes you wonder, doesn't it?"

"I'll see if I can get a story planted about your lawsuit," Ernie said. "In the meantime, you'd better watch yourself."

Miss Shirley reacted ambivalently to news that I'd filed the case. She had been less than excited about the prospect of going to court ever since I first made the proposal the previous week.

"I know you've suffered a lot from the accident," I told her at the time. "A lawsuit will give you an opportunity to get some relief from the people who are responsible."

"Honey, you dreamin'," she said. "Landlord owns the property. They don't pay the tenants for nothin', no matter what happens."

"He's a lawyer," said Fanny, her neighbor, who accompanied me to pitch the idea of suing Kahn. "He knows better than you what Kahn's got to pay for. You listen to him."

Fanny's endorsement notwithstanding, I needed nearly an hour of ardent persuasion to convince Miss Shirley to become my client. Even then, she remained certain I was pursuing a boondoggle in taking Kahn to court.

The case was actually pretty damn solid. The walkway where Miss Shirley tripped was in a state of serious disrepair, a fact that tenants had communicated to Kahn multiple times. The deformity that felled Miss Shirley continued to exist only because of his gross negligence in ignoring it for years on end.

Miss Shirley became the inevitable victim. Her ankle fractured in a particularly gruesome way, such that the success of her surgery was uncertain. The doctors predicted that whatever the result, she'd probably walk with a limp the rest of her life.

Miss Shirley's immobility in the wake of the accident prevented her from commuting to her job as a housekeeper in Shaker Heights. She summarily lost her position as a result, despite ten years of faithful service. Miss Shirley couldn't have worked anyway, given the excruciating pain that constantly shot up and down her right leg.

All of this promised a big potential payday from the litigation. I emphasized that point when I stopped to see Miss Shirley the afternoon I filed the petition.

"We're up and running," I told her. "You can never predict how long it'll take to wrap up this kind of thing. I hope when we're done, though, you'll be set financially, forever."

"From your mouth to God's ears," she responded. "But I worry what Landlord gonna do to me now that I sued him."

"Continue to pay your rent, and you'll be fine."

"I don't know how I can keep paying when I ain't makin' no money."

"We'll keep you afloat," I said. "You have my word. You don't have to worry."

"I still got my doubts, Mr. Gold. A judge ain't gonna make somebody else pay for my misfortune. I hope I'm wrong, but I got a bad feeling."

I didn't succeed in talking Miss Shirley out of her low expectations, but her lack of enthusiasm didn't dampen mine. I still viewed the case as a great opportunity to illuminate Kahn's seamier side, so long as Ernie convinced the *Plain Dealer* to cooperate and the other newspapers followed suit.

I was still in bed the next Sunday morning when I was awakened by the telephone. I picked up after the fifth ring.

"Benny, it's Herb," said the Rabbi.

I hadn't heard from him since the meeting with Braverman at the Temple. No news had been good news, since I made him promise he wouldn't tell Kahn about his role as my client unless he talked to me first. When I heard it was him, I figured he was calling to fulfill that commitment. I wasn't happy. I didn't want to start my day with a heated argument over Herb's misguided sense of truth and honor.

It turned out he had something completely different on his mind. "Benny, have you gone completely crazy?" he asked. "What are you thinking?"

"I'm thinking I have no clue what you're talking about. Why don't you let me in on the secret?"

"The way I see it," he said, "you're fighting for your life in Mendel's defamation case. He's out to destroy you. Why would you pour gasoline on the fire by filing a separate lawsuit against him?"

"So you know about that..."

"Yes, I know about it. And I know you're going to incite him even further with this kind of maneuver."

"I'm not inciting him, Herb," I said. "I'm representing a client."

"Benny, I know you too well to believe it's that simple. You're playing an angle, trying to get some tactical advantage over Mendel."

"So I'm being sneaky, is that it?"

"Quite frankly, yes. And I'm telling you it's a terrible miscalculation. Mendel was already seeing red, and you're going to make him even madder."

"You know what, Rabbi? To hell with Mendel Kahn."

"Benny..."

"To hell with Mendel Kahn, I say. I don't care if he's furious with me. I don't care if his head explodes."

"Benny, that's enough."

"Not even close," I said. "Kahn's a despicable person, rotten to the core, and he knows I know it. He's accused me of terrible things, but what did I do to him, really? I investigated allegations — serious allegations — made against him by somebody else. We didn't have to take him at his word when he denied the charges, not when half of what he tells you is a bold-faced lie."

"I know full well what you think, Benny," said the Rabbi morosely. "I just don't see the need to up the ante in your fight with Mendel. I still would like to see this thing informally resolved. That's not going to happen if you're matching one another, lawsuit for lawsuit."

"How'd you find out about the case against Kahn, anyway?" I asked.

"You obviously haven't seen this morning's *Plain Dealer*. The whole City's going to know about it, which is part of the problem."

I hung up the telephone and hurried to the door to get the newspaper. Ernie had come through in a big way. On one of the inside pages of Section B, the following headline appeared: "Real estate magnate faces liability for tenant injuries at ghetto property."

Ernie himself had written the story, which recounted Miss Shirley's accident and described the Suffolk as "dilapidated" and "barely habitable". A grainy photo next to the article fully captured the building's decrepit condition.

Ernie listed other tenements besides the Suffolk that Kahn owned in addition to the "high-end apartments" he led everyone to believe were the full extent of his real estate holdings. The story featured quotes from Miss Shirley and other Suffolk tenants about the massive crack in the walkway and their complaints about it to Kahn over the years.

Kahn himself wouldn't comment for the article. He did have Braverman deny on his behalf that he knew anything about either the cracked walkway or Miss Shirley's "unfortunate mishap". Braverman pledged that Kahn would "study the situation" to determine "how best to proceed in answering the lawsuit and dealing with the victim's injury".

Only a lawyer could come up with that kind of doubletalk. I had no idea what Kahn and Braverman had up their sleeves, and for the time being, I didn't much care. The plot to assassinate Kahn's reputation had kicked off as planned.

FORTY

BRAVERMAN HAD ALREADY called the office by the time I arrived Monday morning. "The man's not very polite," Evie said after delivering the message. "He was irritated you weren't in yet and said you better call him back as soon as you arrived."

"Don't let Braverman bother you," I said. "He just your ordinary, everyday werewolf. I'll call him when I'm good and ready."

As it turned out, I only waited about forty-five minutes. I wanted to hear what opposing counsel had to say about my aggrieved client at the Suffolk.

Braverman, however, was in an even worse mood than Evie had described. He started right in with attacks on my sanity.

"You know," he began, "your psychosis lets you get away with a lot. You cracked up once, and people worry you'll do so again if they take you to task for all the bullshit you pull. But this lawsuit of your is beyond the pale. I don't care what your impairments might be. You've got to be held accountable for pulling a stunt like this."

"Explain it to me, Braverman," I replied. "Use small words so as not to addle my poor impaired brain. What's so God-awful wrong with the case?"

"Shirley Brown and the other tenants at the Suffolk get exactly what their rent pays for, that's what. The place is a dung-hole, and no one ever claimed it was anything more than that."

"You ought to do Kahn's advertising for him," I suggested.

"How the hell can you hold a landlord responsible for injuries suffered by a tenant in her rented space? That's a complete rewrite of the law."

"That's not what we've alleged, Braverman," I said. "The injury took place in a common area. The landlord has a duty..."

"Duty, my ass!" Braverman said angrily. "This is just another way for you to defame my client, to show that he's owner of shit properties and not just nice ones."

"He *is* owner of shit properties and not just nice ones."

"You plan on dragging this out, don't you? Milk it for all the publicity you can get—punish my client for having the audacity to sue you."

"If that were my deranged plan, it wouldn't be a bad one, you have to admit," I said.

"Well, it's not going to work. The case ends today, once and for all, and so does the publicity."

I started to razz Braverman about his own delusional thinking, but he interrupted to explain what he was talking about. Kahn would fix the crack in the walkway and pay Miss Shirley fifteen thousand dollars, nearly twice what she was seeking in the lawsuit. Once she got her money, there'd be nothing left to litigate. Out of necessity, the case would end.

"Maybe not," I answered when Braverman offered that explanation. "What about all the other terrible conditions at the Suffolk? Are your clients going to fix those?"

"You didn't sue for that, Gold," he replied. "Even a crazy bastard like you knows you couldn't state a claim for that sort of thing."

I didn't know that at all, but I did realize I couldn't do anything to jeopardize Miss Shirley's opportunity to collect the fifteen thousand. She'd probably never seen money like that before. I wasn't going to play around with her payday by drawing out the lawsuit for my own purposes.

"Well, the press won't have a pending lawsuit to report on," I said. "They'll have to stick with stories about how your clients admitted their guilt by paying off two times over."

"That's not what they'll be reporting," Braverman countered. "We plan to publicize the settlement ourselves. It confirms Mr. Kahn's standing as a humanitarian; legal considerations aside, he was concerned for the well-being of his tenant."

"No one's going to buy that hogwash."

"You'd be surprised," he said. "Say something frequently enough, and in the right way, anybody'll believe anything."

"Not everyone's a sucker, Braverman."

"Not everyone's a schizoid, either."

Braverman could really pound away at the personal attacks when he put his mind to it. Just then, I wanted to pound away at his head or his gut — either option would suffice, so long as it ended in a knockout. He'd neutralized Phase One of my plan to do away with Kahn's good reputation, and I wanted to do away with him.

I waited till late afternoon to head over to the Suffolk with the good news about Miss Shirley's case. She was going to receive enough to move permanently out of the apartments and buy a house of her own, if that's what she wanted. I half-expected her to faint when I told her what was going to happen.

But she didn't. Instead, she thanked me profusely and just as profusely denounced Mendel Kahn.

"The bastard," she said. "I could've broke my neck. He knew the goddamned sidewalk was messed up for years, but he didn't do nothing about it. The son-of-a-bitch only cares about his money. It's money and to hell with all of us. Well, now we've taken a big chunk of what he's got from him. Teach the son-of-a-bitch a lesson, maybe."

News about Miss Shirley's payoff spread quickly through the Suffolk. Other tenants wanted the same treatment for the injuries they'd suffered from the building's ramshackle condition. No fewer than five of them approached me about handling their claims. I hadn't planned on spending the evening interviewing prospective clients, but that's what happened. I set up shop at the table in Miss Shirley's kitchenette and spoke to every one of them, writing down their stories in a spiral notebook provided to me by her neighbor Fanny's daughter.

The conversations turned up at least three other solid cases against Kahn. He could settle up with Miss Shirley, but that wouldn't deprive me an opportunity to publicize his status as a slumlord. I was back in business.

The next morning, I called Ronald Blumenthal, Sylvia's brother who wanted me to join his law practice. My balking at the proposition was a lot of what had transformed me into *persona non grata* with Sylvia.

"I see from the papers that you've been a busy beaver," Ron said when he picked up the telephone. "You and Mr. Kahn have become permanent sparring partners."

"You don't know the half of it," I said. "He may have sued me for defamation, but I got him back with the one case, and I've got several more in the hopper."

"What are they, Benny?"

"Several are other tenant claims for failure to maintain a safe common area. It's not public knowledge yet, but the first one's going to pay off to the tune of fifteen thousand bucks."

"Geez," said Ron. "Are the others just as good?"

"Maybe not quite, but I don't think Kahn's going to walk away from them without having to tap his bank account. I'm also planning to sue him for civil assault."

"What's that all about?"

"He sent his goon to beat me up twice while I was investigating him," I said. "Once at the Schvitz, of all places, and again outside the Stadium during a Browns game. I'm going to sue both Kahn and the goon for damages."

"You're going to be busy," said Ron. "What is it that you need from me?"

"I can't handle this caseload on my own," I said. "There's just too much legal work for me to do it competently. I need the support of a law firm, and I was hoping it could be yours."

Ron said nothing for a good long while. Then he asked me whether Sylvia knew I would be calling him.

"Haven't talked to her in weeks," I said. "Listen, I know you wanted me to drop my P.I. business before I joined your firm. Well, I'm not ready to give that up, and I'm not sure I'll ever be. But I can practice law and remain a private eye. It doesn't have to be one-or-the-other. There's no inherent conflict between the two professions."

"I'm sorry, Benny," said Ron. "But I wouldn't feel comfortable having you practice as both a private eye and a lawyer out of our offices."

"I fully understand," I said. "I'd have to keep a separate office for the detective work. But I'd commit to working at least half-time as a lawyer at your place, and I'd guarantee that the firm at least broke even on the cases I brought in."

"You wouldn't have to do that…"

"I'd insist," I said. "Listen, you asked about Sylvia. She might object to my working with your firm. We're still not back together, and I can't say when and if we will be."

"My sister isn't a member of the firm," said Ron. "She doesn't have veto power over what we do. That said, I'll have to discuss this with my partners, Benny."

"I fully understand," I said.

"I'll get back to you as soon as possible," he promised. "This could work. It just might work."

FORTY-ONE

I WENT THE next day to visit Oscar Eckhardt at the West Side Market. Although the place wasn't particularly crowded, Eckhardt was doing a brisk business in anticipation of Valentine's Day at the end of the week. A steady stream of young Romeos paraded to the booth to pick up bonbons for their personal heartthrobs.

"Hello, Eckhardt," I said when I first arrived. "How have you been?"

Eckhardt did not respond. Instead, he stared right past me with the forlorn expression of a puppy dog about to be spanked for chewing up a shoe.

"I stopped by to tell you about a lawsuit I recently filed for a client of mine," I said.

"I think I already know about it," Eckhardt replied. "I saw the newspaper on Sunday morning."

"Good. So you're aware I sued Kandee Incorporated as the landlord at the Suffolk Apartments?"

"Yes."

"And I sued Mr. Kahn as a controlling officer of the company?"

"Yes, I know," he said.

"Well, Mr. Eckhardt, you're a controlling officer of Kandee just as much as Kahn is. I could've sued you, too, had I wanted to."

I expected the puppy dog to yelp. Instead, Eckhardt asked me in monotone why I hadn't included him in the case if I had grounds to do so.

"Because I want to make a deal," I explained. "I think you have more information about Kahn's sister than you let on during our first conversation before Christmas."

"I told you what I know."

"I suspect you didn't. Not entirely. I want you to give me the rest of the story. If you'll do that, I'll keep you out of the lawsuit."

This was a crass, dishonest ploy on my part. I'd excluded Eckhardt from Miss Shirley's case for strategic reasons. The litigation was designed to turn the spotlight on Kahn's status as a slumlord. I didn't want to divert any of the attention to another defendant. And while I hoped Eckhardt might know something more about the lady he identified as Kahn's sister, I had no particular reason to believe he'd held anything back when we spoke in December.

Whatever the situation, I didn't intend to pull Eckhardt into Miss Shirley's case, particularly not after Kahn committed to settle it for twice its potential value. I was offering him a "deal" to see if I could decoy him into providing more inside dope about Kahn's woman in Utica.

I was desperate to find her. If she really was Kahn's sister, that would prove he wasn't really Kahn, since the genuine Mendel had no siblings. Then I would have Kahn dead to rights. People wouldn't forgive or forget his use of a stolen name to punch his ticket into this country. They also would suspect the worst when they considered what he did to get rid of the real Mendel Kahn to set up his turn as an imposter. His reputation would be covered with muck, regardless of any inaccurate accusation that he was Yitzhak Fried in a former life.

Evie and I had done what we could to find "Beryl" in Utica. We got ahold of a city directory but found no listing for anyone having that name. Evie diligently then contacted all the parties identified with a first initial "B." This exercise also proved fruitless.

I called the rabbi at the one synagogue in Utica to see if he had any congregants named Beryl. He did not. I next contacted the Jewish Community Center and the Jewish newspaper in town. Neither knew of any Beryl. I went so far as to call a private detective in Utica to see if he could find Kahn's sister, but I withdrew the assignment before he began. With nothing but a first name to go on, he could've been searching for weeks and months, making a nice living at my expense. The long-distance charges we were accruing in our search had already put Shelly Lipschitz on the verge of a seizure. I decided to avoid unnecessarily accelerating the flow of red ink.

"I have nothing more to tell you," Eckhardt responded to my offer of a deal. "Kahn's sister lives in Utica, or at least used to. She at one time had an interest in our properties. That is all I know."

"Surely there's something more."

"I would not know," Eckhardt insisted. "I would prefer not to be sued, but I cannot make a 'deal' with something I do not have."

Eckhardt effectively called my bluff. To save face, I harumphed about the fairness of the bargain I was offering and the risks he'd be incurring by becoming a defendant in the Suffolk litigation. Eckhardt, however, came across as a shrewd operator and probably realized I was full of malarkey. I wasn't going to sue him, at least not in this instance.

I bought a box of chocolates to give to Sylvia for Valentine's Day, and a smaller one for Sophie Himmel, too. At least my excursion to see Eckhardt wasn't a total waste.

Forty-two

A week passed, and I made no progress on finding the sister in Utica. Another week went by, and then a month, and I was still treading water.

Kahn's lawsuit against me, however, was barreling ahead. During the second week in March, the judge held a conference to discuss the case with counsel of record. Braverman used the occasion to deliver a lurid exposition on the harrowing tortures his client had suffered as a result of my slander.

When the judge turned to me, he wasn't asking to hear a rebuttal. Instead, he wanted to let me know just how strongly he disapproved of my decision to represent myself in the case.

"You're making a monumental mistake, Mr. Gold," he said. "You should know better."

"I think it's the right thing to do, Judge."

"Is it the money?" he asked. "Got a case of the shorts?"

"No, Your Honor."

"What is it, then? You know what they say about an attorney who represents himself in court?"

"I've heard the conventional wisdom," I said. "But I just don't think anyone else can present this case as effectively as I can."

"You're going to regret this, Mr. Gold," the judge predicted. "They've alleged serious claims against you — claims that'll be hard to beat, from what I'm hearing. You're not in a position to make objective, rational decisions on what to do about it."

"I hope you're wrong about that, your Honor," I said.

"I'm ready to set a trial date right now, lickety split. But I'll make a deal with you, Mr. Gold. If you'll hire a lawyer, I'll push the timetable back to give him a chance to learn the case. If not, it's full speed ahead."

"Thanks for the offer," I said. "I really do appreciate your concern, but I think it'll be best if I handle this myself."

"Trial is set for September first," the judge barked in response. "Absent extreme exigencies, that date will not change."

The sand in the hourglass began trickling down. In the meantime, I filed the other cases against Kahn and Kandee Incorporated on behalf of Miss Shirley's fellow tenants at the Suffolk. These lawsuits abruptly ended much the same way the first one did: Kahn agreed to settle for the full amount the plaintiff was seeking. These results attested to the open-and-shut nature of the claims. Kahn had completely ignored the hazards at the building, and people got hurt as a result. But by paying out, Kahn preempted the bad publicity I was trying to generate.

He took the same approach in dealing with the civil assault lawsuit I brought against him and the Hairy Slab. The settlement check arrived before I even had a chance to get the word out about the case. I initially wanted to reject the deal and stay the course. But that wouldn't have bought me much time. No judge was going to allow me to continue litigating when the defendants had already offered to pay every dollar I was suing to recover. I had no choice but to concede defeat, which ironically consisted of total victory.

The flurry of lawsuits I expected to monopolize my time concluded so quickly that I never needed to call upon Ronald Blumenthal's firm for support. Even though the heat was off, I still wanted to pursue the affiliation I'd proposed during our recent conversation. Ron hadn't called me back since then — which was disconcerting, but not overly so. He had to build a consensus among his partners before he could offer me a position. I realized that might take some time.

Ron finally telephoned one morning and asked me to join him for dinner. I happily agreed, fully expecting to receive good news over the meal. I couldn't imagine Ron would take me to a restaurant to tell me the deal was a no-go. Doing so would create the possibility of an extended interrogation on my part about what had gone wrong and what I could do to fix it. No one would easily submit to that kind of cross examination if they could avoid it with a short-and-sweet rejection over the wire.

Ron arranged to meet me at Johnny's Bar on Fulton Road at seven. He showed up fifteen minutes late, which gave me a chance to finish off a rye-and-soda and start on another. When we got to our table, I ordered linguini with shrimp in marinara sauce. I was actually hungry for once, and looked forward to digging in.

At first, all Ron wanted to talk about was how much he loved the food at Johnny's. Then he felt compelled to give me his assessment of the Indians' young pitching staff, and critique what he called the two recent "lawyer movies", *Witness for the Prosecution* and *Twelve Angry Men.*

I had never known Ron to have any interest in our national pastime or the cinema — or in anything, really, other than his law firm and the business deals he engineered for his clients. The chitchat sounded forced, but I didn't get the impression he was using it to put off telling me what I didn't want to hear.

That just went to show how far my head was up my *tuchus*. Shortly after the waiter brought our meals, Ron wielded the hatchet.

"Benny, I asked you here tonight to tell you that our firm is going to pass on the set-up you proposed. The partners just see too many problems in going forward with it."

I had just put a big swirl of linguini into my mouth, so I had to chew and swallow before I could respond. "I'm sorry to hear that," I finally said. "I really thought the idea would've worked to everyone's advantage."

"I'm sorry too, Benny. I really am. That's why I wanted to tell you in person rather than over the phone."

"I appreciate your thoughtfulness, Ron."

"It's the damned defamation case," he said. "That's what drove the partners' resistance, one-hundred percent."

"What do you mean?"

"Our clientele comes mostly from the Jewish business community. Mendel Kahn is a hero to these people — a self-made man, a big donor to all the charities, a temple board member, and all of that. The guys at the firm thought we'd displease a lot of our clients by affiliating with someone in a public fight with Kahn. Particularly when the facts are so sensational."

"There's more to the story than you know," I said. "Trust me: Kahn is not a pitiful victim here, not by a long shot."

"I want to believe you, Benny," he replied. "But things just don't look good. Kahn has made a good name for himself, and you accused him of some heinous things. If they weren't true, he would seem to have a legitimate beef."

Forty-two

Ron's rejection of my proposal to join his firm disappointed me. And his assessment of Kahn's lawsuit had me absolutely distraught. I'd thought I could defend myself by shining the light of truth on Kahn's phony reputation. But the light of truth was obviously sputtering. When even a sympathetic observer figured Kahn had a "legitimate beef" with his defamation claim, I knew I was in trouble.

Ron excused himself and left the table for the men's room. During his absence, I summoned the waiter and paid the check. "Tell my friend I suddenly wasn't feeling well," I instructed him as I stood to leave. "Say I'll be in touch soon."

I was sure I'd done ruder things than ditch Ronald Blumenthal by proxy at a restaurant in the middle of dinner, but I couldn't remember where or when. Either way, I couldn't bear the prospect of making small talk for the rest of the evening. We'd concluded our business and already killed a fair amount of time on topics I didn't regard as particularly pertinent or interesting. I needed to be alone to lick my wounds without having to pretend that everything was peachy.

The next morning, I was sulking at my desk when Evie burst in from the front office waiving a piece of paper.

"We've got it, Mr. G.," she proclaimed breathlessly. "We've found ourselves a Beryl!"

"Huh?" I didn't catch on immediately to what she was telling me.

"Here's a letter we received in the mail from the Jewish Community Center in Utica," she said. "We asked them to let us know if they came across anyone with the name of Beryl".

"Go on," I said, taking the letter as she handed it to me.

"Well, last week a woman named Beryl Guggenheim signed up for a lecture they were offering on some Jewish topic. I couldn't understand from the letter what it was all about, but it doesn't matter, because they sent us her name and address."

"Hmmm," I mumbled as I read the correspondence. "I wonder whether they asked this Beryl Guggenheim's permission to share her information?"

"It doesn't say."

"It also doesn't say how old she is, but we probably didn't ask about that."

"No, Mr. G., we didn't."

"No matter," I said. "A lead is a lead is a lead."

"It certainly is, Boss."

"Book me on a train tomorrow for Utica," I told Evie. "I've got a witness to interview."

Forty-Three

The train arrived at Union Station in Utica just after five o'clock. I'd been thinking I could talk to Beryl Guggenheim that evening, sleep in a hotel somewhere downtown if Utica had a downtown, and hop on the first morning train back to Cleveland. But I was tired from the trek, and I figured I'd better get a good night's rest before turning to the task at hand. Given the difficulty of the mission, I needed to be at the top of my game.

"Hotel Utica," I told the cabbie as I climbed into the back seat of the hack.

"In town for long?" he asked when we got rolling.

"Just a day or two. Anywhere good to eat around here?"

He named a few places, but I wasn't really listening. If I bothered with dinner that night, it would come from the hotel restaurant.

I'd spent the hours from Cleveland to Utica devising a strategy on how I'd conduct the interview of my mysterious possible star witness. It would be a daunting exercise, given all the things I didn't know. Did she live alone? Was she single, or married? How old was she? I had none of this information — I had barely more than her name, really.

I also had no assurance that Beryl Guggenheim was the I-think-it-was-Beryl who had a relationship with Kahn. If she was, she might be his sister or his former lover, or perhaps something completely different. Maybe she'd even been his partner in crime, aiding and abetting the theft of the jewels he brought with him to Cleveland. Maybe they'd met on the boat coming over from Europe.

Before I could resolve any of these questions, I'd have to convince Beryl to talk to me. Doing so wouldn't be easy. I couldn't openly tell her who I was or what I was looking for. That sort of direct approach would almost certainly seal her lips, if she had any inclination to protect Kahn. I needed a plausible cover story, something that made her believe she had no choice but to tell me what she knew.

Reporter? Insurance man? Cop? The usual alternatives wouldn't work in this situation, for one reason or another. I decided to tell her I was an immigration official from the federal government, investigating Mendel Kahn for some unspecified reason. If Beryl asked why I'd come to her, I'd tell her it was an assignment I'd received with little explanation from my anonymous boss in Washington. That sounded semi-plausible, and might even give us a convenient shared enemy to gripe about. Nobody likes anonymous Washington bosses very much.

The Hotel Utica was a decent place. My room was clean and quiet, and I slept reasonably well after downing a good portion of the bottle of scotch the buck-toothed bellhop fetched for me shortly after I checked in. I woke up and bathed at around six-thirty, dressed, and then sat in the hotel restaurant drinking coffee until nine o'clock. I figured that was an appropriate hour for a government bureaucrat to make a cold call on an unsuspecting witness. I could only hope that Beryl Guggenheim didn't have a job and hadn't gone out shopping early that morning.

The taxi needed less than five minutes to get from the hotel to the address I had for Beryl. The cabbie pulled in the driveway and asked whether I wanted him to wait.

"No thanks," I said. "I hope I'm going to be a while."

"Good luck," the cabbie said with a wink.

Beryl lived in a small two-story Georgian with a faded blue paint job and heavy drapes on both downstairs windows that prevented me from scoping out what was going on inside. The lawn was uneven and in need of cutting in those places where grass was growing. As I approached the house, I saw a sign affixed to the front door: "No Solicitors". That warning dimmed any hope that the morning's interview would proceed cordially and without conflict.

I became convinced there would be no interview at all after I rang the bell and stood for a good three minutes without anyone answering. I rang again and still got no response. I stepped off the porch and went up the driveway toward the backyard. The garage was occupied by a maroon Ford Victoria, probably from '52 or '53, if memory served. That meant someone was probably home, so I went back and rang the doorbell again.

"Go away," a craggy voice barked out to me from behind the closed door. "Leave me the hell alone."

"Miss Guggenheim? Miss Beryl Guggenheim?"

"I know who I am. Who the hell are you?"

The door started to open before I could answer. There stood a tall, slender woman in a yellow-patterned housecoat holding an uncorked bottle of wine in her left hand. Beryl appeared to be in her fifties, at least. She wore no makeup and looked as though she hadn't washed or brushed her tangle of thick graying hair for some time.

"Miss Guggenheim?" I ventured.

"I presume you can read. The sign says 'No Solicitors'. No exceptions."

Her voice had the slightest hint of a German accent. The garbled cadence of her words told me she'd consumed a fair amount of the wine bottle's contents.

"I'm not a solicitor," I said. "I work for the federal government, and I'd like to ask you a few questions."

"Federal government?" she slurred. "What do you do for them?"

"I'm an immigration inspector."

"What the hell is an immigration inspector?"

"I investigate cases where people have entered this country under questionable circumstances."

Beryl took a step toward me. "Listen, you," she said, "I came here in 1936, and I've been a U.S. citizen for more than ten years. There's nothing 'questionable' about my circumstances."

"We're not investigating *you*, Miss Guggenheim. If we could sit and talk for a moment, I'll explain it all."

Beryl paused to consider her options. "I'll let you come in, mister," she finally said, "but before I do, I'm going to get my gun. I've got a new thirty-eight, and I know just how to use it."

"Miss Guggenheim, I don't think you have to . . ."

"You may be with the federal government, like you say," she said as she began swinging the door shut. "But if you're not, don't think you're going to get away with any funny business."

As I stood on the front porch awaiting Beryl's return, I found myself checking my shoulder holster to ensure that I was properly equipped to fight fire with fire, if it came to that. The situation was looney tunes. I wanted to interview this witness — very desperately, in fact — but I certainly didn't want to get shot. Beryl Guggenheim's inebriated state raised real concerns about the judgment she'd exercise with a pistol in her hand.

The door creaked slowly open. "Come on in, Mister Immigration Inspector," Beryl said in almost a taunting way.

No interview was worth a bullet in the chest. But I decided to take my chances. I didn't want to leave Utica without finding out what, if anything, Beryl could tell me about Mendel Kahn.

"I'm coming, Miss Guggenheim," I said as I started through the door.

Forty-Four

Beryl Guggenheim led me through the living room and into her small dining room, where she flipped the light switch. "Sit," she directed me as she took the seat at the head of the table.

I couldn't tell you much about the interior of the house. My attention was fixed on the thirty-eight she was carrying in her right hand. Beryl held it at her side while we were walking, then placed it on the table well away from where I sat down. I relaxed a little. I might not be able to grab her gun before she could, but at least she wasn't waving it around or pointing it at me.

Beryl's wine bottle sat on the table directly in front of her, along with two ceramic coffee mugs. "Care for a drink?" she asked as she picked up the bottle.

"No thanks," I said.

My abstinence didn't inhibit her. She poured herself a mugful of wine and took a sizeable sip.

"So what's your name, Mister Immigration Inspector?" she asked after smacking her lips.

"Lawrence Hoaglin," I said. "That's 'Hoaglin' with an H." I had known Larry Hoaglin in the Army. I didn't think he'd mind if I temporarily borrowed his name — he didn't make it back, so at this point he was either someplace beyond earthly problems, or maybe someplace else where this wouldn't even make it onto his list of troubles.

"You live in Washington?"

"I travel a lot for my job, but yes, I do have an apartment in the city," I said.

"So tell me, Mr. Hoaglin — who are you investigating and what's it got to do with me?"

"The gentleman's name is Mendel Kahn. He came over from Italy in 1948 and lives now in Cleveland, Ohio."

"Never heard of him," Beryl blurted. "If he came here in '48, I'd already been here quite a while by the time he arrived."

"You say you came over in 1936?"

"That's right. With my husband, Joseph Guggenheim, the composer."

The possibility of another resident in the house startled me. "Is your husband home right now?" I asked.

"I wouldn't know. He lives in New York City. We're separated."

"I'm sorry to hear that."

"You shouldn't be," she said as she drank another gulp of wine. "He's a goddamned fink."

"About Mendel Kahn," I said. "We're investigating him because we don't think that's his real name. We think he came into this country using another man's identity."

"So what if he did? Why are you asking me about that?"

Beryl's face had suddenly reddened. I noticed beads of sweat glistening on her forehead.

"Mr. Kahn apparently had quite a bit of jewelry with him when he entered the U.S. He sold it off in Cleveland and used the proceeds to invest in real estate. We've received a tip that you had an interest in his properties, Mrs. Guggenheim, and might be able to tell us ..."

"That goddamned fink!" Beryl shouted as she stood up and grabbed her gun. "That goddamned fink ratted us out!"

"Are you speaking of Mr. Guggenheim?"

"That bastard..."

Beryl started pacing behind the table. She again held the gun at her side, but now I noticed her finger twitching near the trigger.

"Please sit down, Mrs. Guggenheim," I urged. "I promise that you've got nothing to worry about when it comes to this investigation. We're trying to find out about Mendel Kahn, and no one else."

Beryl honored my request, but not before ripping off several obscene epithets directed at her husband. "He's a goddamned bastard," she concluded as she sat back down and refilled her mug.

"Why would your husband want to tell the government about what happened?" I asked.

"Joseph's always been disgusted with the whole setup. He's disgusted with the theft of the name and with the theft of the jewelry, and he thinks we should've turned him in the moment we found out about it."

"When did you find out?"

"He landed in New York in the fall of '47 and sought me out. He only stayed with us a day or two, but he told us the whole story."

"Was he asking for your help?"

"Not really," said Beryl. "He just wanted some advice on how he could pull it off."

"But your husband was against it."

"Joseph was being all holier-than-thou," she said. "It was technically a murder — true. But he was my brother. I hadn't seen him in years, but he was still my brother, and he was in trouble up to his neck. I wasn't going to turn him in."

"That's perfectly understandable," I said.

"Well, Joseph didn't understand. He moved out of our apartment shortly after Robert left for Ohio. I wouldn't give him a divorce, but he wanted nothing to do with me after that."

"So 'Robert' is Mendel Kahn?"

Beryl finished off her mug of wine. "Robert F. Oppenheimer," she said. "I was Beryl Oppenheimer before I got married. I think the official records say Robert died in the War, but he's alive and living here — as Kahn. The real Kahn was the one who did the dying."

"Did you give your brother money to buy any of his properties?" I asked.

"Ha! Not at all..."

"Did you give him any money at all after he arrived from Europe?"

"Maybe a few dollars for his trip to Ohio," she said. "But nothing beyond that. He's the one who gave me money. When my husband wouldn't support me, I told Robert I needed help. So he included me in some of his investments."

Beryl had given me the highlights of the story. Now I needed to get the details from her without blowing my cover or wearing out my welcome. I was optimistic about my chances. The wine seemed to have dulled the resistance I would've expected to my inquiries.

Over the next hour, I learned Kahn's background and the true extent of the crimes he'd perpetrated. He and Beryl had grown up in Berlin and lived in considerable comfort before Hitler showed up. Beryl and her husband left for the States relatively early in the Nazi regime. Brother Robert, meanwhile, bounced around Europe, going from England to France and back again in lavish style as he pursued a career as some sort of financier.

Eventually he burned through all the money he had inherited from their parents. When the War broke out, he managed to make himself scarce for the duration, surviving by whatever kind of grift he could come up with. Afterwards, he was just another displaced person, destitute and looking to put down roots wherever he could.

Making his way to a camp in Cremona, Italy, Robert befriended the real Mendel Kahn, a former Auschwitz inmate whose wife and children had perished in the gas chambers. Kahn's health was faltering, but his prospects were otherwise bright. He had made contact with an American relative who was willing to sponsor his emigration. And Kahn had financial means. His father had been a jeweler who stashed some of his merchandise with a Gentile friend before the Nazis overran Krakow. Kahn managed to retrieve the treasure after his liberation from Auschwitz. He planned to sell it before he left Europe, creating a nest egg to start his life in the United States.

Robert Oppenheimer and Mendel Kahn became close friends as they journeyed together to Italy. They spoke extensively about Kahn's background, his family, his plans for the future.

Robert became obsessed with his friend's collection of jewelry. He figured if he could somehow get ahold of what Mendel Kahn had, it would be his ticket back to the life he'd been leading before the War.

Meanwhile, Kahn's health was failing. He had a terrible hacking cough and couldn't walk more than half an hour without stopping for a long rest. Kahn began openly fretting about whether he'd survive long enough to make his trip to America.

Robert made sure that he didn't, one night shortly before they reached the Italian camp. He never told Beryl exactly how he did away with Kahn. All he said is that he disposed of the body as best he could after removing anything and everything that identified Kahn as Kahn.

Robert checked in at Cremona under his friend's name. He introduced himself to everyone as Mendel Kahn and adopted his identity in every respect. Robert already spoke fluent Yiddish, and he made due with his rudimentary Polish when others in the camp tried to talk to him in what they thought was his second native tongue.

The opportunity finally came for Mendel Kahn to emigrate, and Robert seized on it. He figured he could pass for at least a while with Kahn's American relatives, given the education he'd received about Kahn's family history. Robert sewed the jewelry into his clothing before he boarded the ship, and off he sailed.

"It was a daring move," Beryl said as she stood up to take her empty wine bottle into the kitchen.

"He committed murder in order to do it."

"He killed a man who was dying anyway. Robert said Mendel Kahn wasn't healthy enough to make it to America. Better that somebody got the opportunity than no one."

"So you admire your brother?"

Beryl returned to the dining room with a new bottle of wine. "I hate him," she drunkenly declared. "I hate the son-of-a-bitch with a passion."

"Why so, Mrs. Guggenheim?"

"Because he's cut me off. Or practically so. I'm supposed to be a part-owner of some of his buildings, but he sends me barely enough each month to pay the bills."

"Has he told you why?"

"He says it's all he can afford. He's paying me off the books, so it isn't traceable."

"What's he afraid of?" I asked.

"He's deathly afraid someone's going to learn who I am," she said. "It could expose who he really is. So he pays me off the books, and wants me off the books as well. That's why he made me move to this godforsaken place, this . . . Utica."

"I was wondering why you were living here," I said.

Beryl took a large swig of wine. "Robert wants me out of the limelight, where no one can find me," she said. "Well, no one will find me here in Utica, that's for sure."

"Except for me."

"You're his worst nightmare come true, Mister Immigration Inspector. He really is a son-of-a-bitch."

The sloppy drinking became progressively sloppier. Between swigs, Beryl began talking to herself about the various grievances she had against her husband and her brother. She seemed to have forgotten I was even there.

But I wasn't quite ready to disappear. The information Beryl had spilled was dynamite, but it would do me no good unless I could present it as evidence in court.

At the very least, I needed to get a sworn statement from Beryl attesting to the things she had told me. Before doing that, I figured I had to tell her who I really was and why I was really interviewing her. Down the line, any suggestion that I'd procured her affidavit under false pretenses would extinguish its value.

"Hey, Hoaglin," Beryl jabbered. "What're you going to do with my brother, now that you've heard all about him?"

"I don't know," I said. "That's not my decision. The higher-ups will have to figure it out."

"What are the possibilities? Can he be deported? Or arrested?"

"I really couldn't tell you. I've never dealt with a case quite like this before."

Beryl picked up her gun and pointed it in my general direction. "Say..." she said suspiciously. "Are you really a government agent, or are you not? You don't seem to know very much about government business."

"Put that thing down," I said. "Then I'll tell you all I know."

"I don't want anything to happen to him. I thought I made that clear. He's a stinker, but he still supports me, and he's still my brother."

"Put the gun down, Mrs. Guggenheim, and we can talk about it."

Beryl grumbled but did as she was told, placing her pistol back on the table. She must not have been paying attention, though, because this time she put it within my reach. I wasn't going to turn down the invitation — I quickly snatched the gun and shoved it into one of the pockets of my suit coat.

"Hey, that's mine," Beryl yammered.

"Pipe down, Mrs. Guggenheim. There are things I have to tell you. My name's not Hoaglin. It's Benjamin Gold, and I'm a private detective, not an investigator for the government. Your brother has filed a lawsuit against me, saying I've tarnished his reputation as Mendel Kahn. But he's not really Kahn, and I can only save myself by proving that in court. I'm going to need your help..."

Forty-Five

I RECEIVED A call from Doctor Fleischman the morning after I returned from Utica. "I don't know if you saw this," he said, "but the trial of Yitzhak Fried in Tel Aviv finished up last week."

"Do tell. What happened to my favorite Nazi collaborator?"

"The trial lasted three days. A total of five witnesses testified against Fried — three from Bedzin and two from Auschwitz. The only witness Fried called was himself. He claimed he did everything humanly possible to protect his fellow Jews from the Germans."

"So how'd it end up for him?"

"Remarkably well," Fleischman said. "The judge found in his favor on the charges that he voluntarily surrendered Jews in Bedzin to the Germans. The testimony against him, the judge said, was all rumor and hearsay."

"The bad guy wins," I said.

"The judge also cleared Fried on the charge that he'd killed an inmate in Auschwitz. Again, no one witnessed the crime, and Fried testified that the man died from conditions in the camp, not from anything he did."

"So Fried walked away scot-free?"

"Not quite," Fleischman said. "One of the witnesses from Auschwitz testified that Fried beat him with a stick while he waited in line for food. Fried claimed he had no memory of the witness or the incident, but didn't outright deny it. The judge sentenced him to two months in prison for that offense."

"So two months total, for all that Fried supposedly did?"

"That's what it looks like," said Fleischman.

"With that kind of slap on the wrist, Mendel Kahn might prefer to be Yitzhak Fried over who he really is," I said.

"What do you mean?"

I spent the next half hour filling Fleischman in on all that had happened. He hadn't known about either Kahn's lawsuit against me or my strategy for pulling out a victory. I told him how I'd found Kahn's sister, and recounted everything Beryl Guggenheim told me during the interview.

"That's unbelievable," he said. "Her testimony will change the whole complexion of the case."

"It will, if I can figure out how to make her appear as a witness."

"She's not cooperating?"

"No, she's not," I said. "She refused to sign an affidavit corroborating what she'd told me. She refused to sit for a deposition where I could ask her everything under oath. She lives in a different state, so I can't serve a subpoena and compel her to appear at trial."

"What are you going to do?"

"At this point, I don't know. I'll have to come up with something. Quite frankly, I've already done everything I can think of."

"If she's that loyal to her brother," Fleischman said, "she's probably not going to expose him, no matter what."

"I don't think loyalty is the issue," I responded. "She's more interested in hurting me than in protecting him."

"I don't understand."

"I told her at first that I was an immigration official with the federal government. I thought that would convince her to talk to me. Well, it worked, all right, but she didn't applaud my ingenuity when I got around to telling her the truth."

"I see..."

The conversation with Fleischman became awkward after that. He apparently disapproved of the tactics I'd used in enticing Beryl Guggenheim to tell me what she knew.

I didn't think much of them myself, given the way things turned out. Beryl went into an absolute rage when I told her who I really was, and insisted on calling the police. I repeatedly had to wrestle the telephone away from her.

The hand-to-hand combat continued for some time. Then Beryl started grabbing at my coat pocket to retrieve her gun. I ended up standing on a chair and tucking it into the light fixture in the kitchen, where she couldn't possibly reach it.

As Beryl sobered up, she calmed down, at least slightly. I then made my pitch to get her testimony and offered her a considerable amount of cash if she'd play ball.

But she said no. She did so loudly and profanely and taunted me for even thinking that she'd give me what I wanted. I didn't make my getaway until nearly one o'clock that afternoon, walking as fast as I could in the direction of the Hotel Utica. I had no way of knowing for certain whether Beryl contacted the cops after I left, but I'd have been surprised if she didn't.

I spent part of the train ride back from upstate New York thinking of ways to get Beryl's revelations on the record. But as I explained to Fleischman, it was essentially a hopeless situation. There were legal machinations I could try to get the testimony of an out-of-state witness, but before a court would countenance such an effort, I'd have to prove some connection between Beryl and the claims Kahn had brought against me. I didn't see how I could possibly satisfy that burden without first showing what Beryl had to say about the matter. So I needed Beryl's testimony to secure an opportunity to get Beryl's testimony. That formula obviously wouldn't work.

Even so, I eventually realized I still had a hand to play. The lack of admissible evidence wouldn't prevent me from confronting Kahn with the details of his sordid story. He would deny everything, of course, under the correct assumption I couldn't prove what I was claiming. But you never could tell. Hearing the truth might fluster him into making some sort of damning admission that opened him up to prosecution. At the very least, the exercise would make Kahn squirm. That alone was worth the price of admission. Sometimes a bluff hand is a good hand.

I dialed Kahn's office, told his secretary who I was, and asked to speak to him. He picked up almost immediately.

"You're not supposed to be calling me," he said gruffly. "If you've got something to say, tell it to my lawyer."

"Braverman's an asshole, Kahn, and nothing prevents me from contacting you directly."

"So what's so important?" he asked after a short pause.

"I need to speak to you, face to face. I may be in a position to resolve our dispute once and for all, but there are some things we need to discuss first."

"Why can't we discuss them over the phone?" he asked.

"Because they're complicated," I answered. "Things will go much more smoothly if we're sitting in the same room when we go over this."

"Like I said, tell it to Braverman. I don't have time for your nonsense."

"Like I said, Kahn, Braverman's an asshole. He's not capable of understanding what I've got to tell you. If you want to bring him along, that's up to you. But you've got to show up yourself this time."

Kahn hesitated to commit himself. "Braverman thinks you're psychotic," he said. "This may just be some crazy trick."

"Naturally, I can't promise we'll immediately resolve the case, but I'm certain you'll at least want to hear what I've got to say. You've got absolutely nothing to lose, Kahn."

"The earliest I could possibly get together is May the first," he said. "Even then, I've only got a few hours in the morning."

"I get it, Kahn. You're a very busy man. But this won't take more than an hour, an hour and a half. Why don't we meet at nine-thirty in the restaurant at the Statler? You won't have very far to walk, and we can have coffee while we talk."

"Fine," he said. "But expect Braverman, too, because I'm bringing him along."

"He'll be as useful as a rubber hammer. I'll welcome him with open arms."

Kahn hung up without saying goodbye. His lack of etiquette didn't surprise me in the least.

Forty-six

I HAD SEVEN days to kill before my meeting with Kahn. That gave me plenty of time for a return trip to Utica, if Beryl Guggenheim would relent on her refusal to help me.

I called her the next day at eleven o'clock. The thickness of her speech confirmed she'd had wine for her mid-morning coffee break.

"What in the hell do you want, Gold?" she asked me with considerably less belligerence than she'd displayed at her house a few days earlier. "Considerably less" was still quite a bit, though. At least she couldn't shoot me over the phone.

"I wanted to see how you were doing," I said.

"Huh. I'll tell you how I'm doing. It's the last week of the month and I'm short on cash. Again. My goddamned brother..."

"Mrs. Guggenheim, I offered you a considerable sum if you'd just sign a statement repeating what you told me at your dining room table."

"You're a scoundrel, Gold, and I'm no turncoat. I thought I made that clear."

"Your brother's taking unfair advantage of your principles and good will," I said. I didn't know exactly what I meant by that — and I doubted that I really believed it, whatever it was — but it sounded earnest and convincing. "You owe him nothing."

"I don't owe you anything, either," Beryl said. "You're the one who took advantage of me. I hope my brother wins his lawsuit and sends you to the poorhouse."

Again, the sentiment wasn't pretty, but Beryl didn't deliver the line with the rancor she'd previously displayed. I took that as a good sign. I thought maybe I had a shot at turning her around.

"Listen, Mrs. Guggenheim," I said, "I'm going to come to Utica to visit you again."

"Are you crazy?"

"I think we need to talk about my proposal one more time."

"I'm hard up for cash, Gold, but not that hard up. Don't call here again," she said as she hung up the telephone.

So maybe I didn't have a shot, at least not yet. But I knew what I had heard. In her tone if nothing else, Beryl's hard line had softened. I'd call her again in a few days, to see if she'd come around any further.

I was balancing my checkbook later that afternoon when Evie buzzed me on the intercom to say that Sylvia was on the line. I briefly thought about not taking the call. She'd never written or telephoned to acknowledge the chocolates I'd sent on Valentine's Day. At first, I was hurt. I'd hoped we were on the verge of patching things up, but her silence sent the opposite message. Over time, my grief had turned to irritation. No matter how Sylvia felt about our long-term prospects, it wouldn't have killed her to say a simple thank you. I decided to let bygones be bygones as I picked up the receiver.

"Well, hello there," I said. "It's been a while."

"Benny, I was wondering if we could get together for dinner tonight. If you'll come to the apartment, I'll be happy to cook."

"What's the occasion? Are you finally letting me off the hook?"

"I need to talk to you about something," she said. "I thought it'd be nice if we had our conversation over a meal. It seems appropriate."

"Let's go out for dinner instead, Syl. I've haven't done much of that since we stopped seeing each other, and I miss it."

"Benny, it's really not necessary," she said.

"Come on, Syl. Don't be a party pooper."

It took a bit of coaxing, but she finally agreed to Jim's Steak House at seven-thirty. I told her I'd pick her up half an hour beforehand, but she insisted on meeting me at the restaurant.

"Are you sure, Syl? It'll be dark by the time we're finished. I know you don't like to drive at night."

"Please, Benny," she said. "Let's not argue about it. I'll see you at Jim's, seven-thirty sharp."

For a moment, after Sylvia offered a home-cooked meal, I'd thought the ice had finally broken and reconciliation was at hand. The illusion immediately collapsed when she gratuitously refused a ride downtown. I couldn't predict Sylvia's agenda for the evening, but she certainly had one — and I was willing to bet that it didn't consist of sweetness and light. My irritation flared. Given everything else that was going on, I didn't need some complicated tangle with her to ratchet up the tension higher than it already was.

I showed up at the restaurant twenty minutes late, in unspoken protest of what I expected to be a contentious meal. Sylvia already had a table and was sipping a glass of water as I approached.

"Sorry I'm late, Syl," I said. "I just lost track of time."

"I'm surprised, Benny. You're usually ten minutes early."

"We'll eat fast to make up for lost time."

Driving to the steakhouse, I realized I hadn't laid eyes on Sylvia for more than half a year. I was wondering whether there'd be some perceptible change. I was hoping that our separation had been hard on her. I was hoping her appearance had frayed just a little from the experience.

But nothing had changed. She had the same fresh complexion, white teeth, and sturdy posture she'd had when I last saw her. She was still wearing her hair in the pin-curled style she adopted shortly after we started seeing one another. She still wore the same bright shade of red lipstick she'd always used. Even her clothes were familiar. I remembered the purple pleated dress from her spring wardrobe of the past few years.

I had to admit there was something comforting about the constancy of Sylvia's appearance. There was something provocative about it as well, even though I hadn't shown up at Jim's in a mood to be provoked — at least not in that way.

The good feeling didn't last long. Sylvia got down to business shortly after the waitress delivered my rye-and-soda and we ordered the meal I would end up not even tasting.

"Ron told me about your dinner at Johnny's Bar," she started.

"Not the happiest of occasions."

"He says you ran out on him."

"Hey, I paid the tab before I went."

"You left without telling him you were going," she said. "He didn't know what had happened to you."

"Come on, Syl," I replied. "He knew I hadn't been kidnapped or abducted by Martians. He'd just delivered some very bad news on a business proposal. After that, I didn't have it in me to stick around and shoot the breeze."

"That's not how civilized people behave, Benny," she said snippily.

"Let it go, Sylvia. Please."

"All right," she said. "I didn't come here tonight to scold you about your manners."

"You could've fooled me."

"But I do want to talk about your proposal, and why it fell through."

"What do you know about that?" I asked after taking a swallow of my drink.

"I know you offered to come in part-time with Ron while you kept a separate office for your P.I. practice. I know Ron's partners rejected the proposal, and I know why they rejected it."

"Ron told you all this?"

"Yes," she said. "Does that surprise you?"

"Quite frankly, yes. I didn't realize I was negotiating with the whole family."

"Ron and I have always been very close," she said. "It would've been strange for him to talk to you without letting me know about it. Even if you and I are no longer a couple."

"I suppose..."

Sylvia said we were "no longer a couple" as if were an inalterable truth. Her comment killed the feeble hope that the dinner somehow signaled the end of hostilities.

Sylvia prattled on. My mind drifted off for a few seconds but eventually returned.

"...it was at Ron's request that I asked to see you this evening," she said.

"Ron's request?"

"He'd still like to see your proposal go forward, and he thinks I can help make that happen."

"How are you going to do that?"

"Ron's firm said 'no' because of Mendel's suit and the bad blood that's running between the two of you."

"That's how Ron explained it," I said. "His partners don't want to associate with anyone who's fighting with Kahn."

"It only makes sense, Benny. Mendel's an important man in the community, and people sympathize with what happened to him. Ron's firm just can't be on the wrong side of the dispute."

"So what's your point, Syl? They rejected my proposal. That was their prerogative. I don't happen to agree with their thinking, but what would you have me do?"

"I think you've got to mend fences with Mendel," she said. "I think you need to go to him and sincerely apologize for the mistake you made in pursuing your investigation. I think there's a good chance he'll listen, and I definitely can help with that."

"What's that supposed to mean? What's this got to do with you?"

"Mendel and I aren't really seeing each other anymore. We only went out four or five times. But he and I parted on good terms. I think I still have some influence with him and could convince him to drop the lawsuit, if you'll apologize and mean it."

I signaled the waitress as she was walking by. "Another one of these," I said as I pointed to my empty glass.

"Right away, sir."

"What do you say, Benny?" Sylvia asked.

"Let me get this straight. Ron thinks that if I make nice with Kahn, the lawsuit will go away, and we can proceed with our arrangement. Is that it?"

"Ron just wants the deal to go through. I'm the one who told him you could make things right with Mendel, if I helped."

"Well, this has been eye-opening," I said.

"You want to tell me what that's supposed to mean?"

"I didn't realize you and Kahn were so palsy-walsy. I didn't know you'd become so close that you could tell him how to conduct his rotten business, and he'd actually listen. And I certainly didn't know you thought so little of me that you believed I'd grovel in front of Kahn just to get out of the lawsuit."

"It wouldn't be groveling, Benny," she said. "It would be apologizing to a good man for a very serious mistake."

"Good man, my ass! You can't even imagine how despicable Kahn really is."

"Don't, Benny. Don't. It's talk like that that got you in trouble in the first place."

"I can't tell you what I've found out," I said, "and I wouldn't bother even if I could. I don't know you anymore, Sylvia. The woman I was in love with wouldn't cozy up with the likes of Mendel Kahn."

The waitress came by with the drink. I thanked her and asked that she put Sylvia's meal in a doggie bag as soon as it was ready. "The lady isn't feeling well," I explained. "I'll stay and eat, but she's going to head on home."

Sylvia's face turned crimson as she watched the waitress walk away. "Civilized people don't behave this way, Bennie," she said.

"You've already made that point. I'm a barbaric animal. But at least I'm not a killer or a thief. At least I am who I say I am."

"Benny, you're heading for a serious fall."

I ended up having the waitress put my porterhouse in a doggy bag, too. I spent the hours after Sylvia left the restaurant drinking rye-and-sodas and toasting my new life as a man completely without romantic connections.

Forty-seven

I ARRIVED AT the Statler forty-five minutes early on the day of my meeting with Kahn. I had no particular reason for doing so, other than my anxiety about lowering the boom on the man who rightfully went by the name of Robert F. Oppenheimer.

Kahn and Braverman showed up at nine-thirty with ornery looks on their faces. "You shouldn't have called my client directly," Braverman complained as he sat down and squeezed his mammoth belly in behind the table. "I'm his lawyer. Talk to me, if you've got to talk to someone."

"I'm hoping we can wrap this whole thing up, and he had to be here," I said.

The lawyer harumphed. "There's no way we're settling this case," he said. "You don't have anywhere near enough money to buy your way out — not after all the trouble you've caused."

"I don't think money will be a problem," I said as I lit a cigarette. "We'll see."

The restaurant was empty except for us. The breakfast rush had cleared out an hour before we arrived. When the waiter filled our coffee cups, I asked him not to disturb us.

"We're discussing some sensitive business," I said.

"Got it, Boss," he said as he walked away.

We sat silently for a minute. I didn't know exactly how to begin.

Kahn gave me an opening. "So tell me, Mr. Gold," he asked, "what's this tremendous deal you're talking about?"

"I'm offering you a chance to avoid deportation and criminal prosecution. At the very least, I'm offering you an opportunity to preserve what you can of your good name."

"I knew it," Braverman declared as he tried to stand. "This is bullshit. Delusional bullshit. He's wasting our time."

"If we go to trial," I said to Kahn, "evidence of your true background will be fair game, to show that I didn't really malign you too seriously after all. I know the truth, Mr. Kahn. I've spoken to your sister."

"He doesn't have a sister, goddamn it," said Braverman.

"That's right," Kahn said in a controlled tone. "I don't have a sister."

"Oh yes, you do," I said. "Her name is Beryl Guggenheim and she lives in Utica, New York. I've spoken to her and got her story about Robert F. Oppenheimer and what he did to the real Mendel Kahn."

"This is bullshit," repeated Braverman, who'd finally managed to get on his feet. "We're leaving this instant, Mr. Gold, and we plan to make the judge aware..."

"You go ahead without me, Jules," Kahn interrupted. "I can handle this myself."

"Mr. Kahn, you're dealing with a psychotic individual. I don't think it's wise for you..."

"Go on, Jules," said Kahn. "Your services aren't needed here. I'll call you as soon as I get back to the office."

Braverman started to respond but cut himself off, then headed for the exit. After several steps, he turned to bid me a fond farewell.

"You won't get away with this, you crazy son-of-a-bitch," he said. "I'll have your law license before this is over."

"I don't know why you'd want it," I responded. "I thought you already had one of your own."

"So you've talked to someone who says she's my sister," Kahn said to me after Braverman had departed. "What is it that this woman told you?"

I laid it out for him, plainly and simply, in a continuous narrative that went on for a full ten minutes. Kahn said nothing throughout the spiel, though his face took on a distinct pallor when I talked about the murder of the real Mendel Kahn and the theft of his jewelry.

"So where is your star witness now?" Kahn asked when I was finished.

"Presumably at home in Utica. You have the address."

"She's agreed to testify at trial?"

"Our discussions haven't gone that far," I said. "But I suppose if she has to, she will."

"I doubt it."

"Put us to the test, and we'll find out."

"I'm putting you to the test, Gold, because you've got nothing. What you're giving me is unverified hearsay from a woman who claims without proof that she's my sister. Anybody in the world could make this up. You've got nothing, Gold. Absolutely nothing."

"Except, I've got this," I said, reaching inside my suit coat to pull out the envelope that held Beryl Guggenheim's affidavit. "Read it and weep."

The days before the meeting had me on a whirlwind schedule. On Sunday, I'd hopped a train to Utica with two thousand dollars in my suitcase and a new take on how to convince Beryl to give me her sworn statement. The ploy worked, she signed the affidavit, and

Forty-seven

I left town with what I needed to force Kahn's hand.

The inspiration came from analyzing Beryl's reasons for refusing to cooperate. She certainly wasn't resisting out of sisterly devotion. She'd explicitly declared her profound hatred of Kahn. It was understandable — he had caused her marriage to collapse and squeezed her tight with the scanty support he deigned to provide.

But even that stingy support was critical to Beryl. She had to have it because her husband had completely cut her off. The affidavit I wanted would almost certainly make the monthly payments disappear if I introduced it in the slander suit. Kahn's only incentive to pay his sister anything was to buy her silence, to keep her from exposing him for who he really was. Once the truth came out, Kahn would never send Beryl another penny.

Kahn deserved to hang for what he had done to his bona fide namesake. The government would undoubtedly seek to deport him once it found out how he had sneaked in.

I fervently wanted the bastard to suffer these penalties. But I had to accept that it wasn't my prerogative to lead the prosecution. I had a much more self-serving imperative: to avoid annihilation in Kahn's defamation case. If the affidavit could be my ticket to survival without openly implicating Kahn, I'd have to agree to pursue that option before Beryl would even consider affixing her signature.

All of this meant I could never introduce the sworn statement in court. Doing so would make it a matter of public record, and I'd have no way of controlling the consequences that ensued. The affidavit instead could serve only as a negotiating tool — I'd have to use it to threaten Kahn without his knowing that I'd secretly promised never to disclose it publicly. I'd have to hope it scared him enough to dismiss his case.

Even then, the risk of retaliation by Kahn would remain for Beryl. Once he saw the affidavit, she could never again trust him to honor his tenuous commitment to remit her share of the monthly profits. This would be true regardless of whether I presented it as evidence in court, and regardless of whether Kahn abandoned his defamation claim in the face of that possibility. Whatever happened, he'd want to nail Beryl for double-crossing him.

The amount I was offering her to play along would provide temporary financial cover. But inevitably she'd have to look again to Kahn for support.

The affidavit couldn't expose Beryl in this way. As part of the deal I was intending to strike with Kahn, I'd have to secure concessions that covered her indefinitely. Doing so would neutralize Kahn's impulse to beat her brains out once he saw what she'd said under oath.

Beryl was actually sober when I rang her bell Monday morning — sober and forlorn, given the lack of funds available to replenish her stock of chardonnay. She listened to what I had to tell her, then countersigned the contract I'd prepared to document my deal with her.

The affidavit came next. She read over what I'd written up and agreed that it accurately set forth what she'd told me. Beryl was ready to sign then and there, but we drove to her bank so she could do it in front of a notary. After completing the task, Beryl had a teller deposit all but a small portion of the two thousand bucks I'd given her into her checking account.

"The judge will never accept this into evidence," Kahn somberly predicted after he finished reading the affidavit. "The witness needs to appear in person, and what she says has nothing to do with my defamation claims."

"I don't think that's correct," I said.

"You said I was a Nazi war criminal. What this woman says doesn't come close to addressing that."

"You claim I misrepresented your personal history in a way that harmed your reputation. This woman tells the true story, which does at least as much damage. It establishes you as a liar, a fraud, and a murderer, without even the Nazis to share the blame."

If Braverman had stuck around, he would have argued the relevance of that point. But I had Kahn on the run, and I wasn't going to let up.

"Even if this woman shows up to testify, the best you're going to have is her word against mine," Kahn said. "Who's going to believe some woman from Utica who makes claims like this without corroboration?"

"You want corroboration, I'll give you corroboration," I said as I pulled another envelope from the pocket inside my coat. "Here's an affidavit from your brother-in-law, Joseph Guggenheim. He's an esteemed composer. I'd never heard of him, but you have. You met with him and your sister when you got off the boat from Europe under your alias."

"*Vey iz mir,*" Kahn moaned.

"Your brother-in-law will identify you as Robert Oppenheimer, and he'll repeat the admissions you made about the way you took care of the real Mendel Kahn."

Beryl had given me her husband's address in New York City before I left Utica. I got his telephone number right after the train arrived in Grand Central Terminal, from the directory in a public phone booth. He was more than happy to talk to me when I reached him that evening and said I wanted information to implicate his wife's brother. We met at his lawyer's office the next morning, where his affidavit was prepared and executed.

Joseph Guggenheim swore under oath that the man masquerading as Mendel Kahn was a "self-professed murderer, thief, and perpetrator of fraud." I helped with the verbiage. It had a compelling ring to it, if I did say so myself.

Kahn uttered his equally high opinion of Joseph Guggenheim as he read through the affidavit. He threw it on the table when he finished, and looked at me.

"So what's the deal?" he asked. "You use these statements unless I dismiss my lawsuit?"

"That should go without saying."

"So if I dismiss the case, the affidavits disappear?"

"They do, but that's not all," I said. "There are certain collateral terms that are non-negotiable."

"Collateral terms? What in the hell are you talking about?"

I recited them from least to most onerous. Kahn had to fix it so I'd seen the last of the Hairy Slab. He had to settle my tab with Shondor Birns, so I didn't have to worry about being hijacked every time I was out on the street. He had to pay Evie five thousand dollars for the turmoil he'd caused through the early release of Murray Brite. And most importantly, he would have to buy out Beryl's interests in his various apartment buildings at a price I negotiated on her behalf after reviewing Kandee Incorporated's books and records.

"Beryl will get nothing from me," Kahn flatly stated. "I've been very generous with her, and this is the thanks I get? She doesn't own any part of any of my buildings, anyway."

"Beryl has to be taken care of," I said. "I'm prepared to represent her in a lawsuit against you, Oscar Eckhardt, and your company for stealing her interest in the properties and her rightful share of the profits. You don't want that to happen. It could get ugly."

Kahn just shook his head. "You've done it to me again, Gold," he said. "First you hit me with the crap about being Yitzhak Fried; now you're stuffing ancient history down my throat."

"You heard Fried was put on trial in Israel for the crimes he allegedly committed? The court cleared him of almost everything."

"I know all about it," Kahn said glumly. "I paid the bastard's legal fees."

"Huh?"

"Braverman thought it would be better for my case if Fried was acquitted. Make the bullshit you pulled seem that much worse. We got him a very good, very expensive lawyer to improve our chances."

"Did you think he was innocent?"

"I didn't care either way," Kahn said. "I just wanted him to walk away clean."

Kahn didn't have the option of walking away from the deal I proposed. I drew up the papers and had them in Braverman's hands by the close of the following week. When the month ended, Kahn had dismissed the defamation case and paid Beryl the six-figure sum I negotiated with him.

Forty-eight

I saw Mendel Kahn in Temple on Yom Kippur in late September. He sat at the front of the sanctuary, in the second row, with Sophie Himmel at his side. Throughout the morning, a steady stream of congregants approached Kahn to have a word or shake his hand. It was as if he were Master of Ceremonies.

Kahn was back on top. The rumors and innuendo from the incident the previous Yom Kippur had completely vanished. The local press made sure of it with the articles they ran after dismissal of his defamation case. Each of them discussed Yitzhak Fried's prosecution in Tel Aviv and how it closed the book on the local controversy. "Even though Kahn was wrongfully implicated," wrote the reporter in the *Press*, "he has decided to let the affair end without seeking reparations."

That was just the sort of gracious, dignified gentleman Kahn pretended to be. The public resumed its unqualified admiration of his rectitude, munificence, and sterling character.

I personally fought the impulse to gag whenever I thought of Kahn or heard mention of his name. The man was a "murderer, thief, and perpetrator of fraud", as described (with my help) by his brother-in-law. The government should've expelled him from the country for sneaking in as somebody else. He should've been living out his days in a jail cell in Italy, where he'd exterminated the real

Mendel Kahn and stolen his fortune. Instead, under the deal I cut with him, he was sitting pretty.

Seeing Kahn was excruciating. Sophie's presence as his companion made the experience practically unbearable. I'd never stopped thinking about her after that brief interlude at her apartment. The physical attraction that day had overwhelmed me, and it didn't dissipate with cold showers alone. Once I finally got the message that my relationship with Sylvia wasn't coming back from the dead, I became obsessed with finding out whether Sophie and I really might have a "future together" as she had speculated.

Back on the Sunday of the Fourth of July weekend, I'd called her up.

"Happy Independence Day," I began.

"Mr. Gold. It's good to hear from you."

"The pleasure's all mine. How have you been?"

"All right," she said. "I was glad to find out you settled your case with Mendel."

"For better or worse," I replied. "That's my official position."

"You're not happy with how it turned out?"

"It's complicated. I was hoping we could discuss it over dinner."

Sophie didn't immediately respond to the invitation, so I asked again.

"How about it? Dinner tomorrow night, or Tuesday, if you'd prefer."

"I'm sorry," Sophie answered in a subdued tone. "I'd really like to go, but I don't think Mendel would approve."

"Come on. Are you really still seeing that guy?"

"For better or worse, Mr. Gold. For better or worse."

I paid more attention to Sophie on Yom Kippur morning that I did to the prayers. I watched as she stood at one point and headed down the aisle toward the lady's room at the back of the sanctuary. Her path would take her right past where I was sitting. I started to get up, intending to intercept her for a quick hello. But Sophie's expression darkened when I caught her eye. A slight shake of her head told me to stay where I was. I sat back down. She passed my row without even looking over at me.

Sophie apparently didn't want Kahn seeing her consorting with the enemy. But I wasn't much of an enemy anymore — the settlement had eliminated any threat I posed to Kahn. If I'd stopped Sophie to talk, he probably would have thought of it as some pathetic gesture on my part, if he thought of it at all.

I hung around when the service ended just after noon. I was waiting to talk to Herb. He and I had spoken only briefly when Kahn dropped the defamation case, and I wanted to hear what he had to say.

It took Herb almost ten minutes to extricate himself from the congregants milling around the sanctuary. Eventually he made his way to the Rabbi's study, with me right on his tail.

"I'm hungry at the moment," Herb answered when I asked how he was doing. "Otherwise I'm okay. I'm sorry I haven't called, Benny. I figured the less we talked about our adventure, the better."

"Probably so, Herb."

"We had the wrong guy."

"We had the right wrong guy," I said. "Someday when I'm drunk enough to speak out of turn I'll explain exactly what I mean by that."

"All right, I guess."

The room lapsed into an uncomfortable silence, which Herb abruptly broke with an announcement. "Listen," he said, "I have some good news for you."

"Oh, yeah?"

"The board has given me a discretionary fund. Money I can spend however I want, whenever I want, no questions asked. The first withdrawal goes to pay your fees. It's nowhere near enough, but at least it's something."

"You don't have to worry about that, Herb."

"But I do worry about it," he said. "And I insist on paying you. You did a lot of work, at my direction. You deserve the money."

The Rabbi didn't want to transact business on the holiday, so he asked me to come back for payment later in the week. I agreed to do so as we shook hands and said goodbye.

On my way out of the Temple, I had the misfortune of running into Kahn. He was standing just inside the door that led to the parking lot, talking to a gentleman in a dark gray suit whom I didn't recognize. I would've turned around and exited another way if I could've completed the maneuver without being spotted by Kahn. But before I could even pivot, he was gesturing to have me join him.

"Benjamin Gold, ace detective and attorney extraordinaire," he said in a disarmingly cheerful tone. "I didn't expect to see you here today."

"It's Yom Kippur," I responded. "Where else would I be?"

"Today is an unhappy anniversary for all of us. I thought you might be keeping a low profile, just to let it pass."

"I don't think I have too much to apologize for, Kahn. There was some confusion about your background, but all's well that ends well, wouldn't you say?"

"I suppose," Kahn said tentatively. I knew he would've preferred a more biting response, but the settlement agreement had his tongue tied with its confidentiality clause. I myself felt like pushing the envelope.

"After all," I said, "it's not like I committed murder, or robbed somebody blind."

The barb made Kahn's companion noticeably wince, even though he didn't know enough of the back-story to appreciate its full bite. Kahn did what he could to volley back.

"No, you didn't kill anyone, Gold," he said, "but you came close. More than a few times those accusations of yours put me on the verge of a heart attack."

"Fortunately, you pulled through," I replied with a purposeful lack of enthusiasm.

The encounter with Kahn revived all the regret and recrimination I'd felt when I struck my deal with him. I'd really made the case against Robert F. Oppenheimer. With the damning testimony of his brother-in-law (even without his sister's), I probably could've made sure the government gave him what he had coming. But I was facing judgment day, too. Had I followed through in nailing the bad guy, I wouldn't have been able to protect myself from the ruin of his defamation lawsuit. I made the tradeoff that gave us both a reprieve, but not without beating myself up about it.

I had figured I'd gain some perspective over time. After seeing Kahn rule the roost in Temple, though, I knew I'd never be able to live comfortably with my decision to let him walk. There are sins that Yom Kippur does not absolve us of.

Forty-nine

The next morning I called the Immigration and Naturalization Service in Washington. "I've got some information about a man named Mendel Kahn," I told the lady who answered the phone. "He's an immigrant living in Cleveland who sneaked into this country under the name of someone he murdered in Europe."

"Can you repeat that?" she asked.

After I did so, she transferred my call to a staffer whose name I didn't catch. He had me go through the story again, then read me his notes of what I'd said.

"You've got it right," I told him.

"Good. There's someone else you should talk to. Just one minute," he said as he put me on hold.

"One minute" turned into fifteen. I was getting ready to hang up the telephone when a man came on the line and introduced himself as Agent Benedict Purdy.

"Agent Purdy, I've got some pretty startling information about an immigrant who calls himself Mendel Kahn," I began.

"I know all about it," he replied. "And I'm glad you finally felt comfortable enough to give us a call. We have some questions about the affidavits you sent us."

"Affidavits? Which affidavits?"

"Come on, Mr. Gold. You're the only one who could have sent them to us."

"I'm sorry, Mr. Purdy. But I really have no idea..."

"If those statements are accurate, there's a case out there against Mendel Kahn we probably should be pursuing."

Someone, it seemed, had sent the I.N.S. a copy of the affidavits signed by Beryl and her husband, Joseph Guggenheim. My only copies of these gems were attached as exhibits to the settlement agreement with Kahn, locked in my safe at the office. The affidavits would tell the G-Men everything there was to tell about how Kahn wasn't really Kahn, but a killer and thief masquerading as someone else.

The settlement agreement barred me from showing those affidavits to anyone or revealing anything I'd learned about Kahn's true identity. I'd called the I.N.S. now, specifically intending to violate that agreement; without doing so, I saw no way to hold Kahn accountable for the fraud he was perpetrating. Up till now, though, I'd minded my p's and q's — Kahn's secret had been safe with me.

"I know the affidavits," I told Purdy. "I'm the guy who got them from the witnesses. But much to my regret, I wasn't at liberty to show them to anyone who could take the necessary action."

"I guess it doesn't really matter where they came from," said the agent. "What we need to do now is see whether that evidence will hold up. If it does, you can imagine what the consequences will be."

"Deportation?"

"All I'll say," said Purdy, "is that Mr. Kahn is going to need a run of good luck and one hell of a lawyer."

By my estimation, it had to have been Kahn's lawyer who got him into this fix in the first place. Kahn, Braverman, and I were the only three people with access to the affidavits after they became part of the settlement agreement. I certainly hadn't turned them over to the

I.N.S., and Kahn wouldn't have done so either. That left Braverman as the lone suspect for ratting Kahn out.

Still, I had a hard time believing it. Braverman learned about Kahn's ugly history when he and I were negotiating the settlement, but he didn't seem particularly upset by it, much less morally indignant enough to forsake his obligations as an attorney and reveal his client's confidential business to the government. Some people just couldn't abide the type of treachery Kahn had pulled. But Braverman struck me as having a very strong stomach, even for a lawyer. He wasn't the sort to worry about the criminal implications of his clients' conduct.

All of this had me flummoxed. If Braverman hadn't sent the affidavits to the I.N.S., then who could have done so? Completely flummoxed, and a little bit worried. If Kahn ever found out that immigration officials had that proof, he'd have to assume I was the one who leaked it — there simply weren't enough other suspects. I couldn't readily see any means of disproving the accusation if he made it. And if I couldn't do so, this supposed violation of the settlement agreement could subject me to all sorts of misery. I was planning, of course, to let the I.N.S. know about Kahn, the agreement notwithstanding. But I hadn't intended to use the affidavits, since doing so would be tangible evidence of my breach. I wanted to play things more subtly than that. I thought I could turn Kahn in without leaving a paper trail testifying to the unlawfulness of the effort.

Then again, Kahn wouldn't be able to retaliate if he were in some holding cell awaiting extradition. Agent Purdy was clearly hot to move his case along. As our conversation continued, he openly asked me for assistance in assembling proof to corroborate the affidavits.

"I can try to convince the witnesses to sit for interviews," I offered.

"That would be mighty helpful," Purdy replied.

Making the sale to Beryl was not easy. She was keenly aware that Kahn had paid a lot to muzzle her from disclosing who he really was and how he'd slithered his way into the United States. As much as she disliked her brother, she didn't want to see him prosecuted.

But the stakes trumped her personal preferences or any contractual obligation to keep her mouth shut. This was an official inquiry from a federal agency. Beryl simply didn't have the prerogative to withhold what she knew. At least that was the way I presented it.

Beryl eventually fell in line. This time a real immigration agent came to Utica to get her statement.

Beryl's husband presented less of a challenge. He wasn't a party to the settlement with Kahn, didn't like or approve of the guy, had his own income, and remained completely at liberty to repeat Robert F. Oppenheimer's admissions about what he had done to become Mendel Kahn. As a composer, Guggenheim had a flexible schedule. He readily agreed to talk to the I.N.S. and boarded a train for Washington the day after he and I connected.

As an added flourish for the government, I browbeat Harold Feigenbaum into submitting an affidavit that described the cache of jewelry he'd found among Kahn's possessions after his arrival from Europe. Harold undoubtedly caught hell from his wife for allowing himself to get caught up in the investigation, but he could take comfort in knowing he'd exposed the lie of Kahn's rags-to-riches fable. Kahn might have stiffed him when he came looking for a job, but Harold was getting the last laugh.

Purdy called in mid-November to thank me for the work I'd done. I asked where he stood in the case against Kahn.

"You can bank on this," he answered. "Robert F. Oppenheimer isn't going to have a very merry Christmas."

Five minutes after hanging up with Purdy, the telephone rang again. This time it was Sophie Himmel.

"Well howdy, stranger," I said. "It's been a while."

"It certainly has. I haven't seen you since Yom Kippur."

"And I only had a non-speaking role on that occasion. So how have you been?"

"A lot has happened, Mr. Gold," she said. "I was hoping your dinner invitation was still open."

"How about tonight?"

Sophie and I met at the Flat Iron at seven thirty. I chose that location for the same reason I chose it the first time we went there: the unlikelihood that Kahn had any confederates or spies present to give us grief.

"So how is your esteemed boyfriend?" I asked as we waited for our drinks.

"Mendel's not my boyfriend anymore," she replied.

"Since when?"

"Since I told him to go to hell this past weekend."

"Uh-oh," I said. "Kahn is a sensitive soul with such delicate sensibilities. Aren't you worried there's going to be trouble?"

"I think he'll leave it alone," she said. "After I said my piece, the son-of-a-bitch knew his days of pushing me around were over."

"What about the money you owe him?"

"Let him sue me for it. He'll never get a penny out of me."

Sophie's vehemence may me laugh. "I'm glad you're done with him," I said. "That took a lot of guts. Kahn's usually not someone to be trifled with."

"You seemed to have handled him all right."

"Kahn would tell you that *he* handled *me* with the settlement we struck. But I want you to know the truth and what I think is about to happen."

I proceeded to tell Sophie what I'd found out about Kahn's true identity and his sordid rise to respectability. I explained about the affidavits I'd secured from Beryl and her husband and how Kahn settled the defamation case to keep them under wraps.

"It looked like he was going to get away with it," I said. "I'd found out the truth, but I couldn't do anything about it."

"So that was it?" Sophie asked.

"Not at all," I said. "The damnedest thing happened. Immigration officials somehow got ahold of the affidavits. How it happened, I couldn't begin to tell you. But getting them let the Feds know that Kahn killed the real Mendel Kahn and bamboozled his way into this country. I've helped them shore up their investigation, and Kahn's going to be deported. I spoke to an immigration agent today who pretty much confirmed it."

Sophie became tearful as I told her what had happened.

"I know it's a lot to take in," I said. "Kahn's a despicable rat, and he would've gotten away with it if not for the miracle with the I.N.S."

"I'm the miracle," Sophie said quietly.

"Huh?"

"I'm the miracle. I sent the affidavits to the agents in Washington. I wanted them to do something about Mendel. And from what you say, it sounds like they're going to."

Sophie gave me a detailed description of what had happened. My less-than-exuberant endorsement of the settlement with Kahn during our conversation over the Fourth of July weekend made

Sophie curious about the terms of the deal. Kahn wouldn't talk about it and got irritated with her for even asking. One day Sophie turned up at his office downtown for lunch and found that he'd gone to the bank to close on a loan he was taking to buy a pair of two-family homes in University Heights. With an hour to herself, she rummaged through the stacks of paper on his desk and found his copy of the settlement agreement.

"All the legalese threw me off at first," she said. But eventually she got the drift of it: Kahn was dismissing his defamation claims in exchange for my agreement to suppress the dossier I'd put together about his identity and background.

"The affidavits made me absolutely sick," Sophie said. "Mendel lied to me about everything — even his name. He lied about not having any family. He murdered his friend and stole his valuables and then showed up here pretending to be the second coming of King Solomon or somebody like that. I knew I had to do something. The man was a criminal."

Sophie had impulsively unclipped the affidavits from the agreement and folded them in her purse. She begged off lunch once Kahn returned to the office, then set out to turn the hot evidence over to the authorities.

But to which "authorities", exactly? Sophie considered the police, but figured that Kahn's case was out of their jurisdiction. Going to the F.B.I. seemed more appropriate, but the prospect of contacting them was too intimidating for her.

Ultimately Sophie decided to go to Congressman Feighan's office. "The people there were very helpful," she said. She explained what she had and asked what she should do with it. The staff agreed that the affidavits should go to the I.N.S., and one of the secretaries made out an envelope for her. The note she included didn't reveal her name. "I was already way out on a limb with Mendel," she said. "The last thing I needed was for him to know that I was the one who turned him in."

"What happened next?" I asked.

"Nothing. Nothing at all. For weeks I waited for them to come for Mendel, but they left him completely alone. He did discover that the affidavits were missing from the agreement..."

"What'd he do about it?"

"For a while I was sure that he suspected me. That's why I was so careful not to talk to you at Temple on Yom Kippur. I wanted to steer clear of any confrontation with him."

"Did he ever come out and accuse you?"

"No. I think he mostly forgot about the affidavits, since nothing seemed to come from their disappearance. If he mentioned it at all, he blamed his secretary for mishandling his files."

Sophie stuck with Kahn long enough to save the money she needed for the first and last month's rent on an apartment. To fill the coffers, she secretly took a job selling cosmetics at the May Company on the Heights.

"So Kahn has no idea he's under investigation?" I asked. "No one from the I.N.S. has come to see him or called?"

"He doesn't have a care in the world," Sophie responded. "Other than the fact that I never paid him back the money I borrowed. I figured the affidavits got lost in the shuffle in Washington. Some people have all the luck, and he's one of them."

"As it happens," I said, "his luck's run out."

Sophie had taken a cab to the Flat Iron. It was after eleven when we finished our meal, so I drove her home to Cleveland Heights, where she'd leased an apartment in the building next to where she'd previously lived.

"Thanksgiving's in a few weeks," I said as she got ready to get out of the Edsel. "You got plans?"

"Probably a TV dinner and the parade on television," she said. "I think I've told you I have no family in town."

"Well, I do. My brother and sister-in-law are having me over with their two kids, and they said I could bring someone. Would you do me the honor?"

A miracle with the I.N.S. and a date for Thanksgiving. Sophie Himmel and I were off to a promising start.

FIFTY

THE FIRST WEEK of December, I went to the Temple for the check Herb had cut from his discretionary fund for my fees. I'd forgotten all about it until he called to say he'd be giving the money to a charity to be chosen by Mendel Kahn unless I came by soon. That got me moving. Rabbis know how to issue a threat in the nicest way.

Herb wasn't there the morning I stopped by. His secretary was expecting me, though, and handed me a check for five hundred thirty-seven dollars. The amount far exceeded my expectations. "That's one hell of a discretionary fund," I said to the secretary as I folded the check and stuffed it into my shirt pocket.

"You know, you could give that money to the building fund and get your name put up in the new Temple," the secretary replied.

"What do you mean?"

"People donating four hundred dollars or more can dedicate their contribution to someone or something," she explained. "The dedications go on their own plaque for display on a special wall at the new building in Beachwood."

"Interesting," I said. "What are you allowed to say in the dedication?"

"Anything appropriate, so long as it's not too long."

"Kilroy was here?"

"It has to be appropriate."

"Give me an example," I requested.

"Some are made 'In memory of' so-and-so. Some honor the Rabbi. Others are thanking Mr. Kahn for his leadership in getting the new Temple built."

"Interesting..." I repeated.

I hadn't yet contributed to the Temple's building fund, given my aversion to Kahn and his involvement leading the project. But the opportunity to post a commemorative plaque was too tempting to pass up.

Herb's secretary told me how to endorse the check and gave me a form to write out my dedication.

I signed the form "Anonymous". That part wasn't suspicious — even I knew that in Judaism the best contributions are anonymous ones.

"Thoughtful message," the secretary said after I handed her the form. "But who's the lucky honoree?"

"A congregant."

"Hmm... I don't recognize the name."

"You'd know him if you saw him."

The fact was that in short order, everyone would know who I was commemorating. Sophie had received a concerned call from Kahn's maid over the weekend. I.N.S. agents had contacted her boss to schedule an interview. They told him not to leave town and to notify his attorney. Kahn was understandably panicked. His past was closing in on him, and his future was dimming.

Later in the month, after the news about Kahn became public, I received a call from Herb. "You were exactly right about it, Benny," he said. "We had the right wrong man."

"I hope contributions toward the new Temple won't take too serious a hit."

"We'll be fine, Benny, just fine. No one's pulled their money yet."

The same day I got the Rabbi's call, I happened to run into the Hairy Slab on my way into the Theatrical for a drink after work. I figured I was in for a hard time. As part of our settlement, Kahn was supposed to grant me immunity from any further ambushes at the hands of his henchman. With Kahn on his way back to Europe, I questioned whether the Slab would honor whatever instruction he'd received along these lines. And I'd stopped carrying my forty-five. If he started in on me, I'd have no firepower to defend myself.

"Mr. Dudek," I said warily, "I'm unhappy to say that we meet again."

"No funny business, Gold. I'm not looking for any trouble."

"You won't get any from me. Our problems are all in the past."

"Except that I'm unemployed because of you. I've heard that you're the one who turned in the Boss. Now I've got to move back to Pittsburgh."

"It's truly a lovely city," I said.

"I'd like to beat you silly," the Hairy Slab responded.

"Now, now..."

"I'm not going to do it, but I'd like to. You framed the Boss, just like you framed me that night in Cleveland Heights."

"The two cases aren't remotely similar," I said. "Kahn'll be deported, but he'll do it with his pants on."

"You think you're funny, Gold," said the Hairy Slab as he walked away. "What you are is a degenerate lowlife."

I thought about the Slab's diagnosis as I sipped my rye-and-soda at the bar. I was reasonably sure I wasn't "degenerate", though I didn't have to try very hard to come up with a daunting list of other flaws in my character. Just in recent history, I'd played fast and loose with the truth. I'd manipulated witnesses. I'd disregarded my contractual obligations and committed at least some of the sins Sylvia attributed to me. Maybe I was a lowlife, after all.

But I wasn't as low as Mendel Kahn. Calling him a "degenerate" was an insult to the true degenerates of the world. The best you could say for him was that he had devolved from an ordinary grifter into a cold-blooded killer, an incorrigible thief, an inveterate fraud.

Fortunately, Kahn was done getting away with it. The truth had finally come to light, and the multiple expressions of appreciation for his generosity and visionary leadership would never make it to the special wall in the new Temple.

Of course, the snide dedication I'd come up with probably wouldn't make it that far, either. But I had to give myself credit for the prescience of the thing:

To Robert F. Oppenheimer
May light shine on his unsung deeds.

— The End —

ACKNOWLEDGMENTS

MANY PEOPLE HELPED me in writing this book. Ellen Kramer, Pat Cigetich, and Molly Brunner each read early drafts of the novel (Ellen did so twice) and provided encouragement and insights. David Brekke and Melissa Quartner Brekke reviewed later versions and offered incisive comments that helped me cross the finish line with the manuscript.

I relied heavily upon the expertise and guidance of my mother, Maxine Cohen, in writing about the Nazi concentration camps and the Jewish ghettoes during World War Two. Maxine also read multiple drafts of the novel and offered strong opinions on what she liked and didn't like. My wife, Marci, graciously shouldered the burden of reviewing every chapter upon its completion and never uttered a discouraging word. My daughter Abbie and son, Dan, also got into the act by reading parts of the book and sharing their thoughts.

Huge thanks go to Don Radlauer and Yael Shahar of Kasva Press, who motivated me to write *Past Imperfect* and did an excellent job in editing it. I remain forever indebted to them for the opportunity to see my writing in print.

About the Author

Joshua Cohen is the other other-Josh-Cohen. He grew up in San Antonio and attended the University of Texas both as an undergraduate and for law school. For close to 40 years, he has practiced law in Cleveland, Ohio, his original hometown. Josh began writing in the mid-2010s, when the youngest of his three children left for college.

Josh still has his day job as an attorney. His small firm focuses its practice on class actions, employment law, professional malpractice, and other complex civil litigation. A documentary called "Cleveland vs. Wall Street" was made about one of Josh's cases and debuted at the Cannes International Film Festival. It was seen by practically no one in the U.S. but had a big following in France and Switzerland.

Past Imperfect is his second novel, and the sequel to *The Best Assassination in the Nation,* also published by Kasva Press. Josh is currently at work on his third novel.

He lives in the Cleveland suburb of Shaker Heights with his wife, Marci.

Follow Josh at: www.joshuacohenauthor.com